The Other End of the Sea

The Other End of the Sea

Alison Glick

Interlink Books

An imprint of Interlink Publishing Group, Inc.
Northampton, Massachusetts

First published in 2022 by

Interlink Books
An imprint of Interlink Publishing Group, Inc.
46 Crosby Street, Northampton, MA 01060
www.interlinkbooks.com

Cover photograph: Shati (refugee camp Gaza) 1988,
courtesy of Antonia Caccia

Library of Congress Cataloging-in-Publication data available
ISBN-13: 978-1-62371-958-6

Printed and bound in the United States of America

For Tamar

"We are captives of what we love, what we desire, and what we are."
—Mahmoud Darwish

1
Departures

We made our way through the nearly deserted streets, hoping to find a way out of Gaza.

I sensed the rising nervousness of my friends—all of us expats living in the West Bank town of Ramallah. We crossed the main drag, Omar al-Mukhtar Street, and headed toward a parking lot. The sound of the cold winter rain echoed off the metal-roofed taxi stand as we approached. With the weather and the political tension of the first intifada in 1988 combining to keep most people home, we weren't exactly sure what our transportation options would be.

We entered the lot and noted one lone taxi. The sound of its idling diesel engine emitted a distinctive, rhythmic knocking. Known as *serveece,* these seven-passenger Mercedes sedans provided virtually all the inter-city transportation in the West Bank and Gaza Strip of the late 1980s. Normally the *serveece* departed when filled with passengers—three in the middle back seat, three in the seat behind, and one in the front.

There were six of us, so we would need to wait for another passenger or pay for the empty seat. But as the stand where the car stood came into full view, we noticed another man standing there smoking, huddled against the cold. He took one last drag from his cigarette. Squinting through its curl of smoke, inhaling deeply, and sighing a grayish-white stream into the moist air, he flicked the butt downwards and ground it into the cracked asphalt with the tip of his shoe. His heel wavered back and forth, as if he were bidding the cigarette goodbye. At least now the taxi would be full, and the driver would leave for Ramallah.

We were a small group of schoolteachers from the Quaker-run Friends School, looking for a way to be useful since the Israelis had closed down all Palestinian schools in the West Bank. We had spent two days visiting hospitals, houses, and refugee camps, taking statements from victims of Itzhak Rabin's policy of "force, might and beatings"—a failed attempt by the then-Israeli prime minster to crush the Palestinian uprising by literally beating the population into submission. Soldiers set upon people indiscriminately, whether or not they were involved in a demonstration or other political activity. Truncheon-wielding troops crushed the bones of victims whose limbs were held taut by other soldiers. In the fields and olive groves of the West Bank, stones were used to the same effect.

The taxi bumped and splashed through Gaza's muddy streets, making its way north toward the Erez checkpoint. We introduced ourselves to the seventh passenger. His name was Zayn Majdalawi. Born and raised in Shati refugee camp on the western edge of Gaza City, Zayn was a student at Bir Zeit University near Ramallah.

The full taxi buzzed with discussion of Gaza. It was our first time there, and the difference between it and the relative prosperity and calm of Ramallah was striking. Driving north about twenty minutes, we came to the junction at Ashkelon, the first Israeli city on the main road out of Gaza. As the taxi slowed to a stop, Zayn, sitting directly behind me in the last seat, pointed out a building on the left that dominated the intersection: a sandy yellow-colored structure, three-stories tall, with a few high-placed windows. It was set farther back from the road than nearby buildings. A whitewashed concrete wall, topped with a spiral of barbed wire, surrounded it.

"That is Ashkelon prison," he said, "where I was held as a political prisoner."

Our heads turned in unison to take in the imposing compound.

"How long were you in prison?" someone asked.

I glimpsed a courtyard beyond the front gate. Looming above it all was a watchtower with a machine gun trained on the ground below.

"Fifteen years," he stated matter-of-factly.

Until now, I had been content to listen quietly from the middle seat, too tired and absorbed in thought to engage in general conversation, especially with this stranger.

"Fifteen years?!" I blurted out, turning around in my seat. For the first time, I saw his face completely. He had sea green eyes that sparkled playfully.

"*Na'am*. Yes. Fifteen years."

My gaze lingered on him as I struggled for a reply. None came. It was then that I noticed the hint of sadness folded into the lines that edged his eyes.

❧

We had started our first day in Gaza at the office of a well-known human rights lawyer, Tawfiq Salem. From there, my friend Ellen and I were taken to Jebalya, the largest of Gaza's eight camps, then housing over seventy-five thousand refugees in barely more than one square kilometer. Our escort was a camp resident named Abdel Karim. Slight and quick, Abdel Karim spoke through what seemed like a permanently clenched jaw, which softened when he smiled, giving him an impish air. We rode in his bright orange Volkswagen bug and stopped outside of a small cinderblock structure. He knocked lightly on the corrugated metal door and then led us into a room.

It felt like we were entering a hospital ward: A half-dozen men, ranging in age from late teens to perhaps early thirties, lay on foam mattresses arranged on the concrete floor. They were bandaged, in casts, eyes at various stages of bruising, faces swollen and scarred. A few nights earlier a group of soldiers had burst into the house as they played cards and watched television after the eight o'clock evening curfew. Those who could, recounted what happened—the rifle butts, the heavy wooden truncheons—at times wincing with the effort. A single kerosene heater in the middle of the room struggled against the Gaza cold, a tea kettle perched on top hissing a slow simmer. I never before thought human bodies could look like that.

Our last day in Gaza, Ellen and I had visited wounded Palestinians in the two main hospitals. Coincidentally, the man who drove us there was Zayn's brother Lutfi. We wanted to send Lutfi a gift to thank him for his time and set about looking for Zayn to deliver it the next time he went to Gaza. We got word to Zayn via another expat, a tall, blond British guy named Chris who worked at the public affairs office at Bir Zeit University.

A few days later, arriving home from the market, my roommate Nadia informed me that "a man with beautiful green eyes was here for you." It took a moment, but whom she meant finally came to me. Zayn had left a note with a phone number where I could reach him. I bought a bottle of araq—the deceptively clear, anise-based liquor known throughout the Arab world—and set up another meeting with Zayn at my apartment.

The knock on the door of the glassed-in veranda rattled the windows on that half of the porch, acting as a kind of doorbell. I opened the metal door that closed off the house from the veranda and peered outside. I saw the smooth, rounded top of a hairless head. The key clicked in the lock. Zayn turned to face me and stood down from the step as I opened the door.

"*Marhaba,*" I greeted him.

"*Marhabtayn!*" Two hellos he greeted in return, a wide grin lighting up his face.

I could see what Nadia meant about the eyes.

"Please come in."

I gestured him into our small sitting room and offered tea. We drank amber-colored liquid from handleless Pyrex juice glasses, the teacup of choice in the Middle East, and talked—about the indelible impressions my first visit to Gaza made on me, about our now-mutual acquaintances, and Zayn's interrupted studies. When I mentioned my interest in returning to Gaza to hear more stories, he offered me a ride back in a few days, now that his car was fixed.

The earlier taxi conversation and our chat while sipping tea that day told me there was much about Zayn that was not what I would expect. He was deeply anchored by his society, but he both clung to and flouted its customs and conventions. Not many men who had been incarcerated entered university at age thirty-one, further postponing marriage and a family in a society that highly valued both. But his intellectual curiosity was as irrepressible as his wit. A traditional marriage then would have been as confining for Zayn as for his wife.

His looks and his charm were equally unconventional. Bald save for a ring of closely shaved hair on the lower half of his head, Zayn's smooth skin was a shade lighter than the roasted olive hue that was predominant among Palestinian men. His prominent cheekbones rose even higher when he smiled, which was often. And it took me a while to identify perhaps the most unusual feature of his face: he wore no moustache.

Over the next few months, we took many trips in Zayn's tiny beige Fiat. On the road threading between the rolling hills and olive groves of the West Bank, past the nineteenth-century Latrun Monastery, slowly descending into the valley that opened onto the sandy plains of the Strip, he began telling me his story, and I began listening.

❦

Zayn's parents, Omar and Asma Majdalawi, escaped from Simsim in 1948 with the rest of their village. Fleeing the Nakba, or catastrophe, the war that created the State of Israel, they crossed into Gaza with four children, burying two along the way. Two sons were born in Shati refugee camp, the first of whom was my new friend, Zayn.

In 1967 the Israeli Army entered Gaza, an army born of the one that had pushed Zayn's family out of Simsim twenty years earlier. The military occupation created a new generation of resistance in Palestine, tied to the independence and anticolonial movements of those years (the resistance leader in Gaza was nicknamed "Guevara Gaza"). The backbone of the Palestinian resistance was the young men and women of the camps, which were first populated by their parents. Among those fighters was Zayn.

He spent much of his boyhood with his older brother Abdullah, whom he admired and who was already married and on his own. A fervent Arab nationalist, Abdullah was working as a teacher in Saudi Arabia in June 1967, when the Israeli Army entered Gaza and refused to allow him—and most other Palestinians who were outside their country at that time—to return. After the war, he left Saudi Arabia for Egypt, but the authorities there eventually expelled him. So he moved to Benghazi, Libya, where he found a teaching position and raised five children. Abdullah would never see his parents again. He was only able to return to Gaza forty years later.

Zayn was thirteen when the Israelis first occupied Gaza, a star student and the apple of his father's eye. By age twelve, Zayn had memorized half of the Koran, an accomplishment indicative of a sharp, inquisitive mind, able to focus intently. The achievement made his father—an Islamic scholar trained at Cairo's Al-Azhar University, the Harvard Divinity of the Muslim world—immensely proud.

As a teenager, Zayn developed other talents, including exceptional aim with a hand grenade. He joined the resistance and took part in an attack on an army patrol in Shati camp in 1970. The grenade he threw killed a soldier. Zayn was seventeen.

Put on trial in an Israeli military court, he became known as "the laughing accused," so called by the frustrated judge whose gavel couldn't stifle Zayn's laughter throughout the proceedings. It quieted when the sentence was handed down: life in prison.

Zayn was among the youngest political prisoners, whose numbers grew as the Israeli army crushed the Palestinian resistance to the occupation. Years later when I met one of Zayn's comrades from prison, he recalled the day Zayn was brought to the jail to begin serving his sentence.

"We couldn't believe it when he entered the cell," Fathi exclaimed, smiling at the memory. "We asked the guards, 'Who is this child you're bringing us?'"

Zayn sat for the *tawjihi* matriculation exam and was awarded his secondary school diploma in jail. It was then that his true education began.

Palestinian political prisoners, with their tight organization, discipline, and emphasis on intellectual growth, created a subculture that was not only self-sustaining but influential beyond the prison walls. These organizations became known as "University of Palestine." Their graduates are the self-taught intellectuals, writers, artists, and politicians who have impacted the course of Palestinian history, inside and outside of jail, and inside and outside of Palestine. Many prisoners studied Hebrew and English, as it quickly became clear that Hebrew skills would be needed to negotiate with the guards, and English to communicate with the Red Cross. Zayn threw himself into the languages, relishing the cultural idioms anchored in their respective societies and histories. He also became known for his political commentary and analysis, written on tiny scraps of paper, rolled into a capsule size and smuggled out with visitors.

During Israel's 1982 military invasion of Lebanon, three of its soldiers were captured by the PLO. In 1985, they were exchanged for 1,150 Palestinian political prisoners. Among those prisoners was Zayn. He was thirty-one years old. Most of the *muharrareen,* "the liberated," used the compensation provided by the PLO to marry and begin families. Zayn enrolled in the linguistics program at Bir Zeit University, bought a plot of land on the edge of Shati camp, and began building a home.

❦

On our trips to Gaza, from behind the wheel of his Fiat Zayn would point to a tumble of building stones and succulent cacti set just off the road. "*Sawfir, Masmiya, 'Aker*"—mile after mile, he would reel off the names of villages destroyed with the creation of Israel in 1948 as we passed their remnants.

When early spring pushed past the cold, rainy winter, I began rolling down the car window the closer we got to the warmth of Gaza. The lines of *saber* cactus Palestinian villagers had used to mark their land holdings offered up bright yellow blooms.

"You know," Zayn said tentatively during one trip in those first weeks, "you have a very American memory."

I turned to him with a quizzical look and caught his Cheshire cat grin.

"We met before that time at the Gaza taxi stand."

He briefly took his eyes off the road to catch my surprised expression.

"We *did*?"

"Yes. At Chris's house last year in Ramallah. You came to do your laundry, and I let you in because no one else was home."

I remembered now. I closed my eyes as much to focus on the scene as to ward off the embarrassment of my lapse.

❦

Washing machines were a luxury in the West Bank at that time, and renting an apartment that had one was a rarity. Chris, the same ex-pat who had helped me find Zayn to deliver the *araq*, had such an apartment, so I was regularly showing up at his door with a basket of dirty clothes. I remembered knocking on the metal door which flaked the same innocuous butter beige paint that was used, it seemed, in all the interiors and exteriors of Ramallah homes. The door swung open and a grinning bald man stood before me.

"Hello. Is Joel here?" I inquired, about Chris's roommate, a close friend who had invited me to use the machine.

"No. But please come in."

I hesitated, but I had no desire to drag my laundry, still dirty, back to the other side of town.

"Thanks," I smiled as I moved past him and into the kitchen where the machine stood. "Joel said I could use their machine. I won't be long. I'll just put it in to wash and return later."

"Please have tea," he said.

It was a statement more than an invitation.

"I really must get going," I replied as I stuffed the machine too full with clothes.

"Five minutes," he insisted, and by the time I had loaded and turned on the machine, the water was on the boil. This guy was self-assured, but also kind of quirky. Given the scenario we were in—that of a Palestinian man encountering an unknown foreign woman alone in a house without its host—it seemed appropriate to keep our interaction short and perfunctory, even though he put me at ease.

I apologized while walking toward the door, telling him I had other errands to finish.

I lingered in the grocery buying milk and coffee, stopped to visit another friend, and headed back to the house to retrieve my clean clothes. To my relief Joel answered the door. When I entered, my erstwhile host sat on the low sofa sipping tea. Joel introduced us.

"Yes, I know her," Zayn replied. "She is the one who doesn't like my tea."

My eyes widened a bit, as did Joel's. I sputtered an explanation, apologizing again to Zayn.

"Now will you have tea?" he asked, raising the aluminum kettle warming on the kerosene heater.

As if I could refuse.

"I'll have some more, too, BHS," Joel said, pushing his glass toward Zayn, who laughed.

Joel had nicknamed Zayn "BHS"—short for *Baruch ha shem*, "bless the name." A Hebrew response to being asked "How are you?" the expression blesses the name of God for being well and was the standard response Zayn gave whenever he greeted his friend Joel Rosenberg, the Jewish human rights worker from Teaneck, New Jersey. The irony of this so delighted Joel that he had nicknamed Zayn "BHS."

❦

As we left behind the verdant sloping hills and descended into the industrial zone of Ashkelon, I marveled at my American memory, but more so at Zayn's Palestinian one. Soon we came upon the same prison we had passed on that first taxi ride out of Gaza. We caught the red light at the intersection directly in front of it. Zayn shifted into first gear and the car stopped. Our gazes turned to the hulking building on the right. Zayn's eyes narrowed. He was focused on someone near the building.

"*Mish mumkin,*" he said, almost to himself. "No way!" He glanced quickly in the rearview mirror and turned the car suddenly into the right lane and around the corner, driving slowly alongside a long wall of the prison, as close to the curb as he could get. Knowing that the car's blue license plate indicated that it was from the West Bank, I eyed the guard tower.

"What are you doing?"

Ignoring me, Zayn slowed the car more as we came upon a man on the sidewalk making his way toward us. He walked slightly hunched with his hands jammed into his pants pockets that were the same khaki color as his button-up shirt and jacket. When he looked up, Zayn honked the car horn, grinning and waving wildly. The man slowed his pace, ducked his head slightly to see through the car window, and broke into an equally wide grin, waving back.

Zayn hesitated but did not stop the car, instead shouting in Hebrew, "*Mashlom mekh?* How are you?" through my passenger window.

"*Beseder,* OK," came the reply. "*Manee shma?* What's up?" The man caught a glimpse of me and his smile broadened.

Zayn signaled left, made a U-turn and pulled back onto the road to Gaza.

"Who was *that*?" I nearly shouted.

"A guard from the prison," he answered.

"You mean from the time you were a prisoner?"

"Yes."

The facades of gray industrial buildings and white-washed walls blurred past.

"Was he one of the *better* guards?" I finally asked.

Zayn hesitated before responding, "Not really."

The car's engine shifted gears as we reached the outskirts of Ashkelon, making our way steadily to the Gaza border.

2
Crumbling Myths

How did Becky Klein, a nice Jewish girl from the Midwest, find herself on the Gaza border? My American memory of the region first began forming as a seventeen-year-old foreign exchange student. I had been studying Spanish at my suburban Cincinnati high school and hoped to go to Spain. My second-choice country—Israel—reflected an undefined interest in my Jewish roots, and is where I landed in June 1980, the summer before my senior year.

So it was that Palestine revealed itself to me in layers. The first one was Kiryat Yam, a middle-class suburb of Haifa populated mostly by Jews who had escaped from Europe. They lived and worked alongside Jews from across the Arab world who had abandoned communities with deep cultural and historical roots to Judaize a land depopulated of fellow Arabs.

My host family, the Bernsteins, lived in a third-floor walkup, one of the apartment blocks built quickly and on a large enough scale to house unpredictable numbers of immigrants, post-World War II. The parents, Yacov and Esther, were employed in Haifa's industrial sector and were proud Labor Party supporters. They had two children,

Eitan and Tali, my host sister with whom I spent an idyllic summer swimming in the Mediterranean a few blocks away, taking day trips to Haifa, and exploring the country's endless beauty. Tali's friends—Ruti, Hertzl, Rami—became mine, along with the rhythms of her family's life.

The parents' workday ended in the early afternoon, six days a week. Esther usually arrived home first, puffing up the three flights of stairs. She would bustle into the kitchen—her brunette waves dampened into a frame of her glistening pink face—laden with groceries acquired en route from work. Once the schnitzel was in the oven or the potatoes on the boil, she would call to Tali to watch over things while she showered.

One midsummer's day, Esther and I sat sipping iced coffee while lunch cooked. Freshly showered, she lamented having to rush home and bathe after work, even though showers were provided for the workers.

"I don't like to use them," she told me.

"Why not?" I asked.

She wrinkled her nose.

"Because the Arabs use them."

Her words were like the flash of something dark that I didn't want to see—like catching the tail end of a bird in flight, its prey dangling.

In August I returned to the home of my childhood—the home of my oldest American memories of darkness and light. Spending three months abroad had altered my view of the world. Returning to a Midwestern suburb and the trivial concerns of high school life was disorienting after a summer hitchhiking and exploring a place featured regularly in the evening news. My alienation increased when my father was diagnosed with advanced-stage prostate cancer in December. As his once-imposing body withered in our home, so did my relationship to the place and the people with whom I grew up.

All my life I had been a star student, involved in extracurricular activities and with an active circle of friends. But as that last year of high school progressed, I found myself spending more time with my teachers and less time with my friends. I thought constantly of being in Israel, and planned to postpone college to return. I was coming close to being kicked off of the drill team for missing practices, despite having aspired for years to be on it for the badge of popularity it bestowed. In calculus one afternoon that spring, I was greeted with the first "F" of my school career when handed back a test. It took me a moment to recognize the large red letter staring back at me from the white space at the bottom of the last page. I blinked hard and felt as if I were entering a narrowing tunnel, the teacher's voice reviewing the test echoed at a faint distance.

The school year ended with the news that the cancer had spread throughout my father's body. Further chemo and radiation treatments were pointless. He came home from the hospital for the last time in July.

As a father he had been distant and critical, inclined to yell about mistakes and faults rather than to encourage talents and success. But one day that summer, the phone rang to reveal another side of him I never knew existed.

My father was an elementary school gym teacher and one of his students—a young girl in maybe the second or third grade—called to talk to him. He had missed the last several weeks of the school year, and she heard he was sick. There was concern in her innocent voice.

I explained that he was sleeping and couldn't come to the phone.

"Tell him April said hi," she said. Then she added, "I miss him."

Sometimes the people in our lives—those we've always known and those we are just beginning to know—are revealed to us by voices both unseen and unforeseen.

My father's condition worsened throughout the summer. I told my mother that I would cancel my trip to Israel, as things didn't look good. When she informed my father, who was back in the hospital, his response was, "Tell Becky she should go." He didn't want me to cancel.

In my father's waning days, he reached out to my mother and younger sister, the main target of his ire during my childhood, apologizing for his hurtful and often cruel behavior. My well-behaved, straight-A defenses had shielded me, to a certain extent, from the worst of his outbursts, so I got no such apology. What I received instead was permission to explore this part of me—one that in many ways came from him. It was my father's parting gift to me.

He died that August, in 1981.

❧

Late that summer, I boarded a flight for Tel Aviv.

I had signed up for a six-month work-study program called an *ulpan*, which was on a kibbutz nestled in the Carmel Mountains, overlooking the Mediterranean.

Greeting me at Kibbutz Ma'ayan Zvi was a poster peeling from a wall just inside the front gate. With a sky-blue background and white block Hebrew letters, it implored, "*Rok lo Likud*, Just Not Likud." A remnant from that summer's national political campaign, the sign was a three-word editorial on the right-wing party that had, in fact, won the election in June 1981.

I studied Hebrew and worked in the kibbutz's orchards and optics factory, intending to explore further my Jewish heritage, partially funded by the Jewish Community Center (JCC). This is when I met Palestinians for the first time.

On my way to the kibbutz's communal dining room every day, I passed a construction site dotted with Palestinian workers. They moved among the rubble and ladders like specters: faces bronzed by the sun and heads of dark curls dusted white. The scrape of their rubber sandals echoed off the cement as they worked, their collar bones rippling and poking against their skin as they hoisted cinderblocks. They were most likely day laborers from the West Bank or Gaza, hired to build another dormitory to house Jews from the West like me who thought ourselves returning to "*our* homeland," claiming "*our* birthright." But the JCC brochure describing the kibbutz's communal living had said nothing about them.

The group of foreigners participating in the ulpan included some who were considering *aliya*. *Aliya*—to go up, to rise, to ascend to a higher place, in this case the "Promised Land." Those planning to immigrate would talk, slightly breathless, of "making *aliya*" with their Scottish brogues, crisp Queen's English, and Brooklyn accents that drew out consonants into sloshy vowels.

There were others on the ulpan—leftist Americans, feminists from Europe—who had a more critical view of the Israeli government. I gravitated toward three of them in the ulpan's social milieu—Pauline, Dave, and Andrew. They were older and had more serious natures that were closer to my own.

The program was managed by a man named Yitzhak. Shaped like a matryoshka doll, Yitzhak wore a plaid billed cap and ash gray windbreaker, regardless of the weather. He always had his balled fists stuffed into both pockets. This seemed to balance him as he walked, bobbing slightly, to and from his apartment where he lived alone. His froggy voice recited rules he took pleasure in having memorized. "Because that's the way it is," was the only explanation offered to someone questioning him. Announcements of activities on the information board would often be followed by bold, capital letters: "THIS FUN ACTIVITY IS MANDATORY."

One afternoon after first arriving, I returned to the dormitory early from my work detail, sick from the unfamiliar heat. I came upon Yitzhak tacking up one such notice, his shirt sleeves uncharacteristically rolled up against the late summer swelter. As I leaned forward to read the notice, the blur of six numbers tattooed on his left forearm bit through my summer haze. The crudely inked mark, wrinkled and made uneven by the aging of his skin, lay not quite buried under the brush of his arm hair. He hadn't noticed me until that moment. My stare didn't shift quickly enough. He grumbled a question about why I wasn't at work but didn't wait for an answer, turning back toward his office. The door clicked shut, cutting me off mid-sentence.

On a rapidly cooling afternoon that fall of 1981, a lecture called "Being an Arab in Israel" was arranged by Yitzhak. With no other mention of Arabs or Palestinians during the rest of the program, this seemed an attempt by the kibbutz to display its liberal credentials. Rousted from our afternoon naps, we were herded into a kibbutz meeting room by Yitzhak. At the front of the room, a short, mustached man in a brown wool jacket stood next to a chalk board. He nodded and smiled as the group filed in. Yitzhak greeted him and they chatted. Steel-legged chairs scraped against the tiled floor as we took our seats.

"This ought to be interesting," quipped a kid named Todd, from Brooklyn. Draped over his chair was a jean jacket with an extremist insignia—a clenched fist thrust into the heart of a Star of David—stitched on the back.

Finally, the group's chatter gave way to Yitzhak making an awkward introduction. Elias Jabbour spoke about life as an Arab in Israel. I'm sure he must have cited statistics, talked of demographics and democracy, Israeli style. As a teacher, he must have spoken of the education system and the curriculum. I remember nothing of what he said, with one exception. At the end of his talk, he invited anyone who was interested to visit him in his village, Shefa 'Amr.

I don't know exactly why I lingered after the lecture while my classmates filtered out into the twilight, but I did. I had been listening carefully to the criticisms leveled against Israeli policies by some of my leftist friends, although mostly they went over my head or just confused me. Why were they at the ulpan if they had such dim views of the Jewish state? And why weren't they here with me now?

I had also listened carefully to what Elias had said. Now I wondered about what hadn't been said—by Pauline and Dave and Andrew—but mostly by Elias himself.

"So, how would I get there from here?" I asked him.

Together we sat in the empty room as he patiently answered my questions and then gave me directions to his village.

I planned to go on a Saturday morning, early enough so I could make it back before nightfall and for work the next day. Invitations to my ulpan friends to join me were met with awkward silences, or even more awkward reasons why they couldn't go. My roommate Ilana, a sweet, bookish girl from Brooklyn with wiry hair and glasses, kept asking me, "Where are you going?" I repeated the name of the village, and she would murmur it back in a slightly hushed tone, volumes of Martin Buber and Nietzsche lined up neatly behind her on a bookshelf.

❧

On the appointed day I rose early, stopped by the empty kibbutz dining room, and wrapped a couple of boiled eggs in a napkin to eat on the bus. I passed through the kibbutz gate and crossed the road to the bus stop. Waiting for the bus to Haifa to descend the hill from Zichron Ya'acov, the nearest town perched about a mile above the kibbutz, I turned toward the plain below—a patchwork of geometric fields, red-tiled roofs and fishponds spread out toward the coastline in the early morning light. The Mediterranean's foamy lip edged the background; beyond, its gray gaping mouth swallowed the horizon.

In the slow Saturday Haifa bus station, I was to board a Nazareth-bound bus. Elias specified that it should not be one going to "Nazareth *Illit*" or Upper Nazareth, the Jewish part of the city from where it would be difficult to get to Shefa 'Amr. As several shiny Nazareth *Illit* buses came and went, I stood on the edge of a group of Palestinians: thin men in dirty jeans and tattered sweaters hauling home bundles of food and the dust of their construction jobs; waiters wearing creased black pants and shirts once pressed crisp, now stained with remnants of Shabbat dinner specials and sweat; mothers carrying bags stuffed with clothes, and grandmothers grasping children and smiling at me from under brightly colored scarves.

The Plexiglas windows of that Nazareth stop had been broken

long ago, if indeed they ever existed. Sheltering the waiting passengers were pieces of cardboard. Old boxes bearing the logo of Osem biscuits and Lipton tea had been fashioned into "windows," covering the spaces created by the intersecting metal poles of the bus stand and offering a kind of protection from the weather. Low winter clouds began shedding a misty rain. One of the older women nodded toward the shelter and arched her eyebrows at me.

"*Ta'ali jewah.* Come inside," she urged.

As the mist thickened, I moved forward and joined them. When the bus finally arrived, gears grinding loudly and coughing occasional black smoke, the group surged forward and funneled in. The driver hesitated when I gave him my money.

"*Rotze Illit?* Do you want *Illit*?" he asked in Hebrew, confirming my actual destination.

"*Lo*. No, Nazareth."

He shrugged and handed me my ticket.

The ride south and east was accompanied by new sounds and smells: crunchy rings of sesame bread dipped in a mix of dried herbs that was twisted into scraps of newspaper—*za'atar*, as I would later come to know it; the sound of Arabic music on the radio, melodious and warbly to my ear then; and in Nazareth, the bustle of a city not observing a Sabbath.

From the bus station I had been instructed to take a taxi to Shefa 'Amr. Elias had written his address and phone number in Arabic on a piece of paper when we talked after his lecture. I took it out of my bag to give to the driver, unfolding it as I reached over the front seat. Glimpsing it for the first time since that meeting, the slant and curves of the mysterious letters seemed to relax on the paper.

The taxi headed north to the section of the country that is the entrance to the Galilee, with its valleys and hills stretching away from the sea. Soon the taxi was climbing one of the seven hills that dominate the landscape of Shefa 'Amr, its engine knocking loudly as the driver maneuvered through the narrow streets. Not quite at the top of one of the hills, we stopped at a modest house surrounded by a concrete wall. The driver honked the horn, and soon Elias emerged, waving and smiling. *"Ahlan wa sahlan,"* he welcomed me.

I met his wife Siham and we all drank tea together. Elias then suggested I visit the school where he taught. Walking a short distance down the hill, we entered a one-story beige building surrounded by a dusty courtyard. An elderly man with a white scarf folded around his head emerged from the side of the building and opened the door, nodding a near-toothless smile.

The damp, cool air trapped inside greeted us in the classroom we entered. Elias flipped a switch and an anemic glow leaked from a bulb hanging from a ceiling wire. He pushed aside some broken chairs and gestured toward a desk. I sat down and looked around. The blackboard was a slab of slate laid into a space where the concrete had been chiseled out, producing a scalloped frame around it. A few Arabic words were written on the board, and off to the side a couple of names were written in English, adorned with hearts and smiley faces—Tayseer, Munir. I kept squinting to see the glass in the windows that wasn't there.

Soon a young man joined us. Ibrahim was one of Elias's students. They showed me around the rest of the school: several similarly appointed rooms, some of which opened onto the courtyard, with or without doors. Struggling geraniums pushed out of Nido powdered milk cans that lined the schoolyard wall.

I took in the scene around me. When I thought of my host sister's modern, well-equipped school that I had seen the year before, it was hard to believe I was in the same country.

We returned to Elias's house, where his wife had prepared lunch. On a low table that had been covered with newspaper there was a pot of tightly wrapped stuffed grape leaves, glistening in the afternoon light like wet cigars. Aromas suggesting garlic, lemon and olive oil filled the small sitting room. Next to bowls of homemade yogurt and olives, a stack of plates waited patiently. We all took a seat around the table.

About this time the *kibbutzniks* would be lining up for their midday meal: chicken schnitzel and boiled potatoes, tomato and cucumber salad, squares of pale bread spread with margarine the color of creamed corn.

Elias handed me a loaf of still-warm pita bread and invited me to begin the meal. Siham piled a handful of grape leaves on a plate and gave it to me with a shy smile, revealing a gold-capped tooth. Each mouthful of food revealed something new: allspice seeped through the papery grape leaves; the olives hosted the mild tang of the salt and lemon liquid in which they floated. At the end of the meal, the little piles of olive pits and scraps of leftover bread were rolled up into the newspaper, leaving behind a perfectly clean table on which was served delicate cups of sweet Arabic coffee.

In the late afternoon, I said goodbye to my hosts and once again climbed into a *serveece*. Shefa 'Amr lay quiet in the day's siesta. As the car descended a hill, we passed a few people along the roadside—mostly older men walking toward the mosque, fingering prayer beads or smoking, lost in thought. About halfway down the hill, the driver pulled over, yielding the narrow road to a massive truck making its way up. The car idled near the front gate of a small home. On the veranda of the house, a woman stood holding a child—a little girl about two with hair the color of burnished brass, her cheek resting on the woman's shoulder. She shifted in her mother's arms, wanting a better look at the stranger peering out of the window. I leaned forward, my face almost touching the glass.

The truck passed slowly, struggling under its load but making progress. The effort shook the ancient bedrock beneath me.

I smiled at the girl, raised my hand to the glass, and waved.

A couple of weeks later, there was a note in my kibbutz mailbox instructing me to come to the main office for a delivery. I was excited at the prospect of a care package from my mom, if a bit surprised that she'd send something so large that it couldn't fit into my mailbox.

An "x" had been slashed across a box next to a line explaining why it hadn't been delivered. What the explanation was, I didn't understand. After lunch I took the paper to the office. A middle-aged woman was sorting through letters when I walked in and handed her the note. She went into a back room and emerged with a regular envelope.

Before I left she looked at me and asked, "Ulpan?"

I told her yes.

Her eyebrows arched slightly.

I thought she would continue, but she said nothing else. Turning to close the door behind me as I left, I noticed her looking at me even as I walked away.

Back in my room I opened the envelope. The return address was written in two languages: the city, Shefa 'Amr, was in English, and the rest was in Arabic. It was a letter from Ibrahim, the contents of which I've long ago forgotten. It must have told me how happy he was to meet me, about his activities in the village—soccer perhaps?—and ended with a fervent wish for me to write him back. The appearance of the letter, though, is still vivid: Framing the entire page were tiny, hand-drawn flowers—green stems and leaves hosting red-petaled blooms, with miniscule dots in the center made with the faintest sweep from the tip of his pen.

I felt my face flush. Without knowing why, I tore the kibbutz notice into pieces and hurled it into the pink plastic trash can at the foot of my bed.

In the spring of 1982, I returned to the U.S. and enrolled at the University of Cincinnati. There I met Nadia—a Palestinian-American and my future Ramallah roommate. She was just finishing her undergraduate studies and preparing for graduate school at Temple University in Philadelphia. She introduced me to other Arabs and international students, and to the works of writers like Noam Chomsky and Edward Said, whose books on Palestinian history and U.S.-Israeli relations helped explain what I had seen on the kibbutz and in Shefa 'Amr. An entirely new view of the world was opening to me.

And then that June, Israel invaded Lebanon. In September, the Sabra and Shatilla massacre of over a thousand Palestinian civilian refugees in less than forty-eight hours shocked the world. As Israel's culpability in the slaughter came to light, public opinion began doubting its victim role in the region, not to mention its much vaunted "purity of arms." The unquestioning loyalty accorded the Jewish state was being questioned by many American Jews for the first time. The myth was beginning to crumble.

Nadia introduced me to a progressive Middle East historian at Temple, and I transferred there to finish my degree. In many ways, my undergraduate education was a re-education of almost everything I had been taught, not only about Middle East history but American history and politics as well. My political activity on behalf of Palestinian rights and progressive causes defined my time at Temple, and there was no question in my mind what I would do as soon as I graduated: return to the region, but this time to live in the Palestinian community.

Living in Philadelphia—the birthplace of American Quakerism—facilitated making contacts with the Quaker school in Ramallah. The school had a sizable Palestinian-American population: teenagers (and younger) whose parents had sent them to Ramallah from the States to finish high school with the dual goal of strengthening their knowledge of Arabic, and escaping (their parents thought) the sex, drugs and rock-and-roll culture of U.S. high schools. There was a parallel English language curriculum to accommodate these students.

In September 1986, the Friends School hired me to teach social studies.

3
A Garden Blooms

The first time I visited Zayn's house, a cement mixer greeted me as I walked through the metal gate surrounding the yard. The opening of the contraption where the ingredients were fed gaped empty. Black buckets of gravel and sand were abandoned around the machine, and a dusty water hose snaked around its feet. Opposite it—separated by a path leading from the street to the front veranda—was the garden, verdant and intricate with its bushes of fragrant basil, plain earthy potatoes, and showy trees of lemon and almond. I hadn't intended on going there, but with Zayn one's intentions could dissipate like drops of water in a hot skillet that dance on the surface and sizzle away.

Our sojourns between Ramallah and Gaza had taken on a certain pattern through the winter and into the spring of 1988. I would contact him in Ramallah through friends or in Gaza through Tawfiq, the human rights lawyer.

"You can leave me at Faiza's," I would casually remind him about my plan to go to a friend's house as we merged into the bustle of Gaza traffic.

"I'm inviting you to drink coffee," he would reply, as if this had slipped my mind.

"But I have an appointment. She's expecting me."

At first I could talk my way out of his car relatively easily. But with each successive trip, this push and pull became a ritual of our Gaza drives. So I tried being more strategic in my rationale for going straight to my friend Faiza's.

"She asked me to bring her some medicine from Ramallah that she's been waiting for."

"Really, just ten minutes," he would reply lightly, almost laughing.

Every time I saw Faiza's apartment building fade into the rearview mirror, I silently swore that I would never accept a ride with him again.

But with each trip, Zayn's plans, sprung on me as we got closer to Faiza's, grew more elaborate. Having coffee became lunch with friends I just had to meet. A brief errand morphed into visits that stretched out into the late afternoon. On one trip, I mentioned that I hadn't been to the seaside in Gaza. So he drove me to a remote swath of beach where I stood and watched the waves break along the empty shore while Zayn stayed in the car, watching me nervously. In the midst of the intifada, Palestinians did not go to the beach.

Then one day he insisted on showing me the house he was building, and the garden of which he was so proud. Zayn made tea and we sat on the veranda and took in the view. Shati camp, home to fifty thousand refugees and where he was born and raised, spread out before us fifty meters away. Beyond the camp, the Mediterranean shimmered. This was his Gaza.

❧

Not long after that, I was back in Ramallah at a gathering of the expat community at the home of an American couple. We were planning a demonstration at the U.S. consulate in East Jerusalem, and we spent the morning warming ourselves with tea and strategizing with the human rights lawyers who would monitor the action. Our strategy was to stay within the grounds of the consulate, considered United States property, so we would need no permit and the Israelis could do nothing. Then-Secretary of State George Shultz would be visiting, and our goal was to protest the U.S. military aid to Israel that was being used against the civilian population—our neighbors, colleagues, and students. Despite my knowledge of U.S.-Israeli relations, it was still shocking to pick up a spent tear gas canister and see imprinted in large red letters: MADE IN JAMESTOWN, PENNSYLVANIA, USA.

With most of the plans in place, Ellen, her husband John, and I left for their home to have lunch together. John was an artist and carpenter who taught art at the Friends Girls School and used his manual skills as the campus caretaker. Carrying a bag of rolled-up poster board and markers to use for making signs with the names and ages of Palestinians who had been killed by the Israelis, we walked into the sun that cold, late-winter day.

We walked down Ramallah's main street past merchants shuttering their shops in observance of the noon strike time called by a coalition of the local Palestinian leadership. At the beginning of the intifada, most businesses were closed because demonstrations and army violence brought everyday life to a standstill. Within weeks of the uprising's spontaneous outbreak—triggered by the death of four day laborers from Gaza who were killed when an Israeli truck rammed into their car at the Erez checkpoint—the coalition formed and began issuing calls directing the nonviolent actions that became the strength of the intifada. Demonstrations, the boycott of Israeli goods, popular education committees to counter Israel's closing schools—these were tactics that were called for in the leaflets one would find fluttering in the quiet morning streets every week. When food distribution became problematic and merchants complained of the economic impact of a near-constant general strike, local groups responded with a revised call for shops to be open three hours a day. Each community could decide its own hours, and in Ramallah the hours were nine to noon.

On our way, we stopped at the home of another American teacher to update her on our plans. Ellen left to check in with others, while John and I continued toward their house. It was well past noon, and the only movement in the street was the swaying of the lonely-looking Lebanese cedars scattered among the neighborhood homes. As we descended a hill, I detected the distinctive whiny sound of a jeep's engine approaching from behind. It passed us and slowed, pulling over to the curb just ahead of where we were walking. Then it stopped. I heard the click of changing gears and the crescendo sound of an engine in reverse. Our conversation dwindled as the open back of the jeep approached. The midday sun glinted off two rifle barrels pointed outward. At the other end of the guns, two helmeted soldiers sat expressionless. The plastic bag of poster board rustled in the crisp air, as John shifted it from his outside hand to the other. The silent message exchanged between us was to keep walking, eyes straight ahead. But a few steps later we heard a loud, "Hey! Hello!" We glanced at each other, stopped, and turned.

The driver climbed out from behind the wheel. His sidekick riding shotgun slid out of the other side and stood looking up and down the street.

The driver slowly approached, pushing his Polaroids to the crown of his buzz cut as he stopped in front of us.

"What are you doing here?" he asked, his weight shifting into a near-slouch.

Without waiting for an answer, he looked over our heads and shouted to the back of the jeep.

"*Bo! Ronni! Uri!* Come!"

The two in the back extended their legs out of the jeep and strode toward us, adjusting their gun straps as they turned their heads to spit sunflower-seed shells that skittered and spun across the sidewalk. Loose-limbed and clean-shaven, they looked like they could be my secondary students.

"Passport," the driver refocused his attention, thrusting his palm toward us.

We hesitated, not sure of the wisdom of handing over our U.S. passports to soldiers. Any Palestinian who refused such an order would be beaten or arrested or both.

We handed him our passports.

The driver slid mine between his thumb and index finger, and quickly flipped through the pages, looking for nothing, then back to the photo page. He turned it so my picture and name were right-side up. His eyes flickered between the photo and me.

"Klein?" he finally asked me.

I looked at him but said nothing.

He took a similarly cursory look at John's passport then saw our bags.

"What's that?" he demanded, pointing toward them.

"Art materials," John replied, obviously having thought ahead.

The driver moved toward the bag and gestured to John to open it. As his hand reached in, I noticed a few fine, golden hairs crisscrossing his knuckles. Fishing around, he pulled out the paper and list of Palestinian names. He turned toward me and ordered me to open my handbag, retrieving from it a newsletter, *News from Within*, that I subscribed to from an Israeli human rights organization based in Jerusalem. He took the items and turned back to the jeep.

The two-way radio inside suddenly crackled to life as he began talking rapid-fire Hebrew to someone, presumably a superior, on the other end. The soldiers from the back sat on a low stone wall in front of a house and returned to their sunflower seeds, steadily cracking the shells with strong white teeth, heads cocked, taking us in. I saw the curtains in the house's living room window move and a young man's profile slide barely into view.

The driver returned after a few minutes, barking a quick order. The seed eaters stood up and came toward the jeep. The guy riding shotgun appeared from the other side.

"Get in," the driver motioned toward the jeep.

"Give us our passports," John snapped.

"Get in," he repeated, locking his gaze on John, his jaw tightening.

"Why are you detaining us?" I interjected.

The curtain moved again, but no one was there.

The soldier from the front suddenly spoke, a smile slowly spreading across his face.

"Because the sky is blue," he almost laughed, shifting his eyes upward and spreading his arms in mock reverie.

John took the first step toward the jeep, and I followed. As he climbed in the back, I heard someone call our names. Ellen was running down the hill, having come upon the scene while returning from her errand. Her face tightened as she lurched toward the jeep. One of the seed eaters put himself between me and her, as she snarled at him to get the fuck away from her husband. John was already in the back of the jeep. I locked eyes with Ellen and mouthed the words, "Al-Haq, Al-Haq"—the name of the human rights organization in Ramallah just up the hill. The worst thing that could happen was for the soldiers to arrest all three of us, without anyone else knowing we had been taken.

Ellen's eyes glistened—steel blue eyes that always seemed to sweep the situation before her with an analytical assuredness—and her breathing came in shallow gasps.

"Al-Haq," I repeated, my voice barely a whisper, my eyes pleading.

She bit her lip and took a step back from the jeep. She white-knuckle clutched the strap of her leather shoulder bag, as if it were holding her up. I got into the jeep, and the last of the seed eaters slid in next to me.

The radio squelched again. I could hear the low rumbling tone of the soldier riding shotgun talking into it. The jeep shifted into motion as Ellen receded from view, the look on her face as wan as those lonely cedars. As the jeep rounded a corner, I caught a glimpse of her turning and running up the hill.

We took small side streets I had never been on, cruising past shuttered, silenced homes. The view from the back of the jeep was like looking through a tunnel, the black asphalt moving out from under us as if we were on a treadmill. I wondered what would happen if the jeep was stoned. The soldiers sitting with us said nothing. I could sense their occasional stolen glances, but they looked away when I met their gaze.

Within a few minutes, we were at the Ramallah police station, next to the Friends Boys School where I taught. A guard was waiting for our arrival and opened the metal gate that blocked the driveway. We climbed out of the jeep and were led into the building. As we stepped inside, a young man in jeans and a tee shirt sauntered down stairs that led from the second floor to the front door. The guard who had opened the gate, one of the few Palestinian policemen who worked with the Israelis doing low-level tasks, was seated at the entrance. He rose when he saw us, muttering to himself; his eyes widened and blinked.

A soldier from the jeep took us up the stairs and into a room on the second floor. It had a weathered wooden table with a few chairs scattered around it. A single barred window looked out onto Ramallah's main street. Glancing down, I glimpsed the dry cleaners on the corner that I passed nearly every day. The sign above the shuttered front read "Rami cleaners." *So that's the name of that place!* I thought to myself.

We were told to sit at the table. About fifteen minutes later, a middle-aged man in a pressed army uniform with stripes on his shoulders walked straight-backed into the room. He sat at the table and opened a folder he had in his hand, not yet acknowledging our presence. He shuffled through some papers and pulled out our passports.

John looked at him.

"John Lanzatella," the officer grumbled.

Expecting a reply, his eyes lingered on John.

"Rebecca Klein," he said as his gaze fell on me.

I shifted in my chair.

"What are you doing here?"

"They brought us here," I nodded at our guard, who shifted uncomfortably in his chair.

"No," he refocused on me. "What you are doing *here,*" he insisted, leaning forward and thrusting his hand toward the window that overlooked my dry cleaners.

"I'm a teacher," I blurted out.

"We want to talk to the American consulate," John interjected.

He put down our passports and closed the folder.

"We want to talk to the consulate," John repeated.

He took in John's words and spoke slowly.

"You can talk to me," he said.

My thoughts slowed. And then something began spinning in my mind's far recesses, like one of those seed shells left forgotten, but not unseen, on the afternoon sidewalk.

"Who do you know here?" the officer pressed on.

At that moment a realization burst forth: my address book was in my purse. I hadn't taken it out since my last trip to Gaza, during which I had put in the names and numbers of people I met under the heading "contacts for Zayn Majdalawi." I could feel a small ring of sweat form under my arms as I thought of the officer finding it and punishing us by punishing our Palestinian friends.

"We know lots of people," John retorted. "We are teachers."

"What are their names?"

"Mohammed. Ahmad. Hussein." John began reeling off the most common names in the Arab world. The equivalent of telling someone you know Mary or Bob.

"Mohammed what," the officer's voice rose slightly.

"Don't know," John shrugged.

The sound of a honking horn from the street below resounded slightly in the room.

"We want to talk to the American consulate," I managed. "We're American citizens and we want to speak to our consulate."

The officer replied with a glare.

"We have rights as citizens," John chimed in.

"This isn't a democracy!" the officer shot back, loud enough so that the guard slouching in his chair sat up straight.

A slight smirk curled slowly on John's lips.

The sound of footsteps on the stairs shifted the officer's attention. The Palestinian policeman who had let us in the gate entered and whispered something to him. He stood up and walked to the window.

He looked out for a moment and then turned and disappeared down the stairs, leaving us in the room with the policeman, who smiled weakly. A moment later the officer returned.

"Your wife is here," he announced, indicating John. "She has food for you both. You go first," he nodded toward me.

I grabbed my purse and walked down the stairs.

Ellen stood at the bottom clutching two plastic bags. She turned and smiled.

"Where is John?" Her brow furrowed.

I hugged her and whispered in her ear, "He's upstairs. We're okay. I'm putting my address book in your pocket, keep hugging me."

I quickly unzipped the purse I made sure was wedged between our embrace, slipped out the address book, and found her coat pocket.

"Here are some provisions," she said. I opened the bag and saw a rolled up *shwarma* sandwich, a Cadbury's chocolate bar, and a pack of Marlboro Lights. I smiled and gave her one last hug and hurried up the stairs.

John went to see her when I returned. I looked out of the window and could see several of our expat friends and colleagues crowding around the front gate below. A few Palestinians stood on the side street directly across from the station, wisely keeping their distance.

"Move away," the officer rumbled.

I sat down at the table, and a few minutes later John returned.

The plastic bag John had been carrying was now on the table. The officer carefully laid out the contents on the table.

"What is this?" his eyes moved from the poster board and markers to us.

"Poster board and markers," John replied.

"And this?" he asked, grasping between his thumb and index finger the list of dead Palestinians, holding it up as if it were a dirty rag.

"Names of Palestinians killed during the intifada. It's part of an art project I'm doing," John said and relaxed back in his chair. "I'm an artist."

"An artist," the officer repeated, his chin tipping up.

He shuffled through the other papers before him, briefly looking at the *News from Within* they had plucked from my bag. He slapped the file closed. Dust from the table was caught up in the late afternoon sun that struggled through the window.

"*Beseder,* okay," he muttered, pushing his chair back hard, the metal legs screeching against the tile floor. He exited without another look at us.

We sat for some time, watching the guard half watch us, the light outside fading quickly into a winter's evening. After nearly an hour, the Palestinian policeman came into the room with the officer.

"Come. We're taking you to the Russian Compound. You'll be brought back here for more questioning tomorrow," the officer ordered.

The Russian Compound—so called because the buildings were constructed by an Orthodox society in the nineteenth-century originally to serve Russian pilgrims to the Holy Land—was a notorious West Jerusalem prison. We were being taken there because the Ramallah police station had no separate holding cells for women. And what cells they did have were full.

We were led back out of the station. By now the crowd of friends out front had dwindled with the fading light. Only Ellen and someone from Al-Haq remained. We were taken directly to the lot in back where we were put into a police van. Before shutting the door, another Palestinian policeman tied John's wrists with the white plastic handcuffs we had seen on so many detained Palestinians kneeling in the streets or lined up against walls. The policeman looked at me and shrugged. Later, John told me that the policeman had whispered an apology as he cuffed him.

Ellen ran over to the gate as we pulled out of the lot. I could see her face reddening as she fought back tears. I smiled and waved, trying to look encouraging. John raised his tied hands and blew her a kiss.

The main road between Ramallah and Jerusalem was one we knew well. So when the van veered off onto a side road just outside Ramallah,

I looked over at John, who shook his head. The Palestinian homes of weathered stone and arches appeared fewer and farther between. As the van navigated up a winding road, I looked from side to side, hoping to recognize something in the quickening nightfall. Eventually we stopped at a dark, concrete house. A few minutes later, the young, jeans-clad Palestinian man whom I had seen when we first entered the police station emerged. He slid open the van door hard; it bounced off the side hinge and ricocheted back in his direction. He climbed into the back with the policeman, smiling at me as he did.

An informer...it dawned on me who he was.

The van continued its ascent, and the young man started speaking in Arabic.

"*W'allahee hadoleh ajnabiyat zakiyat kthire.* Those foreign women are really attractive."

My back stiffened and I turned my head from the sound of his voice, leaning as far into the door as I could. He continued talking in hushed tones to the policeman. I could feel beads of sweat forming on my upper lip.

As we crested a hill, the Jewish settlement of Beit El loomed beneath the nearly full moon. Under construction and sparsely inhabited, the settlement's apartments sat on the lip of a huge foundation hole that gaped open like a hungry mouth. The van stopped near one of the buildings, and the driver got out and opened the door. Looking out, I could see half-used bags of cement and tools scattered in the black pit. My breath started coming in shallow heaves. A muffled ringing rose in my ears, and everything suddenly seemed bathed in a harsh white light. For a moment, I thought I might faint. All I could think of was the picture I had seen a few years earlier of the American Maryknoll Sisters in El Salvador—the nuns who worked with the poor in that country and were targeted by government death squads—their bloodied bodies lying in dirt after being raped and killed.

Should I try to run? My mind spun with the limited flight-or-fight options. I realized I could hardly move let alone run, so I climbed slowly out of the van. We started walking toward one of the buildings—a townhouse-style apartment with a red tile roof that could have been in the suburbs of Minneapolis or Tampa. Passing the front window, I saw the flash and twitch of a television lighting up a room. A barrel-chested man with shorn black hair opened the door and a *swoosh* of air made us all look up. For a moment, no one said anything. The man looked past the policeman and the informer to John and me. He barked a quick word in Hebrew to the policeman, who responded with a shrug. He apparently wasn't expecting us.

"*Bo,* come," he grumbled.

We followed him into the house. The collaborator stayed outside. As we crossed the threshold, I glanced up and saw a *mezuzah* nailed at an angle on the doorpost. *May God guard my going and my coming, now and forever.*

We walked into a living room. The two men crossed into an adjoining room, but John and I hesitated when we saw a woman sitting and watching television. She looked up.

Seeing John's handcuffs, she muttered in Hebrew, "*Mazeh?* What's this?" clutching her pink velour bathrobe tighter around her.

A laugh track from an American sitcom swelled into the room. She looked over at her husband, saying something in an unmistakably urgent tone. I noticed that her slippers matched her bathrobe.

"*Beseder,* okay," the husband said from across the room in the same tone he might use if she were asking him to take out the garbage or walk the dog.

A few minutes passed with the lady in pink, John, and I taking in one another, along with snippets of *Diff'rent Strokes.*

The two men finished their conversation and led us out of the room. The man with the buzz cut stopped and turned to John and me.

"I will see you in Ramallah police station tomorrow."

The halting tone of his accented English contrasted with the authority of his Hebrew. He tried to compensate by speaking a little too loudly. With no reply from us, he opened the door to the still night.

We all climbed back into the van and started down the hill. When we reached West Jerusalem, the main drag of Ben-Yehuda Street was crowded with cars and people—kids eating falafel sandwiches, mothers pushing strollers, and young couples kissing while old men watched and smoked. If I could have reached out of the window, I could have touched them. No one even glanced our way.

We finally turned into the Russian Compound, the massive gate shutting with a mechanical *click* behind us, controlled by an unseen guard. The van door opened, and we were led across a lot, past military jeeps, police cars, and an armored personnel carrier. We entered a low building where a sharp-faced man in an Israeli police uniform stood in what looked like a coat-check room. One of the Palestinian police officers handed him our passports. He ordered over our shoestrings, belts, jewelry, and my purse. We were allowed to keep the bags of food that Ellen had brought us. The Israeli jotted down information from our passports into a large log book. Another uniformed man was buzzed in through an adjacent door. They exchanged a few words, and the second man led John away through the secure door. Just before the door clicked behind him, John turned toward me and raised his cuffed hands halfway up and flashed a quick "V" sign. I caught his eye and mustered a smile.

The first officer emerged from behind the "reception desk" and unlocked the door with a set of keys dangling from his belt loop, just like the sheriffs in spaghetti Westerns. As he led me down the hall in silence, we passed a few cells. Weak fluorescent lights flickered off bunk beds and gray cement walls. He stopped, fingered through the keys, and turned the lock in one of the cells. The metal bars groaned open. There was movement inside. Two women sat cross-legged on a bottom bunk. They stood up as we entered.

One of them walked over to the guard and greeted him as he brought me in and shut the door behind us. She threw me a look that settled somewhere between disbelief and curiosity. The woman cocked her head at the guard and before she could ask anything he began talking, his voice rising in rapid, angry Hebrew. Every so often I could make out words like "Ramallah" and "Falesteeni." The inmate said nothing, her dark bed-head curls bouncing as her gaze swiveled between me and the guard.

Finally, he stopped. A rustling came from a far corner bunk bed and then a muffled moan. The guard seemed to make a joke at which only he laughed. He left and slammed the cell door behind him.

The clang hung in the cell for a few moments, uninterrupted. The curly-haired woman stepped toward me and said, "I'm Daphne."

I realized I had been holding my breath. I exhaled and replied, "I'm Rebecca."

The other woman came over and introduced herself as Eva. When she smiled, I noticed one front tooth was missing.

Daphne said something to Eva in Hebrew, pointing to the bunk from where the earlier sound had come. Eva gathered up some blankets and a pillow from the bottom bed. It was then that I noticed the faint outline of a human form wrapped in a dark blanket in the top bunk, curled in a fetal position with its back toward us.

"Our other friend over there," Daphne said, indicating the bunk, "puked in the bottom bed. Sorry."

Daphne and I stood in silence, looking at each other and then at Eva, who was making a pallet on the floor for me. Unable not to ask any longer I said, "So what did the guard say to you?"

She made a face and shrugged.

"Oh, something like you are helping terrorists in Ramallah. You hate Jews. And that they're going to throw you out of the country or put you in prison for two years. Something like that."

The faint light hanging above us seemed to dim further.

She waved her hand in the air.

"Don't worry," she said, almost chuckling, "this is how we Jews think."

I blinked hard. My head, inclined slightly forward as she talked, retracted involuntarily a few inches.

She moved past me back to her bunk. "Why *are* you here?" she asked, settling her back against a pillow that she had propped against the concrete wall.

"Well, the truth is I'm a teacher at the Friends School in Ramallah. Another teacher and I were picked up by the army when we were walking in the street."

It was then that I remembered I was still clutching my bag from Ellen.

"Do you want some chocolate?" I offered, opening the bag and picking out the contents one-by-one.

"*Sigareeyot!*" Daphne exclaimed, grabbing the pack of Marlboros. Eva rushed over as Daphne rummaged through the bag, asking if there was a light.

"Inside the cigarette pack."

I pulled out the matches and lit her cigarette. They puffed away, giggling and licking chocolate off of their fingers.

"Thank you," Eva said through a mouthful of chocolate.

"She is here because she likes to take things that aren't hers," Daphne looked at Eva, who laughed nervously, covering her mouth full of chocolate. "I sold drugs to a fucking police," Daphne snarled through a hard drag.

Blowing the smoke out in a silver stream, she pointed the cigarette toward the bunk across the cell.

"She killed her boyfriend. And took too many drugs."

I stopped eating and put my sandwich back in the black plastic bag.

After a while I bedded down on the pallet Eva had made and tried to sleep. Despite her best efforts, I could feel the cold hard floor through the blankets, which reeked faintly of vomit. The toilet—more like a porcelain bucket without a normal toilet's lid, seat, and tank—was a few feet away from me and open on three sides. The only way to avoid the odor wafting my way was to bury my face in the pillow, making it hard to breathe.

After about an hour of lying there in the dark, the incongruous sound of a man's scream seeped through the walls like an aural specter. My body stiffened and I sat up straight. I looked around, but Daphne and Eva were asleep. A few minutes later, another wail. A wave of nausea rolled through me. I turned on my side and pulled my knees to my chest, opening my mouth and gulping air. I lay alert and motionless. The rest of the night passed in silence.

How had Zayn endured fifteen years?

It seemed like I had just dozed off when the metal clank of the door jolted me awake. A new guard yelled at the other women to wake up. Groaning and muttering curses, they slowly came to life, using the toilet and splashing water on their faces.

We were led down the hall and into a small room with bolted-down metal tables and benches. At one end of the dining room was a serving window. Next to it were stacked orange plastic trays and boxes of white plastic spoons and napkins the consistency of tissue paper. About half a dozen other women lined up at the window where a young man served food: hard-boiled eggs, white bread, and small cups of yogurt. Thin coffee served in plastic cups was available upon request. When my turn came, I pushed my tray forward in the window and a paper plate of food was set on it. The boy looked up as he was about to push the tray back to me and stopped mid-gesture. He angled his head and smiled sheepishly, the faint beginnings of a moustache arching above his full lips.

He turned to someone in the kitchen behind him and said in Arabic, "*Tal'a!* Look at this!"

Waiting for him to push the tray within reach, I hesitated but then said, "*Marhaba.* Hello." His smile almost became a laugh and he handed me my tray.

"*Stanee.* Wait," he said quickly, and reached to one side. He placed an extra slice of bread and second cup of yogurt on my tray.

"*Shukran.* Thanks," I smiled and took a seat.

As Daphne, Eva and I ate, another woman was escorted into the dining room by a hulking female guard. Daphne and Eve jumped up from the bench when they saw her.

"Rula," they waved her over. She acknowledged them as the guard unlocked her handcuffs. She cheerfully greeted the young man serving food and made her way to our table, shadowed by the guard who stood against a wall about a foot and a half away.

"This is Rula," Daphne introduced us. She immediately focused her attention on Rula, peppering her with questions in Hebrew. Rula answered succinctly, smiling the whole time. Every now and then her eyes shifted to me. Daphne finally got up to get more coffee, and Rula scooted closer to me on the bench. She was the only one in a prison uniform—a gravel-colored jumpsuit that hung off of her petite frame. Her jet-black hair fell in shoulder-length curls. She had bright eyes the color of toasted almonds.

"Where are you from?" she said in perfect English.

Recognizing her Palestinian name, I told her in Arabic that I was American but lived in Ramallah, where I was a teacher at the Friends School.

"Ramallah?" she responded in surprise.

Before we could continue, both her guard and the one who had escorted us to the dining room walked toward us, giving an order. Everyone stood and shuffled toward the garbage cans, emptying their plastic trays and tossing them up on the counter.

She smiled at me and whispered, "Take care. I will see you later."

Her guard wrapped her delicate wrists in the plastic cuffs and yanked hard.

Back in the cell, Daphne and Eva were preparing themselves for a court appearance, hurriedly washing, brushing teeth, and helping each other pick out clean clothes from a pile on Daphne's bed. Soon the cell door opened again and in walked Rula with her guard. Daphne and Eva rushed toward her, leading her over to their beds. Daphne pulled out a black plastic bag from under hers and laid out a hairbrush, comb, make-up compact, and tube of lipstick. Rula went to work first on Daphne's hair, expertly braiding her unruly curls into a relatively smooth French braid. Eva's hair—smoother and a lighter brown than Daphne's—was pulled tight at the nape of her neck and twisted into a soft bun. While Rula worked, the girls used the mirror of the compact to swipe face powder over their skin, blemished and scarred by a life which I had barely glimpsed. They traced pink lipstick over their chapped lips as the finishing touch.

Before they left, the guard from the night before reappeared and motioned for me to come with him. I said a quick goodbye to my cellmates and wished them luck.

"*Diri balik 'ala halik.* Take care of yourself," I bid Rula goodbye.

"*Inti kaman,* you too," she smiled back

I learned later that Rula was eventually convicted of killing a soldier in Jerusalem and sentenced to life in prison. In 1997 she was released in a prisoner exchange.

John and I were reunited at the "reception desk," our shoelaces and other possessions returned to us. John had spent the night in a cell with Hasidic Jews who had been arrested for stoning cars breaking the Sabbath.

We were taken directly to the Ramallah police station, where the man we had surprised at the settlement—Major Yossi—waited. The conversation soon turned to him trying to talk John into signing a confession in Hebrew, a language he did not understand. After about ten minutes of John refusing to sign, one of the Palestinian policemen rushed into the room and whispered to the major. He rubbed his temples and stood up, pushing the page of Hebrew aside. He headed toward the door but stopped suddenly at the window and shouted something down the stairs. A few minutes later he returned with a man in a suit and wire-rim glasses who offered us his business card: David Schneider, United States Consular Officer, East Jerusalem.

The consul asked us some cursory questions about our detention and treatment, jotting down notes in a small notebook he pulled from his breast pocket, like someone making a grocery list. He produced our passports, which we hadn't seen since the Russian Compound, and explained that the Friends School had posted a five thousand shekel bond, in case we were ever called to court to answer the allegations against us: inciting the population to riot. Palestinians had endured over two decades of military occupation in the West Bank and Gaza. But it was a young Jewish teacher from Cincinnati and an Italian-American artist from Rochester who apparently were responsible for inciting them to revolt.

After handing us our passports, the consul turned to Major Yossi, who had been pacing between our conversation and the window, nervously eyeing the street below.

"Just get them out of here before there's a riot," he said to the consul.

Emerging from the building I saw what he meant. A group of about thirty friends, colleagues, and people I didn't know were milling about the front gate. As we emerged, I saw Ellen and Nadia push up against the metal barrier and stick their hands through the bars. I took Nadia's and Ellen grabbed John's as we waited for someone to unlock the gate. As it opened, I heard a voice shouting through a bullhorn for everyone to disperse.

We did. Gladly.

The AP wire story from the Occupied Territories that day led with our arrest. It identified us, our lawyer, our employer, and even quoted family members and our congressmen, who were demanding the Israelis apologize. Buried next to the last paragraph was another news item from the same day: two Palestinians, unnamed, were shot dead by Israeli troops in the West Bank town of Jenin.

To be sure, those twenty-four hours were frightening and the charges against us utterly ridiculous. But that in the U.S. media our experience overshadowed the death of two Palestinians elicits in me a mixture of shame, embarrassment, and anger to this day. I know how their loved ones mourned.

My becoming acquainted with Gaza was like the blossoming of a romance—the more I saw and got to know, the more I wanted to know. One hub of it was Tawfiq Salem's third floor law office. The dust and sand that blew in from Omar al-Mukhtar Street below collected on the wooden coffee table that sat in front of Tawfiq's desk. The table was perpetually littered with half-empty Arabic coffee cups, their powdery remnants drying in the Gaza heat. They competed for space with ashtrays overflowing with cigarettes—some smoked down to the butt and others crushed out almost whole. The breeze that would occasionally blow up from the sea sifted the ashes onto the tabletop.

Rarely would I find Tawfiq in his office. Karim, Tawfiq's partner, was who I came to expect sitting behind the desk. Perhaps in his late twenties, Karim's cherub face suited him well in what seemed to be his primary role—doling out scraps of information to detainees' families in various stages of distress. Tawfiq would often arrive from military court, if I waited long enough, case files bulging under his arm, black barrister robes billowing in his wake, and sweat condensing on his brow.

As Karim relayed phone messages and reported who had stopped by, Tawfiq rifled through his desk drawer.

"*Endek* Panadol? Do you have any Panadol?" he asked Karim, searching for the local Tylenol equivalent and not giving any indication that he was listening.

"*Bajeeblek*. I'll go get you some."

Karim turned and disappeared down the hallway, his quick steps echoing on the stone stairs before Tawfiq had the chance to call him back.

My first visit to this office was the trip with my Friends School colleagues. But on this late spring day in 1988, there would be others coming with a slightly different agenda. A group of Israeli peace activists, intellectuals, and writers would be visiting. Zayn and a friend had arranged to meet the group at Erez checkpoint, a few miles north, and bring them to Tawfiq's office. Zayn had asked me to join them.

As the late morning meeting time passed, I smoked and paced between the coffee table and the window overlooking the street. They appeared early afternoon—Galit, Shai, Ilana, Dorit—chattering in Hebrew, a language whose once-familiar staccato had been largely nudged aside in my brain by the thick rise and fall of Arabic. The sound of Israelis speaking Hebrew in that room unsettled me like a stray bird darting through the window. I followed its sound and trajectory as it bounced off the walls, trying to orient it in a place that it didn't belong.

We all introduced ourselves, and Karim served coffee on the table that was unusually clean. Hebrew swirled low among the Israelis; they spoke mostly English with the Palestinians, with Zayn translating Hebrew words that the Israelis couldn't. The flow of the conversation took on the aura of a collective onion peeling.

"Tawfiq, how many political prisoners do you defend?" "Do any actually face charges?" "When is there curfew?" "How is life in the camps?"

Subsequent layers were more tender and harder to get under, the separating out having to be done just so to avoid damaging what lay beneath.

"Have you ever been arrested? Do you believe in a two-state solution?"

In the car on the way to lunch at Tawfiq's home, they all perched on the edge of their seats, heads swiveling to take in the street scenes of Gaza. The crush of humanity—street vendors, shoppers, schoolchildren, day laborers and businessmen on their way to work—mixed with donkey-drawn carts and the occasional army patrol. Seeing the surge of activity in Souk al-Fres, the main open-air market, it was easy to discern Gaza's place as one of the most densely populated on the planet. The same scene could be cleared in less than five minutes with the thud of a stone against a patrolling jeep and the subsequent crackle of gunfire.

During the ride back to Erez after lunch, the Israelis were quiet.

"What a place," one of them murmured. He registered a passing army jeep with a sigh. "What are we doing here?"

Before departing, invitations were extended by the visitors to their Palestinian hosts to visit them where they lived—Jerusalem and Tel Aviv. When I heard Zayn give the standard, noncommittal Arabic reply, "*Insha' allah.* God willing," I thought, *There's no way*!

I was wrong.

Within a couple of weeks as the summer heat bloomed, Zayn and I were in yet another *serveece,* this time headed for Tel Aviv. Taking Zayn's car with Ramallah license plates into an Israeli city for an extended time was problematic. Cars from the Occupied Territories had blue plates, easily distinguishable from the yellow Israeli ones, making them an easy target. The *serveece* dropped us at the Tel Aviv central bus station, from where we were to take a local taxi. Before we hailed one, Zayn warned me not to speak Arabic. He instructed our driver in Hebrew, based on Galit's directions, and soon we were ringing her doorbell.

Galit and her husband Shai were journalists at the liberal daily newspaper *Ha'aretz.* Before leaving the bus station, Zayn had bought several of the largest candy bars he could find for their four-year-old son Daniel. His face flared into a smile when Zayn handed him the chocolate. There was Arabic coffee and Gaza sweets for the hosts.

In Tel Aviv the coffee of political conversation was Nescafe. Zayn's was black, two sugars. With most of the Hebrew conversation eluding me, I could only follow the outlines of what was being discussed by observing intently and catching words like "*keebush*" (occupation) *khamas* (Hamas), and Arafat. At one point Galit seemed to tense. She kept repeating a phrase, her voice rising a bit each time she intoned the words, "*ata...khilofee hashovim.* You...prisoner exchange?" After the second or third repetition, Zayn began giggling and nodding, his laughter rising with Galit's voice until he was gasping for air. Her face finally broke into a smile as she reached for a cigarette. She inhaled deeply and sighed.

"Oy vey!"

As the sun traced its path along the white walls of their airy flat, the only lull in the conversation was when Galit rose to boil more water or Daniel checked in from the television playing loudly in the next room. When Shai excused himself to prepare for his overnight editing shift at the newspaper, Galit suggested we go to the nearby city center for dinner. When Zayn hesitated, she at first assumed it was a matter of money.

"Don't worry," she insisted. "You are our guests!"

Nervous laughter delayed Zayn's response.

"*Ma?* What is it?" Galit asked.

I could hear someone in Danny's cartoon screeching to a dramatic halt.

While I couldn't understand his explanation in Hebrew, the evolving expression on Galit's face told me Zayn was explaining to her that Palestinians from the Occupied Territories weren't allowed overnight in Israel without a pass. Being on the street at night could be dangerous for him, if we were stopped and had to show an ID. Galit's brow knit together over her narrowed eyes. She was at an unusual loss for words. Then she wasn't.

"*B'emet*. Really?"

She stomped down the hall to find Shai, her hands flying in arcs around her head as if batting away the sudden annoyance, anger, and confusion.

They had literally invited a Palestinian to break the law. And he had accepted.

"Shai! Have you heard of such a thing? What are we going to do?"

Zayn and I looked at each other but said nothing. Their voices bounced down the hall in an odd sort of dance: Galit's loud words, quick and sharp, leading the softer, even tone of Shai's response. After several minutes, Galit came back down the hall, veering off into the kitchen from where there soon emerged the sounds of cupboards opening and pans rattling.

In the *serveece* on the way back to Gaza the next day, Zayn relayed to me some of the conversation from the night before, he and Galit having stayed up talking long past my attempts to understand what they were saying to each other.

"Some of the things she said were so naïve, silly even," I said, shaking my head. "How do you have the patience to talk to her about the most basic realities of the occupation?"

He turned to look at me, his head at a slight cant. Behind him I could see the morning sunlight reflecting off the high rises of Tel Aviv.

"Who else are we going to talk to?"

❧

As the intifada intensified, schools remained closed despite sporadic efforts to open them. That spring of 1988, I got word while in Gaza that the Friends Schools were going to defy the Israeli military's orders and reopen.

I returned to Ramallah and arrived at the school early the next day, unsure of what I'd encounter there. Students were filtering into the main entrance, arriving individually or in small groups from the various surrounding villages, but I could tell by their numbers that attendance was light. The headmaster, Khalil Mahshi, stood on the stone steps leading to the entrance's archway, nervously working a string of prayer beads as he eyed the street in front of the school. It had the geographic misfortune of being located next to the Ramallah police station.

The ring of the school bell signaled the beginning of first period. Its shrill, relentless sound, normally irritating, both startled and comforted me after so many months. A handful of ninth graders settled into my social studies class, greeting me with the customary, "Hi, Miss Rebecca." The students talked excitedly—some of them hadn't seen each other since December, when the intifada had erupted and the Israeli authorities had closed all schools. They began regaling each other with tales of demonstrations in their villages and raids by soldiers. I heard one of them recount the chilling details of a seventh grader who had been detained and beaten. Spotting him in the hallway later, I could see the bruises and cuts on his arms and face still pushing shades of red and blue through his olive skin. When I smiled at him, he lowered his head.

After a few minutes of sharing stories, I began reviewing the last lesson on the civil rights movement in the U.S. Less than halfway through the period, the sound of a siren pierced the air. A muffled voice crackled through a bullhorn. The only words I could make out were *mantaqa mughlaqa askaria*—closed military zone. The army had arrived.

For an instant the students and I froze. I turned from the blackboard and looked at them. Then all at once we rushed toward the classroom door. Looking beyond the scattering pupils and teachers already in the hall, I could see through the open main door two army jeeps parked in front of the school, blocking the entrance. Khalil, the headmaster, was on the front steps, calmly arguing with a soldier who was shoving a piece of white paper in his face—the order declaring the school a closed military zone. As the soldier gesticulated, the M-16 slung over his shoulder swayed, the barrel grazing Khalil's thigh with each forward motion. Students started surging for the door. Some of the elementary kids were crying. Khalil yelled to the teachers to take the students back to class.

While Khalil negotiated with the soldiers, small groups of students were released from the classrooms and escorted by their teachers past the soldiers at the front gate. Outside of the school there was already a pile of cars, *serveece,* and buses sucking in groups of children as horns blared. One woman abandoned her car half-parked in the traffic lane, jumping out and yelling her children's names. Her waving arms clattered with gold jewelry and her high heels clicked furiously as she rushed to the sidewalk to scoop up her kids. It was on this day that my teaching career effectively came to an end.

❧

With schools still closed, my teaching contract expired in June. By then I was spending most of my time in Gaza and was hired as a researcher for Save the Children to work on a report about the status of children during the intifada. Soon afterwards, I gave up my apartment in Ramallah and moved into a flat on the top floor of what was then, at seven stories, the tallest building in Gaza—*amarat al mohendesseen,* the engineers' building. In exchange for my flat, I gave English lessons to the building's owner and his wife.

After the trip to Tel Aviv, Zayn and I spent more time together. I began to notice things about him that had escaped me before. The first of these was his fingers. Slim and supple, almost the color of caramel, there was a delicacy about them that struck me one day as I observed him talking with a friend. Those fingers didn't hold a cigarette; they gently curved around it, appearing to caress it as he moved it to and from his mouth. When he spoke, they fanned through the air with the lightness of palm fronds in a breeze. But I could see their strength when he worked in the garden or held a pen. I had never seen a man with such beautiful hands.

In the weeks that followed, he introduced me to his Gaza. There were friends from prison to meet, along with the extended families of those friends and other political comrades. Accompanying it all was the food special to Gaza: fish baked or fried a dozen different ways, the sumptuous *qidre* made of rice, lamb, and chickpeas, and of course the *shatte* hot sauce Gazans were rumored to put on everything.

Without warning one day, I was taken to the home of one of his sisters who lived in Sheikh Radwan—a neighborhood that had been built specifically for Shati refugee camp residents to persuade them to move out of the camp. Sheikh Radwan also became the second refugee home to those whose first camp shelters had been destroyed in the early 1970s, when the Israelis crushed the armed resistance to the occupation and bulldozed large swaths of the camp. But the vast majority of camp residents refused to move, because in doing so they would abandon their right to return to the villages from which they had been expelled in 1948.

Zayn's sister Fatima was an older, taller, female version of Zayn. Quick to laugh and to joke, she had a broad, strong face that seemed the perfect frame to her easy smile. She married barely out of high school and had four children. The easy interaction between Fatima and Zayn was more like that of buddies rather than siblings, cracking jokes at each other's expense, each one's voice louder than the other's. With his younger, gentler brother Lutfi, Zayn was harshly and relentlessly critical. But somehow with Fatima there was an emotional parity that Lutfi—who was university educated, politically involved, and in many ways had more in common with Zayn—would never achieve. Up until then, I had spent more time observing Zayn's interaction with Lutfi, so seeing him relax and joke with his sister—an expression of love on his own terms —brought out another dimension of him that I hadn't yet encountered. Her face lit up when he entered the house to visit, and I could hear the twinge of concern and sadness in her voice when he rose to leave.

"*Deer balak alla' halak.* Take care of yourself," were always her parting words.

Even though I had my own apartment, we returned to Zayn's house next to the camp more frequently after these visits with friends or relatives. Lutfi was often there too, escaping his wife after their recurring quarrels—but not always. When Lutfi was there, the three of us would spend the evenings watching television—reruns of *Dallas* interspersed with Israeli news broadcasts. When he wasn't, Zayn and I would bring chairs out onto the veranda that gave us a view of the camp and the Mediterranean beyond, watching the crimson sun sink into the sea. We would drink tea and talk—about politics, our families, mutual friends—studiously avoiding the unspoken feelings developing between us. After the TV program ended or our conversation reached as far as it could for the evening, it was often after the eight o'clock curfew so we would retire to our respective beds—his being the sofa and mine a mattress on the floor in one of the two bedrooms.

One day after work, Zayn picked me up and we had yet another Gaza lunch with friends. We returned to his house earlier in the afternoon than usual. The neighborhood had the stillness of the midday siesta, when people slept through the heat in order to survive it.

As I washed my hands in a sink that stood outside the bedrooms, I noticed that the room where Lutfi usually slept was empty. I dried my hands and as I turned to walk back down the hall, there stood Zayn.

Without a word he embraced me and kissed me hard, the softness of his mouth surprising, given the passion that was suddenly exploding between us. After the initial kiss I pulled back a bit and looked at him, not quite knowing what to say. He looked at me with a mixture of fear and longing. Saying nothing I leaned into him, and the awkwardness of the first embrace relaxed as our bodies consciously pressed closer.

We moved into "my" bedroom and down onto the foam mattress. For several minutes we lay together fully clothed, kissing and adjusting to the feel of each other's body so close. Our clothes came off, already wet by the heat outside and inside the room. There was an ease with which our bodies fit together, like a puzzle piece locking into place. There was a smoothness, a naturalness of the rhythm between us that remains, until today, a surprise to me.

❦

The temperature rose in Gaza with each passing week that I walked the path separating the garden from the gravel at his house. Zayn gave me a key and I would often go there after work.

One oppressive August day while peeling potatoes that I intended to fry for lunch, I was startled by the rattling of the high metal gate that closed off the walkway to the house. It was a harsher sound than the usual clank and scrape I was expecting with Zayn's arrival. I headed out of the kitchen and onto the porch, where I came face-to-face with a soldier.

I'm not sure who was more shocked at seeing the other standing there in the midday Gaza sun—the awkward teenager with bad acne, or the Jewish Midwesterner wondering if I was going to be arrested again. Looking at the M-16 slung over his shoulder, I imagined the sound it made banging against the metal gate when he scaled his way over. He looked down and his brow knit. I followed his gaze. There I stood, facing the world's third strongest army, potato and peeler in hand.

Beyond him the gate was open and at least half a dozen soldiers flooded into the garden, trampling the eggplant and basil. Others ran into the house and up the stairs to the roof, searching for Zayn. In the midst of them was an older man dressed in a tangerine polo shirt and blue jeans: the Shin Bet intelligence officer. He barked something in Hebrew to the soldier still staring at my potato peeler. The soldier moved into the house as Major Polo Shirt calmly asked me where Zayn was.

"He's not here. I don't know where he is," I managed in reply.

He clearly wasn't expecting this. Intelligence reports apparently had said nothing about the American girlfriend of the Palestinian, who, from that moment, was a wanted man.

Major Polo yelled more orders and stepped away to talk into his walkie-talkie. I was torn between heading toward the sound of the banging closet doors and crashing furniture coming from inside the house and staying outside to see what his next order would be. After finishing his conversation, he shouted one final time, and moments later the soldiers filed out, guns swaying and bumping against their thighs. Still on the veranda, I listened to their jeeps speed away.

Silence filled the neighborhood. I turned and walked back into the house.

In the living room, papers littered the floor, and the crunch of glass followed me into the bedroom. The broken door of an armoire squeaked pitifully in protest, swinging on its remaining intact hinge and holding on for dear life. The few things I had brought to Zayn's house were undisturbed, save for two missing music cassettes. I imagined the patrol singing along to Springsteen's *Born in the USA* and belting out Cat Stevens's *Peace Train* between house raids.

❧

After the army raid, Zayn stopped going to his house, spending most nights at my apartment to avoid arrest. The Israelis were rounding up masses of men in their attempt to quell the uprising; it was estimated that ten percent of the male population was in prison at the time. Because of his past, Zayn was a target. Another arrest could mean an indefinite time in prison without charge or trial under the Israeli military justice system.

A daytime curfew had been imposed during one particularly turbulent week in late August. Lying in the bedroom of my seventh-story flat, I tried to sleep away the midday heat. Zayn lay next to me, his head propped against the headboard, smoking and listening to an Israeli news broadcast. A reporter began interviewing a woman, and suddenly Zayn started muttering repeatedly in Hebrew, "*nachon,* correct," as if she were talking to him. I asked him to translate.

"She is saying that we, Palestinians and Israelis, need to stop killing each other's children."

Some of us are lucky enough to have etched in our memories, decades later, the moment we know not only that we've fallen in love but also the reasons why. What kind of man is born and raised in a refugee camp, lives his entire life under foreign military rule, spends nearly a decade and half as a political prisoner, and still thinks about the children of both the occupier and occupied? The answer, I would learn over the years, is a very complicated one. What I saw that day was a man who had not let the devastating, scarring events of his life so far narrow his vision of the future. A man whose suffering had in some ways opened him up, rather than closed him down. That was the man with whom I fell in love.

A couple of weeks later we sat on the veranda of his house, waiting for twilight to usher in something like cool air. Earlier in the day, I had received a message from Zayn asking me to come there. I couldn't understand why he wanted to meet at the house, given the risk that posed. As we sat at an angle to each other, our knees close but not touching, I noticed he looked almost sad—the lines around his mouth drawn slightly downward, his eyes stilled of their usual playful bounce.

"It is time for me to marry," he finally managed. "I hope that person will be you, but if not I need to know."

For Zayn, proposing marriage was more like making a closing argument.

"There may be someone better for you out there, but you may never find him," he posited, his turquoise eyes darting.

He had been born and raised until age seventeen in a refugee camp, followed by fifteen years as a political prisoner. Romantic gestures weren't exactly his thing.

More convincing for me was the unit of Israeli soldiers that had come crashing over the garden wall a few weeks earlier. *It would only be a matter of time.* When the inevitable happened and he was captured, I would need a way to stay connected to him that was recognized by both the military authorities and Palestinian society. Over the past several months, I had begun to realize what a unique, complex person Zayn was.

I wanted to know more, to be part of whatever fate awaited him, I would need to be his wife.

In a way, you could say it was a shotgun wedding.

4
Shotgun Wedding

With three older sisters, I had lots to feed my imagination of what my wedding would be. My oldest sister Paula had converted to Catholicism to marry in a cavernous church on the west side of town. I was the obvious pick to be her flower girl: I was six years old at the time and took directions well.

I wore a robin's egg blue dress, with a slightly darker blue satin ribbon that encircled me above the waist and ended in a flat bow in front. It had never occurred to me that a bow could, or should, be tied in the front of a piece of clothing and have nothing to do with keeping it fastened. It was an utterly superfluous accessory, and I loved it.

Donning satin shoes dyed to match my dress and white gloves, I was charged with carrying a small woven basket of rose petals and scattering a dainty trail before the bride. This was harder than you might think. I had to accomplish this while walking at an unnaturally slow pace, executed by taking one step forward, bringing the lagging leg to settle next to the front one and then moving it forward, simultaneously leaving a sprinkle rather than a clump of petals behind. This deft move was to be executed on a sheet of satin laying a snowy trail from the church vestibule to the altar. Satin, I soon learned, when walked on by anyone weighing more than a pound, wrinkled and caught one's shoes.

No one told me that a Catholic wedding also included a full mass before the actual marriage ceremony. So, not counting the time it took all the bridesmaids, groomsmen, and finally the bride to make it down the aisle, I stood an hour and a half at the altar holding that dainty basket in my gloved hands—and trying with all my six-year-old might to hold my bladder. The Latin proved a distraction for a while, not having heard many foreign languages at that point in my life. I fixated on the huge, bleeding Jesus on the cross hovering above us, but only in an accident-by-the-side-of-the-road kind of way. The disappointment of each Hail Mary and sign of the cross that I thought would signal the end of the ceremony, but didn't, only intensified my urge to pee. As the ivory-robed priest recited something in the general direction of my sister and soon-to-be brother-in-law, a warm trickle made its way down my legs, soaking my lace ankle socks and pooling in my dyed-to-match shoes. I don't know if I was more horrified or relieved.

I stood as still as I could, hoping the puddle wouldn't spread and that no one would notice. When the ceremony ended, my mother noticed my hesitancy to walk back down the aisle. Then she saw that look on my face. Whisking me out a side door next to the altar, we beelined to the nearest bathroom. She snapped brown paper towels, one after the other, out of the white metal wall dispenser, wet them under the running faucet, and dabbed at my legs and the hem of my dress. The dyed-to-match shoes and lace anklets landed with a *thunk* in the trash can. Fortunately, the wedding reception was about ten minutes from our house. I sat silently in the back seat of our old Ford Fairlane as my aunt drove me home for dry underwear and shoes.

By the time my third sister, Jan, married, I was almost sixteen, had started dating, and occasionally indulged in fantasies about my own wedding. Jan's wedding dress and veil hung in my parents' closet in the weeks leading up to the September ceremony, the stiff protective plastic rustling loudly every time the sliding door was opened or closed.

Bored one summer day, I was in my parents' bedroom, quietly sliding open the closet door. Her lacey mantilla veil hung separately from the dress on its own miniature hanger. I carefully reached in one hand and slid the veil off the silk-wrapped hanger on which it lay, not daring to actually take out the entire ensemble. Standing in front of my mother's dresser, with its half-length mirror, I held the rough-edged veil between my thumb and forefinger on each hand and lifted it onto my head. It fluttered slightly as it settled on my dark hair. The cream-colored lace contrasted nicely with my late-August tan. It kept sliding off, so I found a couple bobby pins in my mother's dresser drawer and fastened the veil to my hair. Turning, I admired my image in both left and right profile. *Simple lace,* I thought to myself, smiling at my image in the mirror. *Yes, simple lace.*

❧

When my time to marry came ten years later, satin and lace weren't an option. I had been thinking about what I would wear since we had decided a few weeks earlier to marry. In Gaza, standard bridal attire consisted of layers of poufy white polyester and dramatically beaded taffeta —outfits I could no more picture myself wearing than I could picture myself showing up naked. But there would be no wedding dress shopping, since we had to keep the marriage secret given Zayn's circumstance.

A few days before the wedding, I was visiting Dr. Riad and his wife Um Ayman, close friends of Zayn who were among the first people he introduced me to in Gaza. They had agreed to host the ceremony, and Um Ayman had offered to lend me her wedding dress. Initially, I declined, muttering something about not wanting to bother her. She had three boys and was pregnant with her fourth, so I couldn't exactly use the excuse that she should save it for her daughter's wedding. But she was persistent. Shortly after arriving, I was following Um Ayman up the stairs and holding my breath while she excitedly dug through her closet. Soon she emerged beaming at me and offering up an incandescent mass of material that exuded the unmistakable aroma of mothballs.

I don't know if it was the thought of what I would feel like encased in what was essentially several yards of white plastic wrap in ninety-plus degree heat or what I would look like in it, but I immediately began to sweat. I struggled into the dress, which consisted of an hourglass bodice sporting beaded flowers, flowing into a skirt that trailed snowy layers that seemed to shimmer in the harsh fluorescent light. I turned to face the mirror so Um Ayman could zip me in, taking in the image of me as a dollop of melting whipped cream. While she struggled with the zipper, for the first time in my life I was grateful for those ten pounds I had always wanted to lose.

❦

Our wedding day dawned clear, as do most days in Gaza. But in the air there was already a hint of the sweltering heat to come. It was October 6, 1988. I would soon turn twenty-six. In choosing this day for our marriage, my husband-to-be—a longtime political activist—somehow had forgotten it was the anniversary of the Yom Kippur War, which would mean a general strike. No vehicles other than ambulances and UN cars could be on the roads. I would be walking to my wedding.

The longer I stood staring into my open closet, the less sure I was about my decision. I hadn't the time or ability to think this through and just went with my gut. My favorite outfit at the time was a red cotton skirt with a black striped pattern woven in, edged with a smattering of white and yellow. I paired this with a black shirt and a wide black belt that cinched through a large silver ring. It had that late eighties "ethnic" look—progressive chic. It was, I realized when I later saw the look on Um Ayman's face upon arriving for my "big day," the anti-Gaza wedding dress.

Accompanied by Lutfi, my soon-to-be brother-in-law, I set out around mid-morning for the mile plus walk. Trudging through the sandy streets of Gaza, I immediately regretted my color choice as I came to understand why you shouldn't wear black in the sun. The scent of jasmine and bougainvillea wafted through the deserted streets, eerily quiet except for the occasional flapping sound made by the large blue-and-white UN flags planted on the agency's vehicles that crept through the streets, monitoring the tension. In an attempt to avoid army patrols, Lutfi led the way through unfamiliar backstreets. Trusting his knowledge of the area, I just followed, not knowing how we would end up where we were supposed to be.

I hadn't seen much of Zayn since his proposal. To protect me, he spent less time at my apartment, sleeping in a different place each night. He was to meet us at Dr. Riad's house. I pushed away the thought that Zayn might not show up and what could happen to prevent him from doing so, as I hopelessly attempted to keep up with Lutfi and to keep that damn black shirt from plastering itself to my body.

East across the expanse of two-story cinderblock buildings that formed the middle-class neighborhood of Gaza City, a plume of thick black smoke drifted into the startling blue sky— charcoal on pastel. As if on cue, minutes later the gunning engine of an army jeep could be heard before it could be seen roaring toward the barricade of burning tires. The deep thud of a fired tear gas canister was followed by the acrid scent of the fumes that carried on the wind. I picked up my pace to avoid the effects of the gas and wound my way deeper into unknown territory.

The jasmine vine reached down over the large metal gate to greet us as Lutfi and I pressed the intercom button and waited for Um Ayman to buzz us in. The gate was part of a privacy wall that was standard for most middle-class houses in Gaza, and like many this opened onto a well-tended garden, small patio and driveway. Passing through the garden and entering the house, we could hear the dialogue of an Arabic soap opera spilling into the hall. Dr. Riad's mother lived on the ground floor and could usually be found watching TV from her sofa, which was strategically placed for her to observe the comings and goings of her son's and daughter-in-law's visitors. The door to her apartment was closed only when she was upstairs with Dr. Riad's family.

"*Sabah al kheir, ya hajee.* Good morning," Lutfi and I greeted her in near unison.

"*Sabah al noor! Tefudulu.* Good morning! Come in," Um Riad's cigarette-deepened voice replied.

Smoke from her skinny brown cigarillo curled up from the ashtray and seemed to dance in the late morning light. She looked up from her show and grinned widely at us from under a thin scarf. Her large gray eyes never hesitated to meet one's gaze. Even seated alone watching an afternoon soap opera, she conveyed the authority of a family matriarch.

"*Shukran.* Thank you," we nodded, continuing up the stairs to Dr. Riad's flat.

We rang the doorbell, and Dr. Riad's middle son opened the door, grinning knowingly at me and extending his hand in greeting. We moved into the living room, past the blaring television with the other two boys gathered around it and into the more formal sitting room. Um Ayman emerged from the kitchen, wiping her hands on a dish towel, her sweet, cherub-like face beaming. She greeted us and motioned for us to sit while she returned to the kitchen to get us something cold to drink.

"Where is Zayn?" I asked.

Dr. Riad came down the stairs, an ever-present cigarette dangling from his lips.

"He's gone to get the sheikh," he managed without removing the Marlboro. Islamic law was the default jurisprudence for family legal matters under the occupation, so all marriages were performed by religious clerics in Gaza.

"But how?" I wondered aloud, knowing that Zayn couldn't drive our orange Peugeot on a strike day.

"In an ambulance," replied Dr. Riad.

No doubt he had used his connections at Shifa Hospital to facilitate things. My husband-to-be, thirty-five years old and on the lam from the Israeli military, was to be married to me, a Jewish woman from the Midwest, in Gaza, on a strike day, in the middle of the intifada, by a sheikh who was arriving in an ambulance.

Soon Zayn appeared with the sheikh, an older man with a spotty white beard and thick, square glasses so large they seemed to announce his presence a step or two before his actual arrival. He was cloaked in a sand-colored *jebbeh* and sported a matching *emma,* the robe and skullcap worn by Muslim clerics.

The sheikh took me in, his eyebrows arching above his massive glasses. He turned to Zayn and started to say something but stopped. Dr. Riad shook his hand and guided him to a chair. The sheikh hoisted his briefcase onto the coffee table that had been pushed close to him and ceremoniously began pulling out sheaves of paper and, finally, a pen.

He began completing the marriage certificate, directing his questions to Zayn. In Arabic he asked my name.

"Ra-bek-ah Klin," Zayn replied, over articulating the foreign words so they could be transliterated into Arabic.

"Gaza is full of women but you could only find a foreigner to marry, Zayn?" the sheikh muttered in Arabic. His gaze remained on the papers as he pondered whether the "ei" in Klein should be represented by the Arabic letter "ya" or "*ayn.*"

Zayn chuckled and glanced at me. Lutfi shifted in his chair.

The sheikh looked up suddenly from his paperwork and shot a question at Zayn.

"*Khaberet abuk an hathe*? Does your father know about this?"

"This is not the concern of my father, *ya* sheikh. Do you want to perform this marriage, or shall I bring someone else?"

He glared at Zayn a moment and returned to his writing.

"*Ism abuha.* Her father's name?" the Sheikh all but demanded of Zayn.

"*Ism abuee Marvin*. My father's name is Marvin," I answered.

At the sound of my voice the sheikh's head once again jerked up. His eyes—sweeping between me and Zayn—grew larger with each look at the bride and groom. I caught his gaze and smiled. He quickly turned back to scribbling.

I looked at Zayn, who was shielding his face with his hand and laughing noiselessly, his body heaving with the silent effort.

According to Islamic law, I was owed a *mahr*—a payment from the groom to the bride at the time of the marriage to show his intent to be a responsible husband. In order to complete the marriage contract, we agreed on the spot that mine would be one thousand Jordanian dinars (about fifteen hundred dollars at the time), one dinar of which was payable immediately, with the rest to be paid "at a future date." Zayn had no cash on him, so my about-to-be-brother-in-law took out his wallet and handed over the marriage's downpayment.

The ceremony proceeded.

"*Bismallh, al rahman, al rahim.* In the name of God, the most gracious, most compassionate," the sheikh intoned, indicating the beginning of the ceremony.

But with each vow we made before God and the sheikh, Zayn seemed to lose it a little more. As I affirmed that I was the daughter of Marvin Max, Zayn's body slid a little farther down in the red crushed velvet chair. A loud giggle escaped him. The sheikh's face flushed from pink to crimson. Between muffled bursts of laughter, Zayn managed to squeeze out that he was indeed Zayn Omar Seif Majdalawi. Then the sheikh turned to Lutfi to affirm his identity as our witness, giving Zayn a chance to collect himself.

The sheikh focused once again on me. At his instruction, I turned to Zayn and said, "I wed myself to thee."

With those words Zayn's shoulders hunched. He squeezed back the tears in his eyes and opened his mouth wide, the laughter escaping unrestrained. The sudden burst of his voice reverberated off the sunlit walls of Dr. Riad's living room. Riad, chuckling himself, tried to shush Zayn. At that point I began giggling as I watched the man who I think was my husband by then convulse in laughter. Even the face of quiet, subdued Lutfi broke into a wide grin.

We exchanged no self-written vows, nor lit a unity candle that day. But a ceremony ending with peals of laughter from Zayn—his expression of love, nervousness, fear—with me learning to laugh along, was the truest beginning of our marriage there could be.

Zayn regained some control, and we finished the brief ceremony, proclaiming our faithfulness before Allah and signing the marriage contract. The sheikh quickly gathered his papers, waving off Um Ayman's invitation to stay for lunch. The ambulance was called to take him away.

Kufta (spiced meatballs in a tomato sauce) over rice, salad, and homemade pickled vegetables were followed by tiny cups of thick Arabic coffee. Then it was time for us to go home.

I had avoided thinking about the walk home in the blazing afternoon sun, hoping that the bride would be offered the same courtesy of a ride home as the sheikh, but not daring to ask. Relief rushed up in me when we walked out of the house and I could see the emergency lights shimmering in the mid-afternoon sun.

As we emerged into the blinding sunlight, the driver hopped out to open the back door. Lutfi held out his hand as I stepped onto the ledge and then into the ambulance. I squeezed in against the stretcher occupying most of the small space and clutched the low metal fold-down bench. As the vehicle jostled and bounced over the rutted, sandy streets of Gaza, I peered quizzically at the medical accoutrement lining the walls: bottles of antiseptic were stacked next to various-sized gauzes and bandages wrapped in the crinkly white paper that could be clenched in the mouth and ripped opened with one hand while the other hand stemmed a bleeding wound. Closer to the stretcher were tubes, oxygen bottles and square metal boxes marked with large red crosses, presumably opened when things got really bad.

The worse the roads got, the more the aluminum frame gurney shook and bounced, straining against the wheel locks. One particularly nasty rut bounced the metal frame into my knee. As I leaned over to push it back in place, the ghostly outlines of blood stains seemed to rise up from the otherwise white ironed sheets stretched across the gurney.

We honeymooned in my apartment. The veranda, where we made love on a foam mattress, did have a view of the Mediterranean, after all.

The second day, Lutfi appeared. He and his wife had moved into Zayn's house, so my apartment became the place he came when they argued. The three of us spent much of that day under curfew playing an Arabic version of Monopoly. The setting for the game was Cairo, not Atlantic City, the properties for sale being ones like Tahrir Square and the pyramids. My man-of-the-people husband crushed us, quickly adopting a strategy of buying everything he landed on and building on his property as soon as he could.

❧

I suppose I was carrying on a fine family tradition of unconventional marriages and homemaking. Four decades earlier, my disapproving grandmother—a migrant herself, who escaped the crushing poverty of Depression-era Appalachia—had objected to her daughter marrying a Jew. Of course my nineteen-year-old mother did what countless young women have done when forbidden a love: she eloped with my father.

Initially, they lived with my father's parents in a neighborhood—named, ironically, English Woods—populated by his Russian immigrant extended family. Their whole-hearted embrace of my mother came to represent the moral core of our family values. The family, which would have been more extended if my grandparents hadn't been first cousins, included my two paternal great-grandmothers, Ida and her sister Anna, and their respective husbands. When Anna went blind, she and her husband Samuel also moved in with my father's parents. Her condition rendering her conveniently unaware of nocturnal imperatives, Anna would invite Ida for late-night visits. Amid the dark hush of the sleeping household, they would sit at the kitchen table, gossiping in Yiddish and giggling like schoolgirls as they drank tea through sugar cubes held in their teeth.

Anna spoke only Yiddish and Russian but communicated with my mother through the language of food. At Anna's side my mother mastered matzo ball soup, knishes, kugel, borscht, and potato pancakes. Anna could twist the Sabbath *challah* dough by feel alone, weaving a perfect braid of bread like a magician performing a trick; it was then brushed with egg white and baked golden brown. Never converting to Judaism, my mother proudly declared herself a "Jewish hillbilly" on the strength of her culinary skills alone.

My parents eventually moved out of my grandparents' house and into one of their own. It was not until years later that I realized how different our welcoming home was from our neighbors. Jan and my brother Greg brought home Black friends and gay friends during the seventies. As a young adult I added to the mix with visitors from a half-dozen or so countries, and my younger sister got an early start in her social-service career, inviting over a variety of addicts and runaways. On any given holiday, I could look around our ever-expanding dining room table and see someone whose face and story were vastly different from my own.

After Anna's death, Samuel moved into an Orthodox Jewish retirement home. A curmudgeon with distinctive culinary tastes, he set up a clandestine dill pickle operation in his closet that my mother discovered one day while collecting his dirty laundry. During his Sunday visits with my parents, he complained of the "old people" food served at the home while sitting at the kitchen table, wolfing down bacon by the pound.

The home I would eventually make with my husband in Gaza would also serve as an epicurean refuge of sorts. During the Ramadan month of daytime fasting, Fathi, our neighbor and Zayn's long-time friend from prison, would sneak over midday to grab a quick bite and a smoke. Surviving several years in an Israeli prison was not enough, apparently, to prepare him for his wife's reaction if she knew he wasn't fasting. The doorbell rang about the same time every day. Fathi was over six feet tall with a layer of hair that ringed his bald head, giving it the appearance of an egg set in an egg cup. When I opened the door he always greeted me with the same sheepish grin.

"Welcome to *beit al haram*, the house of the forbidden," I would joke with him, his surprisingly boyish laugh revealing tobacco-stained teeth.

❧

A few days after our wedding, Zayn resumed sleeping elsewhere. Concerned that the Israelis would discover that we were married and come after me, he suggested I do the same. I began spending the night with Lutfi, Sawsan, and their two young daughters at Zayn's house. By then I was working at a local human rights organization in Gaza City, documenting the cases of women political prisoners.

Near the end of October, a thunderous banging on the front door woke us. It was sometime after midnight. Rushing out of my bedroom door, I met Lutfi in the hallway pulling on a sweater. Sawsan was not far behind him, carrying two-year-old Leen.

"*Ifthakh! Jaysh!* Open! Army!"

Soldiers had once again hopped over the garden wall and were banging the butts of their rifles against the front door. Leen began screaming. Lutfi reached the door first and unlocked it.

"*Besder,* okay." he responded in his usual calm voice. He seemed to be the only one not surprised by the night visit.

There were three soldiers on the patio. I could hear the running motor of a jeep just outside the garden wall. The periodic squelch of its radio and the murmur of voices echoed in the sleeping neighborhood, making it sound haunted.

"Where is Zayn?" one of the soldiers asked while two more pushed past Lutfi into the house. Sawsan followed, warning them that there was a sleeping baby inside.

"I don't know," Lutfi shrugged.

They did a cursory search of the downstairs and headed upstairs to the roof.

Sawsan emerged with a bathrobe and handed it to me.

"*Ilbisi.* Put this on," she urged, almost giggling.

I realized then I was standing in my flannel nightgown.

The soldier who had asked about Zayn was at least fifteen years older than the others. He paced once from the veranda to the garden wall and back. When the other two emerged shaking their heads, he looked at Lutfi.

"*Bo.* Come." His voice seemed strained with control.

"*Ya allah!* Oh, God!" Sawsan yelped, her usually girlish voice suddenly raw. One of the soldiers who had searched the house moved toward Lutfi, pulling out a pair of white plastic handcuffs from a large pants pocket.

"*Khalee ilbis dafee*! Let him put on some warm clothes!" Sawsan cried.

Both Lutfi and the soldier looked at her, unmoving.

The older soldier said something in Hebrew and nodded at Lutfi. He went into the house followed by one of the soldiers. The older one resumed his pacing.

The third soldier looked at me. His gaze shifted to the garden and then to the camp beyond. I could see his eyes widen. He was maybe nineteen years old, pale and gangly. The large automatic rifle slung over his shoulder seemed to teeter between balancing him out and pulling him over. Judging from the new growth of his buzz cut, he had probably just finished high school a few months earlier and was doing his first compulsory army duty.

He turned again to me.

"What are you doing here?"

"I live here," I responded. I could hear the crash and murmur of the tide behind me. "What are *you* doing here?"

He paused and looked down at his feet. I could see a pink tinge rise under his wispy teenage beard. After a moment, he regained his composure and crossed his arms in front of him.

"Having fun," he tossed out with a half-laugh.

Lutfi emerged from the house clad in a jacket, jeans and sneakers. Pulling Lutfi's arms behind his back, the soldier tightened the plastic cuffs around his wrists. Before turning to go, Lutfi took two steps toward Sawsan and kissed her. Then he bent over Leen, who was crying softly into her mother's chest, whispered something and kissed the crown of her head.

Before leading him out the door, the older soldier turned to me.

"Tell Zayn to come get his brother."

❦

A few days after Lutfi's arrest, Zayn sent me a message to meet him at my apartment. I arrived first and soon heard the elevator door open and the click of the key in the front door. Zayn walked over and put his arms around me. I pressed my face into his shirt, which was moist with sweat; he must have walked far from wherever he had been.

"*Marhaba,*" he said, his voice just above a whisper.

"*Marhaba*," I replied to his shirt. After a few more moments, I let him go.

"Have you had lunch?" I asked.

He nodded and lit a cigarette.

"I'll make some tea."

I retreated to the kitchen, and Zayn followed me. I filled the kettle and set it on the stove.

"Rebecca, you know Lutfi has a family…"

"I know, I know, Zayn," my voice broke in, louder than I expected. "I know."

He closed his eyes and exhaled a stream of smoke.

I took some fruit from the refrigerator and washed it. The kettle boiled to a frenzy. I put everything on a tray, and we moved into the living room.

"Do you know where they took Lutfi?" I asked, spooning the usual *wahad wa nus*, one and a half teaspoons of sugar, into his glass.

"Gaza Central," he replied, referring to the main prison in Gaza.

We ate fresh figs, breaking open the golf ball-sized fruit to reveal the crimson pulp inside.

He reached into his pocket and took out an envelope.

"If you need more, just ask Riad," he said. I looked inside and saw a wad of folded dinars. "If you need anything, just ask him. You know he and Um Ayman are ready to help you with anything."

I nodded and asked him for a cigarette. We smoked together in silence and drank our tea.

Finally, he stood up.

"I need to go."

My eyes burned. The lines around his mouth trembled as he pulled me to him.

"I love you," he spoke into my hair. "*Diri balik 'ala halik.* Take care of yourself."

"I love you too, Zayn." My wet face flushed with heat. He kissed me one last time, put his key on the tea tray and walked out the door. I could tell he was trying not to turn around again.

His footsteps echoed on the stairs. I went into the bedroom and out onto the veranda where we had made love on our honeymoon. He emerged from the building into the street below. I watched him look up and down the street, and then turn and walk toward the center of Gaza to exchange himself for his brother.

Lutfi was released within an hour of Zayn turning himself in to the Israelis. The next day the first place I went was Tawfiq's office. It was oddly comforting to sit at that dusty table and drink coffee out of those glasses dull with use, as the families of other detainees milled about. I listened to Tawfiq discuss Zayn with the prison authorities in the same way I had listened to him discuss the fates of others so many times.

After several calls, Tawfiq finally learned that Zayn was under "administrative detention," military legalese for detention without charge or trial, and had been taken to a prison camp in the Negev desert. He would be there for at least six months, although the military order was renewable indefinitely.

I began to realize that life with Zayn would often be life without Zayn.

My first order of business was to visit Zayn's parents, meet his father, and tell my in-laws that they were, in fact, my in-laws. I had met Zayn's mother at his house a couple of times before we married, but his father never ventured out of the camp. So the Friday after Zayn's arrest, Lutfi borrowed a friend's car and we drove the short distance from the house to Shati camp. Bouncing over the ruts and around the scorched remains of burned tires, we made our way to the alley where Omar and Asma lived.

The labyrinthine blocks of one-story cement shelters gave way unexpectedly to wide swatches of sand that stretched for several meters. In the camp they were known as "Sharon Boulevards" after the young commander Ariel Sharon, who in the late 1960s burnished his rising military star by razing hundreds of refugee homes, depriving resistance forces of the ability to attack and take cover in the winding, narrow streets where tanks could not navigate. Thousands of refugees were once again scattered and made homeless.

We turned off one of these "boulevards" and rounded a corner where a closet-size store stood selling candy, cola, tins of meat stamped "Food Aid: Not for Resale," and the occasional lonely-looking vegetable. Four houses in was a door consisting of a piece of corrugated metal that thundered when we knocked. It reminded me of the Tin Man's chest when Dorothy verified his claim of having no heart.

"*Meen?* Who is it?" she called out.

"*Ana Lutfi.* It's me, Lutfi."

Hearing her voice on the other side of the door reminded me of her surprising response to me, the first time we met.

Asma had come one afternoon to visit Zayn. He hadn't gotten home yet, so she and I sat together on the veranda, drinking sweet, dark tea and watching the last of the sun's rays descend in a blaze of fiery reds and golds. Then, like clockwork, the sound of army jeeps seeped into the hush, as the evening patrol of the camp began.

"What do they want from us?" she'd asked of no one in particular. "*Bifhamesh,* I don't understand."

I didn't expect to hear her bring up politics, just having met me. But what she had to say turned out to be more about family, and welcoming me.

"I remember what life was like in our village, in Simsim," she continued. "We had Jewish neighbors and Christian neighbors and Muslim neighbors. But they weren't Jews or Christians or Muslims—they were our neighbors."

I could hear her rubber sandals shuffling toward the door. The door creaked open, and my mother-in-law peered out.

Asma was perhaps five feet tall. Her simple, embroidered Palestinian *thobe* dress covered her legs, skimming the ground when she moved so that she seemed to rock forward rather than walk. Her age was a mystery, like others of her social background and generation whose births were documented not by pieces of paper but weather cycles or historical events: you were born in the year of the great rain or the departure of the Turks. She was surely well into her seventies, but the girl she had been would at times eclipse the old woman she had become. When she smiled, her wrinkled skin would pull taut over cheeks that unexpectedly rose round and smooth. She would occasionally readjust the sheer white *mandeel* that covered her hair, sliding it off to reveal waist-length hair hennaed a blood orange red.

We stepped into the open-air courtyard, and Asma reached up to greet her youngest son for the first time after his release, cupping his face in her thick hands. She asked for news of Zayn, which Lutfi relayed matter-of-factly. Tears welled in her eyes, magnifying their aged opaqueness. She called to her husband, Sheikh Omar, who was finishing his afternoon prayers in one of the three rooms off the courtyard.

He emerged clad in a white Nehru shirt, drawstring pants cinched loosely at the waist, and a skull cap perched atop his smooth head. Blind since boyhood, he began guiding himself toward us along the courtyard wall; with a few strides Lutfi was at his father's side. I could see my father-in-law's once statuesque physique, now bowed with age and the labors of blind perambulation, reflected in Lutfi's.

"There is someone I want you to meet," Lutfi said loudly. He took his father's hand and led him toward me, past the lone fig tree that grew defiantly in an old olive oil tin.

As they approached, a moist circle sprouted under my arms.

"*Ya ba, hathee marat Zayn.* Baba, this is Zayn's wife, Rebecca."

Sheikh Omar had begun extending his hand in greeting, but when the sentence ended his arm froze. The words *marat Zayn* bounced off the cinder block walls, playing with the dead silence that echoed even louder. Omar's mouth twitched and he cocked his head.

"Zayn tjawaz? Zayn married?" His voice soft in a wave of confusion edged with another growing emotion.

"Hathee marat Zayn?!" Asma croaked.

She struggled to her feet and steadied herself by throwing her arms around my shoulders and planting innumerable moist kisses on my cheeks.

I turned back to the sheikh, who still seemed to be taking in the news. I could hear the distant sound of the sea pounding itself along the camp's beaches.

"*Marat Zayn,"* he repeated.

A smile formed from the center of his lips and spread itself across his face, lifting the corners of his salt-and-pepper beard. His mouth opened into a toothless grin. He released Lutfi's grip and reached out to me, taking my face in his hands so he could find my cheeks and kiss them.

My father-in-law led me into the room in which he had just prayed. We sat on floor cushions arranged against the wall. Lutfi brought us tea.

"*Keefik?* How are you?" he asked.

He offered me a cigarette and while we smoked and drank tea I told him about myself: my family, my work, where I was living.

"What do you need? Money? Food? *Aya hajee, bas eselee!* Anything, just ask!" he commanded.

Between questions about my siblings and where I had gone to college, he suddenly had me repeat the *shahada*, testifying: *la elah illa allah wa Mohammed rasul allah.* There is no God but God and Mohammed is his prophet. I did so and went back to telling him about the Friends School in Ramallah. Lutfi grinned and shook his head. It was then that I realized the reason for Sheikh Omar's request: repeating the *shahada* was how one converted to Islam.

I helped his fingers find the cup so he could pour me more tea. Then he took my hand in his and turned my palm upward. With his other hand he began gently rubbing the tips of my fingers with a smooth, circular motion, slowly moving from finger to finger.

"*Ya binti. Ahlan wa sahlan.* Welcome, my daughter."

In the late 1980s, it was still possible to travel relatively easily in and out of Gaza on an American passport. So during the December holidays through the beginning of 1989, I visited my family in Ohio. While there, my siblings threw me a belated wedding shower, including household gifts and the requisite negligée. It would be a while before I would wear that. They even included Zayn in the celebration by way of constructing what has come to be known in our family lore as "broomstick Zayn." A photo of him that I had given my mother had been blown up to eight by ten, taped to the bristle part of a broom and a black-and-white-checked *kufiyeh* draped around it. He spent the party propped in a corner observing the festivities when he wasn't posing for photos with various family members.

In January I returned to Gaza and resumed living in Zayn's house with Lutfi and Sawsan, having given up my apartment in Gaza City.

I found the house in shambles. Many things amazed me about this part of the world, but among the most astonishing was the ability of women, who bore the brunt of housework like everywhere else, to keep their homes spotless. Whether they lived in upper-class villas or in refugee camps, the floors gleamed, the furniture was dust-free and everything—*everything*— was ironed. How was it, then, that I managed to marry into a family that was the one rare exception?

I could deal with the dirty clothes strewn about and the dishes piled in the sink, but there was a bigger problem. Lying in bed my first night back, a sudden scampering noise was followed by a fluttering movement across the top of my pillow, within an inch or two of my hair. I leapt from the bed and hit the light switch screaming, "Oh, shit!" and bounded out of the room. Lutfi and Sawsan emerged from their room in time to see me bang out of the kitchen wielding a broom. I had been cleaning up all day, trying not to seethe too much in the direction of Sawsan, knowing that her housekeeping strike was part of the ongoing marital discord that plagued her and Lutfi. But feminist solidarity only goes so far when faced with a fifth column of mice.

I shoved the large bed back with one deft move and immediately saw the enemy's tiny brown droppings. To my left I heard faint scratching sounds and blindly brought my weapon down with an *ugh!*—my opening salvo in the *Harb al Furan*, the War of the Mice. It was a quick one, aided as I was by compact Styrofoam trays containing a caramel-colored resin, innocuous-looking enough to the unsuspecting rodents, who would stray onto the tray looking for food. And like the notorious roach motel, they wandered in, but never wandered out.

❧

By the spring Lutfi and Sawsan had moved back into their house in Shati camp. Late April marked the sixth month of Zayn's "administrative detention." The authorities would either renew the detention order or he would be released.

Given his record, I was not optimistic. Though they didn't say it directly, I could tell that neither was Tawfiq, or Amira Pardo, an Israeli human rights lawyer who had represented him in prison.

Amira had fled Belgrade and the Nazis with her parents and became involved with leftist politics in Israel. She made a late-life career transition, started studying law at age fifty-four, and was one of the first Israeli lawyers to defend Palestinians from Gaza jailed during the intifada. Amira was a compact woman with a bob of blonde-gray hair that she habitually brushed behind her ears while talking. Despite being barely five feet tall, she walked with a stride that took effort to match.

She had visited Zayn often in the Negev prison camp that was dubbed Ansar III (Ansar I and II were notorious prisons established in southern Lebanon after the 1982 Israeli invasion) and would come to Gaza every couple of weeks to confer with Tawfiq on cases. I would meet her in his office and we would talk about how Zayn was doing and her Kafkaesque encounters with the Israeli military justice system. She had gotten to know Zayn during their chats through the chicken wire that separated detainees from their lawyers.

After talking to her last client one day, a family member who had waited hours to see her, Amira slipped off her shoes and curled her legs under her, sipping her fourth coffee. She asked me for a cigarette.

"Like you, Rebecca, I came to Gaza during the intifada."

She looked out of a window where a breeze ventured in.

"The people here never cease to amaze me—their sense of humor no matter what, their warmth and generosity toward newcomers like you and me, their creativity in figuring out how to survive such disastrous circumstances."

Amira shook her head slowly and took a long drag.

"Even though I officially represent Zayn in this insane system, I feel I'm the one who has really benefited from the relationship. The hours I've spent talking with him at Ansar have been a gift."

She finished her cigarette, contemplating the softening light. I smiled at her, and she smiled back.

"Do you know what I mean?..."

I knew exactly what she meant.

❧

On the morning marking Zayn's six months in prison, I went to work just as I did every other day. The disappointment and sadness that kept creeping in I would chase away by keeping busy. I returned home mid-afternoon and made a simple lunch for myself—fried eggs and potatoes. After a short nap I started with a broom at the back of the house, sweeping sand that would accumulate again in the places I swept, before I had even emptied the dustpan. Making my way into the kitchen near the front of the house, I heard the rattling of the front gate and the familiar scrape of metal-on-concrete from the door being opened. Lutfi would be considerate enough to ring the bell before he let himself in. No one else had a key, and there was no one left for the Israelis to take. I approached the front door slowly and stopped in the hallway when I heard voices. I leaned forward and peered through the door open to the afternoon air. Zayn was making his way up the path between the outer gate and the front stoop. I stepped into the doorway, still clutching my broom and dustpan, just as he ascended the stairs.

"*Keefik, ya hajee?* How are you?"

His smile lit up his entire face, as it always did. I noticed that his teeth were more tobacco stained, but his eyes were still that disorienting Mediterranean blue-green.

I smiled but couldn't move.

Behind Zayn walked Tayseer, a long-time friend from prison who had also been released in the 1985 prisoner exchange. Another metal scrape announced Ali, Tayseer's little brother, who was closing the outer gate.

Zayn arrived at the top step and looked at my broom and dustpan.

"So you've become a good housewife?" His voice lilted.

I let go of the broom and dustpan and wrapped my arms around his neck. His lips were surprisingly soft and his face moist.

"Are you okay?" was all I could say.

"I'm fine," he whispered. His arms tightened around my waist and I could feel his nose lingering in my neck.

Looking over his shoulder, I could see Tayseer averting his gaze. Not so Ali, who beamed at us.

"*Nuttet al heitan!* I jumped over the wall!" Ali exclaimed.

He had climbed up the outside wall and opened the door from the inside, apparently thinking he was the first one to have ever done so. I didn't tell him otherwise.

Zayn released his embrace and smiled. He then reached his hand into his pants pocket and pulled out a cigarette pack, his eyes still on me. Dipping a finger carefully into the pack, he slowly pulled out a tissue folded many times and handed it to me.

"A souvenir from Ansar," he chuckled.

I took the tissue and looked at him.

"Actually, I made these for you," he said softly.

I carefully unfolded the tissue to reveal two tiny, carved stones. One was sculpted in the shape of a heart with an "R" and a "Z" etched in relief on each side. The other, also bearing our initials, was a meticulously chiseled map of Palestine, so detailed that even the Dead Sea was carved into the West Bank.

I looked up. "*Yislamo ideek*, bless your hands," I offered, overwhelmed.

He beamed at me.

"*Shukran, habibi*," I said, "thank you, my love," wrapping my arms around him again, his gift clasped in my hand…

The next morning, Zayn rose early and went to the market in Shati camp while I slept. He returned laden with plastic bags full of fresh fish—*lukus*, St. Peter's fish, my favorite—tomatoes whose skins burst with their own juice, lettuce whose oversized leaves flapped over the plastic bag like giant tongues, and fruit, including melons approaching the size of basketballs.

He sat the bags on the kitchen counter, pulled a knife out of the drawer and carried the melons, a garbage can, and a straight-back chair from the kitchen into the hallway that ran the length of the house. In the late morning light, juice the color of a harvest moon ran in rivulets down his smooth arms as, one after the other, he sliced through the fruit's flesh, scooped out the seeds, and quartered them, methodically eating each one down to the rind. The waiting garbage can registered each fruit with a *clunk*.

The melons gone, he slumped back in his chair, closed his eyes and heaved a sigh. After a moment's pause, Zayn opened his eyes, stood and arched his back with a groan, and disposed of his feast's debris.

The flood of well-wishers welcoming Zayn home had begun the night before, as word of his release spread. The eight o'clock curfew ensured that we had some time alone each night after serving countless cups of coffee, along with the sweets people brought to celebrate the "sweetness" of Zayn's release.

We resumed our evening watches on the veranda, observing Shati camp prepare for another night. Lights went on and off with the rhythm of fifty thousand people who normally would be visiting neighbors, gossiping, and enjoying the relief of the wind blowing in from the sea, but instead were confined inside this one square kilometer of cement blocks. When an army patrol would rumble by the homes on the camp's edge, lights went out in succession like falling dominoes.

On one of those evenings together, I asked Zayn why he thought he was released, when Tawfiq and Amira had been so pessimistic.

"They had nothing on me," he replied.

The rhythm of the evening's tide played like a soundtrack.

"It's only because of my past. They don't know what to do with the intifada, so they are just arresting anyone they think may even *think* about doing something."

He lit a cigarette and the smoke traced blue against the night sky.

"Were you interrogated? You know…hurt?" I asked, not really wanting to know the answer.

"They didn't touch me, but I was interrogated by a Shin Bet officer. I think the same one who came here before we got married. Abu Salem."

Shin Bet officers would often take Arabic monikers, naming themselves in the way Arab men do after they have children. They then become "Abu Salem"—the father of Salem.

"He asked me about you, where you were from. When Amira told me that you had gone to visit your family in Cincinnati, I was afraid they wouldn't let you back in the country. So I said I wasn't sure, that the place was something like Connecticut." He chuckled at his feeble attempt to cover up the name of my hometown.

"Did they say anything to you at Ben Gurion?" he asked, referring to the Tel Aviv airport.

I shook my head. He nodded in response.

"What else did 'Abu Salem' say to you?"

I leaned forward and took a drag of his cigarette.

"Nothing, really. He just wanted to talk about the situation. The intifada." Zayn laughed and shook his head. "At one point he said to me, 'Zayn, I wouldn't be surprised if one day you are in my position and I am in yours.'"

Out of the corner of my eye I saw a bat swoop down over the garden and flutter away in its loopy flight.

I looked at Zayn.

"I told him that whatever happens, I would *never* be in his position."

We finished his cigarette in silence. Then he stood up, stretched, and yawned.

"*Yalla?*" he looked at me.

"*Yalla,*" I responded, and together we walked into the house.

5
A Broken Map

After a little more than six months of marriage, we began living together as husband and wife. I began a new job as a consultant for a local NGO, arranging visits to Gaza by international delegations and journalists. Through my human rights work and friends who were involved in the Palestinian women's committees, I had made many contacts that proved useful. One particularly memorable afternoon, I arranged for a French journalist named Juliet to interview the founder and spiritual leader of a leading Islamist political party. I translated her questions about the group's founding at the beginning of the intifada (as an offshoot of the Muslim Brotherhood), the role of women in Palestinian society (a version of separate but equal), and his vision of the country's future (Islamic, but open to all).

I was not expecting the quiet tone of the sheikh's answers and his mild demeanor. His voice was high and raspy, barely audible at times, possibly related to his being a quadriplegic since age twelve. His classic aquiline nose mirrored the shape of his long beard, which grew dark around his mouth and faded to white as it descended his chin and chest. He had high cheek bones and small round eyes that seemed to smile before his mouth could. A simple white shawl was draped over his head and shoulders; it creased and flattened with the movements of his head, the only part of him that moved as he spoke.

We sat on floor cushions in his modest home in Gaza City. His wife served us tea.

"We do not fight Jews because they are Jews," he said at one point. "We fight whoever steals our land and deprives us of our legitimate rights, regardless of religion."

He swallowed with some effort.

"Before 1948, we lived with Jews in my hometown of Asqalan. Like all people of the Book, we have no problem with them or their religion." Blinking slowly, he continued, "It is the occupation we cannot live with."

The group became focused on building clinics, schools, and charitable institutions that served the impoverished Strip. Its efforts eventually paid off in 2006 when they swept the Palestinian legislative elections, backed by voters desperate for a change from the corrupt and repressive Fatah leadership brought by the Oslo Peace Accords. But the sheikh didn't live long enough to witness those election results: He was assassinated in 2004 by a missile fired from an Israeli helicopter gunship as he was wheeled out of a mosque after dawn prayers.

In the taxi after the interview, Juliet expressed surprise at what the sheikh had said.

"I certainly don't agree with most of his views, although I understand the logic behind them."

She was silent the rest of the ride. Back at her hotel before exiting the car she turned to me.

"I was expecting him to be different," she said.

She then handed me a thank-you gift—a sweet-smelling bar of French milled soap.

❦

Learning to live together as a married couple came in fits and starts. After the initial euphoria of Zayn's release, we were faced with negotiating who did the dishes and who cooked dinner. Laundry was done on Friday, the only weekend day off from work. On one such morning I was in the hallway where we hooked up a small washing machine wheeled in from the kitchen to drain into the sink outside the bathroom. Zayn came in carrying groceries as I was taking a load out of the washer to hang on the rooftop clothesline.

"*Ya, Allah.* Oh, God!" he shouted, dropping the bags of food and running toward me. A few stray apricots rolled out of a bag, like fuzzy, meandering baby chicks.

"*Wein al haweeya?* Where is my identity card?"

Zayn kept repeating as he rifled through the soggy clothes. He seized a pair of pants—an odd ochre-colored pair of corduroys—and dug his hand into one of the back pockets.

My grip tightened on the laundry basket I had cradled against my hip, my hands sweating on the plastic rim.

"*Yallan…* "

An aborted string of Arabic curses fell into the silence of the hallway. I watched as Zayn extracted from the pocket the red plastic cover that held his *haweeya*. He turned it over, exposing the transparent sleeve that held the identity card. A round bloom of fog was all I could see. His fingertips slid under the sleeve's open end and, with the delicacy of a surgeon, gently removed the card.

The *click, click, click* of the living room clock's second hand was unrelenting.

The card went limp when it was out of the sleeve, and Zayn's face fell. He mumbled something and turned from me, cupping the ID card in his hand as if it might explode.

"Let me see!" I lunged forward, dropping the clothesbasket.

"There's nothing to see!" Zayn burst out. "It's ruined!"

He thrust the card toward me. Water marks streaked across his photo on the card, and various lines of Hebrew type faded from black to gray to nothing.

"What are you going to do?" I whispered.

Every Palestinian over a certain age had to have an Israeli military government-issued identity card and had to produce it on demand by any soldier. Not having one was simply not an option.

"What am I going to do? I'm going to go to the *muqataa* and try and get a new one!" he boomed, referring to the military government building.

"Who doesn't check pockets before washing?" he queried, his eyes narrowing on me as he gestured toward the laundry.

I looked at him and blinked.

"You leave your ID in your pants and it's my fault that it gets washed?"

"Everyone knows, Rebecca, that you check pockets first!" His words quivered, and he started to say something else but stopped and stalked off.

I followed him into the living room.

"Zayn, I'm really sorry that your ID got wet, but this isn't my fault. It was an accident."

He was opening and closing drawers of the credenza and desk in the living room, looking through papers. Without answering he turned and went into the bedroom. I stood in the hallway and listened to him rifling through our bedside table.

"What are you looking for?" I asked through the door.

After a few minutes, the door swung open and Zayn brushed past me. Sweat gathered and glistened on his wrinkled forehead and at the corners of his eyes. Papers that had fallen from the drawers skittered under the bed with the rush of air from the door's opening. I stood still and closed my eyes. A few seconds later I heard the front gate bang closed, its shudder echoing in the empty garden.

After hanging out the offending laundry, I spent the day wandering aimlessly around the house. It was late afternoon when Zayn returned. I was sitting in the living room when he walked in the front door. I started to speak but stopped when he continued silently past me down the hallway. Something thick and gray hung in the air, something beyond anger.

I went into the hall and saw he was limping. He bent over the sink outside the bathroom and turned on the water full force. As he bent over the basin and cupped the water in his hands, I noticed the back of his pants were streaked with dirt and that one side of his shirt was torn.

He took several drinks of water in between rinsing and washing his face, then his arms, and finally the top of his head. He turned off the faucet and the final drips from the spigot—always three no matter how tightly one turned the handles—made their slow, final descent.

Zayn straightened up slowly and looked at me in the mirror above the sink.

"*Fee bashkir?* Is there a towel?"

I rushed into the bedroom and brought him one.

"*Shu sar?* What happened?"

"I got my *haweeya*," he replied.

He finished drying and walked slowly into the bedroom. I followed him and stood at the foot of the bed where he was sitting, taking off his shoes.

"Zayn?" I said.

He unzipped his pants and gingerly slid them down his legs. A rectangular mark rose crimson on the back of one thigh. A few streaks of blood revealed themselves on his shirt along with more bruises on his back.

"Jesus…," I muttered.

I had seen injuries before. In fact, it was during my first trip to Gaza that I originally saw victims of army violence. And I had documented more injuries than I could possibly recall as a human rights worker. But seeing the physical evidence of this violence on the body of someone I loved pushed the act of seeing into the realm of disbelief.

My husband's body doesn't look like this, I thought. Where did this blood and these bruises come from? How did they get into my house?

Zayn lay back on the bed, his face locked in a grimace.

I could picture the rifle butt coming down, but to this day I cannot picture Zayn lying on the ground.

"I'll get you some ice." That was all I could say.

Retreating into the kitchen, I opened the freezer door and a cloud of frozen air rolled out. It stilled me for a moment, and I breathed it deep into my lungs.

I wrapped some ice cubes in a kitchen towel and took them into the bedroom. Zayn rolled to one side. As I gently pressed the cold cloth to his skin, his entire body winced.

After a while Lutfi showed up. When I heard Zayn ask Lutfi to run a bath and help him in, I flinched with guilt and bewilderment.

Zayn never took baths.

With Zayn leaning on the taller Lutfi, the two brothers shuffled slowly into the bathroom. Lutfi emerged after a short time and smiled at me as I sat on the edge of the bed.

"Don't worry," he reassured me. "You know how some of the soldiers like to be tough guys in front of the others. This happens. He'll be okay."

I nodded.

I listened to the odd sounds of water rolling and splashing against the porcelain tub when he moved, accompanied by the low murmur of groans.

Throughout that summer of 1989, I remember amid everything else times of lightness and indeed joy: extended "siesta" lunches—the norm in that part of the world—with friends and family; evening visits with

Dr. Riad and Tawfiq that became nights spent eating, talking, and watching television; and countless evenings together on the veranda watching the sun dip beyond the camp into the Mediterranean.

Then, in August, Zayn announced that he was going to be sleeping elsewhere for a while. "A precautionary measure," was his only explanation. There was a new head of the Southern Command, and as often happened when there was leadership turnover, army attacks on Shati and other camps had intensified, as had roundups of "suspects."

Near the end of the month, one night around eleven, I had just fallen asleep when a cacophonous rattle and banging jolted me awake.

The army. Again.

I wrapped a robe around me as I peered around the corner of the front door and saw two soldiers on the veranda.

"*Iftach.* Open!" one of them said.

"What do you want?"

When he heard my English, he turned and said something in Hebrew to someone behind him. An older man, apparently the officer in charge, came to the door.

He peered through the door's metal bars and took a half step back. I thought I heard him sigh.

"There was someone writing graffiti on the wall, and they jumped over it into this garden. We need to look."

I moved out into the hall and unlocked the door. Two soldiers went into the house, did a cursory search, then came out and tromped around the garden a bit. I stood my ground on the veranda with the officer. The search didn't take long, and as they headed for the outside gate, the officer turned to me and started to say goodnight or maybe apologize or something.

"I don't want to hear it." I cut him off.

On they went to the surrounding houses, and the banging continued into the night.

Not long after that, Zayn's friend Fathi suddenly appeared at the home of my friend Yara in Shati camp, where I often spent afternoons. I was used to seeing Fathi's lanky frame come up the steps of our veranda, always dressed in a freshly pressed white *dishdasha* that fluttered around his ankles. Seeing him at Yara's wearing a button-down shirt and slacks, I sensed something unusual.

Yara offered him coffee, which he declined. He asked to speak to me alone. The only other room in the small camp house was Yara's and Tayseer's bedroom, so we went in and he shut the door. Tayseer, the man who had brought Zayn home after he was released four months earlier, had himself been arrested recently. Fathi looked at me, and I felt that he was thinking very carefully about what to say.

"*Hadri halik t'aishee bara.* Prepare yourself to live outside," he said in his hushed baritone voice. Zayn would be going into exile.

So the army visit a couple of weeks before hadn't been just about a graffiti artist. My breathing became slightly shallower. My head felt like it was filling with sand. He couldn't give me any details, other than to tell me that I should not say a word to anyone. Once Zayn was safely out of Gaza, he would let me know what to do and where to go.

My mind raced. A hundred questions that I knew couldn't be answered came and went. What I didn't know then was that Tayseer had confessed under interrogation about Zayn's political activities, so if the Israelis caught him he would likely face another lengthy prison sentence.

I looked around the room to collect my thoughts and saw propped on the ledge above the door the wedding photo of Yara and Tayseer. They stood smiling down at us—he handsome in a dark suit and with green eyes even more striking than Zayn's; she surrounded in a cloud of white with her natural beauty hidden under layers of makeup. Not knowing what else to do, I smiled back.

Yara had busied herself in the kitchen while we talked but emerged quickly as Fathi opened the door, her face taut with the worry we both knew she couldn't express. Fathi left immediately. I turned to her.

Finally she asked, "*Tishrabi 'ahwah?* Would you like some coffee?"

"I need to go."

She didn't bother responding with the customary, "No, it's early. Stay longer."

As I moved toward the door she reached out her hand. I stopped.

"Is Zayn okay?" she murmured.

"Yes," I responded, "he's okay."

We moved toward each other for our usual one-kiss-on-each-cheek goodbye. As our faces touched she encircled me with her arms, whispering in my ear, "Please let me know if you need anything, *habibti.*"

I nodded and blinked back the burning in my eyes, stepping out into the narrow alleyways of Shati.

❧

My life retained a veneer of normalcy: I continued working and visiting friends. An odd weight hung in the room during those visits, like the air preceding a storm, but before the birds begin to flurry. Some seemed to know the plan for our future; they were extra cheerful and generous to me. I left those lunches with pillowcases stitched with colorful mazes of Palestinian embroidery, or with fragrant boxes of dried dates and nuts. Others knew nothing. These visits were the hardest. The burden of acting as if nothing was different rested solely on me. We ate, drank coffee, watched television. I lost track of how many people I didn't say goodbye to, and how many I said goodbye to without their knowing.

August passed into September as I waited for word on Zayn and what my next move would be. I was invited to the wedding of Fatima's oldest son Ziad. I arrived at her house and found my mother-in-law, Asma. Ziad's wedding, such as it was in the midst of the intifada, consisted of the bride coiffed and smiling in all her wedding finery—Ziad's gifts of gold jewelry encircling her neck and wrists, and a shimmering, ornate dress in the style I didn't dare try to wear—sitting next to her husband. Electrified Arabic pop music played as the ebullient Fatima danced for the bride and groom. Guests were served cola and *mansaf*—sweet chunks of lamb on a bed of subtly-spiced rice and pine nuts, topped with dollops of yogurt separating into camps of fat and liquid as the heat from the rice curlicued around them.

After finishing my meal and washing my hands, I emerged from the bathroom to find Zayn standing just inside the door. I hadn't seen him in weeks. I was shocked that he would risk being at a family event—one the Israelis would surely be monitoring if they knew about it, in the hopes that he would appear. He congratulated the bride and groom and ate quickly, his eyes flitting toward the window every few minutes.

"I have to go now," he turned to me and said. He rose from his chair and walked toward his sister. She was standing next to their mother, who was seated *diwan*-style on a floor cushion. When he kissed his sister twice on both cheeks, a display of affection I had never seen before, a tingle swelled at the back of my throat. At that moment I realized the true reason for his showing up. He then stood before his mother, who started to rise.

"*Khalleeki.* Stay where you are," he responded to her, his voice eerily calm.

A sudden weight pressed deep into my chest as I struggled to maintain composure. Zayn gently took his mother's head in his hands. As she looked up at him, he bent forward and kissed her forehead three times. His furtive, final farewell.

He then turned from her quickly and slipped out the door.

I didn't see Zayn in Gaza again. I continued to wait for the instructions Fathi said would come. In the evenings, I would prepare a simple dinner and sit on the veranda, watching what was left of the sunset. Stars appeared in the sky one-by-one like shy, celestial debutants, and by ten I was in bed for my last nightly ritual——listening to the Israeli radio news in English.

One night as I listened to the usual cycle of Knesset reports and pronouncements from the prime minister's office, a report from "Judea and Samaria"—the biblical name the government-controlled media prefers for the Occupied Territories—caught my attention. A "suspected militant" had been shot in the Negev near the Egyptian border. I knew that the plan was for Zayn to cross into Egypt. I felt suddenly dizzy as I listened for a name to come over the airwaves and into our bedroom. None did.

"Tomorrow will see a high of 38 degrees Celsius."

I sat up and swung my legs over the edge of the bed and realized I had been holding my breath. When I let it out, what emerged was part groan, part cry. I reached over and grabbed my cigarettes off the desk, my fingers managing to light a shaking Marlboro.

"Maccabee Tel Aviv will be playing Haifa this weekend," the sports news reported.

With the end of one cigarette, I lit another and another. I turned on the television, hoping to catch any version of the eleven o'clock news, since I would recognize the name in any language.

"Nurses are threatening to strike, and the jellyfish count is abnormally high for this time of the season."

The wave of panic that night came in at least two layers. First, the visceral terror that accompanies the possibility that someone you love has been taken from you. It is the precursor to denial, because the death, the loss, still floats in the ether as a mere chance. Then the panic of confronting another kind of loss: What would I do here without Zayn? I came to this land without knowing him, but he had become an anchor, an interlocutor, a translator of all things Gazan and more. Could I be here without him?

I smoked and cried until just before dawn, dozing off for an hour or two. I awoke nauseous and with a pounding head. With no phone in the house, I would need to get to Tawfiq's to confirm any news. I dressed quickly and was startled by the whiteness of my face and the dark circles under my eyes. It was still early when I got to Tawfiq's house, so chances were good that he had not left for the office. I rang the doorbell.

"*Meen?* Who is it?"

The voice of Tawfiq's wife Nour came through the intercom with a note of surprise that someone was at the door before eight. She buzzed me in, and I apologized on the doorstep for disturbing them so early.

"*Mish mushkeela,* no problem, Rebecca," she reassured me, the look on her face reflecting what she saw in mine.

"Tawfiq is in the kitchen eating breakfast."

Tawfiq's wide, warm smile faded as I collapsed into a chair across from him. I sputtered out what I had heard on the radio the previous night, but before I could finish he put his hand on mine and held it tight.

"It's okay. It's okay. He's alright. It wasn't him."

I put both hands on Nour's perfectly polished kitchen table, laid my head down and sobbed.

He patted my shoulder, muttering, "*Mat Khafeesh,* don't be afraid."

I sensed Nour's presence in the kitchen doorway, so I collected myself. Tawfiq quickly explained why I'd come over. She moved to my side and stroked my hair.

"Have you had breakfast?" she asked, smiling down at me.

I shook my head and managed to smile back.

Nour walked to the refrigerator and began pulling out eggs, vegetables and bread. I rose to wash my face. As I passed him, Tawfiq whispered to me to come to his office in about an hour. He stood to leave and when I looked at him he smiled at me in the way that I had seen him do dozens of times with clients seeking news about missing sons or just-sentenced husbands.

"It's going to be okay," he said, and turned toward the door.

I tried to relax as Nour fed me breakfast. Trying not to be rude, I chatted with her—keeping one eye on the kitchen clock. When an acceptable amount of time had passed, I excused myself and drove to Tawfiq's office.

Walking up those now-familiar stairs, I could hear his voice echoing in Hebrew down the hallway as I approached the office door.

I entered and Tawfiq gestured for me to sit. I declined Karim's offer of coffee and after a few minutes Tawfiq hung up the phone. He rubbed his closed eyes with the thumb and index finger of one hand, and when he opened them again he smiled and stood up, gesturing for me to follow him.

Once in an adjacent room, he closed the door and we sat at a wooden table dotted with cup rings and ashes. From his pants pocket, he pulled a piece of paper that had been tightly rolled into a capsule.

"Keep this with you in a very safe place," he said, looking directly into my eyes. "This is where you will find Zayn."

I slowly unrolled the paper, flattening it gently with the palm of my hand, careful not to set it on any of the coffee rings.

"The address is in Arabic and English," he continued. "You know how to get to Cairo on the Israeli tour buses. Once you're there you can give the Arabic address to a taxi driver and he should know the area. It's in *Masr al-Jadeeda*, on the outskirts of Cairo."

I looked at the handwriting to make sure I could read the address.

"Keep this in a place where it would be difficult to find if you are searched."

I knew that this would take some creativity on my part, but in the end it fit nicely inside a Kotex pad I wore in my underpants.

"Prepare yourself to leave as soon as possible. Fathi will come by the house to give you money for the trip. It's probably best if you don't call or come by my house or office again before you leave."

For the second time that morning I felt my eyes brimming with tears in front of Tawfiq. He stood quickly as his eyes did the same. We embraced and said goodbye, two kisses on each cheek.

"Say goodbye to Nour for me," I managed. He nodded, turned toward the door and strode back into his office. I could hear the phone ringing as he did.

❧

How Zayn made it out of Gaza I only fully learned years later. It was a departure aided by some Bedouin, a few camels, and a field of summer squash near Rafah.

After a month of hiding in Gaza City, he managed to get to Khan Yunis, about fifteen miles south of Gaza City, with two others who were fleeing. Here they encountered an army checkpoint on the road to Rafah, the southern-most town straddling the Gaza-Egypt border. They hid among date palms set back from the road to avoid the soldiers, sleeping when they could and waiting for the checkpoint to be moved. It was September and by then the nights had grown cold. Zayn spied a field of *cusa* summer squash not far from their clump of trees, so when night fell they made their way toward it. The wide leaves and thick, long stems of the *cusa* would provide both cover and warmth, he surmised. He was right. They spent the night there, blanketed by the earth and the foliage.

The weeks of hiding and the patently absurd situation he now found himself in proved an inspiration of sorts. At some point Zayn began singing into the darkness:

We are fedayeen in the cusa patch!

Guerillas in the cusa patch!

After a few minutes of his serenade and his traveling companions' hysterical laughter, they begged him to stop for fear of someone hearing them.

With the checkpoint cleared they proceeded south, first into the Negev and then into the Sinai desert. There they were picked up by a Bedouin man in a jeep and taken to a gully, where they spent the night. After crossing into Egypt, they were met by another Bedouin, this one with camels, which they rode to a highway and a waiting car. After one more car switch, a Palestinian driver took them to Cairo.

What does someone with a gun at her back decide to carry from her home and into a diaspora? My family of Russian Jews had to think twice about it. When Cossacks descended on their shtetl in the early twentieth century, my great-grandmother Ida didn't think about the family silver hidden behind the stone fireplace. Not immediately, anyway. They fled into the nearby woods and watched their village being emptied and burned. Once the flames had subsided, Ida gave my Grandpa Bill his mission: retrieve the silver left behind. Perhaps she calculated that his youth—at ten, he was the youngest of the family—would bestow upon him an air of inculpability if caught. Knowing my grandfather many years later, I think it could have been his ability to talk himself out of (and, alas, into) sticky situations, which won him the job.

He waited at the edge of the woods for night to come. Lingering smoke was borne above the trees by an evening wind. Absent hearth fires and oil lamps, the stillness of the village merged with the forest's darkness. My grandfather made his way through the remains, plucked the box from its hiding place, and returned to his family.

His success landed the family with the means to buy itself out of Russia, and it left Grandpa Bill (his Russian name lost at the border by the bureaucrat who couldn't be bothered with such a peculiar collection of consonants and vowels) with an impressive piece of family lore. The family immigrated piecemeal, the older men coming first, establishing themselves and sending for others, until the family reassembled itself from fragments.

❧

It had been a while since I had to fit so much luggage into the trunk of a Gaza taxi. As Lutfi transferred the two suitcases from our orange hatchback to the *serveece* that would take me to Ramallah, my first destination on this journey into the unknown, I wondered if I had packed the right things. What do you carry into exile from a country that is your home but not your homeland? The bare essentials were obvious—bras and underwear, sensible shoes, a jacket for the oncoming winter. But what of the things I could live without but didn't want to: the negligée my mother gave me as a wedding present, my favorite American shampoo, the treasured books shipped from the States not even a year ago? The calculus of exile packing included size, necessity, cost, and emotional value. There was a risk factor as well: Anything that might raise suspicion with the Israelis if my bags were searched at the border had to be eliminated. Taking the negligee was a no-brainer, as was the skirt and blouse I wore to our wedding. The shampoo didn't make the cut, but books that steered clear of Middle East politics and that were not written by Arab authors did. Howard Zinn's *A People's History of the United States* and Alice Walker's *In Search of our Mother's Gardens* accompanied me out of Gaza. Edward Said's *The Question of Palestine* remained.

There were some things that required a little more ingenuity. Especially the two tiny precious stone charms Zayn had hand carved for me during the six months he had been in prison immediately following our marriage.

I plucked the stones from the drawer of our bedside table. The smooth sandstone felt surprisingly cool in my palm. I gently traced the grooves of our carved initials with my finger, contemplating if I dare pack them and how I would explain such things to an Israeli security official if my bags were searched. Having crammed in as many things as possible, I stood looking at the bulging suitcase, holding the stones in my hand. By then it was clear that I could give no explanation of the stones to satisfy anybody who expected one. I jammed in one last item and closed the suitcase. Sandwiched between a pair of Keds and wrapped in flannel pajamas, those stones made their way out of the Promised Land buried at the bottom of a tampon box.

Back at the taxi stand, the last passenger had settled into the *serveece*, and the impatient driver and car full of riders gawked at the foreigner holding up their departure. I could no longer put off saying goodbye to Lutfi. Standing in the middle of the bustling Gaza taxi stand, I knew that our farewell not only had to be quick but subdued. The unacknowledged and unknown goodbyes to friends and family over the past few weeks were necessary on the theory that the less that was known about our plans, the better the chances I would make it out of the country without problems from the Israeli authorities. But Lutfi knew where I was going and that I might never return, so there was no imperative to hide my feelings. This made doing so all the more difficult. Yes, he was my brother-in-law, but he was more than that. He was among the first Palestinians I had met on my initial trip to Gaza, that fateful day not quite two years ago when I first began to experience the endearing charm and perpetual heartbreak offered by this tiny strip of land. And now he was my final goodbye.

Lutfi slammed closed the packed trunk after wedging in my bags and turned to me. I extended my hand in what I hoped would be an emotionally easy handshake that would also not shock the audience peering through the Mercedes' window. Lutfi took my hand but used it to pull me closer, saying, "*Salme kteer ala Zayn.* Many greetings to Zayn."

As he wrapped his other arm around my shoulders, I felt his chest heave a heavy sigh.

"*Allah ma'ik.* God be with you," he whispered.

I could only whimper and feel the tears trace hot down my face, warmed in the Gaza sun. He released me, kissed both cheeks, turned and walked back to what used to be our car.

Squeezing into the taxi's back seat, I turned my face to the window as much to hide my tears as to watch Lutfi pull away. The candy-colored car made its way back into the chaos of Gaza. An older woman sitting next to me pushed a Kleenex into my hand and muttered, "*B'ayn Allah.* We're in the eyes of God."

I viewed the passing landscape as if under water: date palms blurred and waved; sand dunes were magnified in size then suddenly shrunk. I had made countless trips on this same road, yet it was as if I was seeing everything for the first time. The landscape gradually transformed from Gaza's dominant browns with spots of green into the dominant greens with stripes of brown as we neared Ramallah. Panic unfolded in me as the taxi circled the *manara,* Ramallah's main square. *What if the Israelis stopped me at the border? What if I got through and couldn't find Zayn? Where were we going to end up?*

Then the *serveece* jolted to a stop and the passengers climbed out. I unloaded my bags from the Gaza taxi and into a local one that would take me to Joel's house. I was leaving Gaza in stages and his house was my first stop, where I would check off my "to do" list: make a reservation on an Israeli tour bus to Cairo that left regularly from Jerusalem; exchange my remaining Israeli shekels for dollars; edit out Palestinian names and phone numbers from my address book in case it was searched; mail information and papers I wanted to keep to my mother in Ohio from the West Jerusalem post office across the Green Line, from which delivery was more certain and mail less scrutinized by the military authorities.

On the morning of my departure for Cairo I woke early. I would first need to take a taxi to East Jerusalem, and then find another to the western part of the city where the Israeli tour buses departed. I did a final "security check" through my things and pulled the bundle of flannel pajamas holding the two stone charms from their hiding place. As I unfolded the Kleenex in which the stones were wrapped, the etched stone map of Palestine slipped from the fold and skidded under the bed.

I dropped to my knees. Sweeping my left hand across the cool tile floor, searching, I brushed something and, relieved, scooped it up into my palm. But as I began drawing my hand out from underneath the bed, my wrist jutted into something else small, hard, but slightly sharp. Pressing my wrist against it into the floor, I carefully steered it out. From beneath my hand emerged the broken-off stone carving of the southern half of Palestine—from the Negev desert almost to Jerusalem. It clung to my wrist as if holding on for dear life to an invisible bracelet. I uncurled my clenched fist, and resting in my palm was what remained of the map—a shrunken rectangle enclosing a bit of the Galilee and the Dead Sea.

6
Guests of Hosni Mubarak

Most of the passengers on the Egged public transit bus were European tourists moving on from Israel to Egypt. From my window seat in the middle of the bus, I watched young blondes in shorts and dirty tank tops shuffle down the aisle, their pale, bloodshot eyes indicating that this early morning hour of the day wasn't one they were used to seeing.

The few Israelis who boarded were more awake but had a certain obliviousness about them. They appeared neither concerned nor interested by the fact that they were about to enter former enemy territory. This group mostly seemed bored, occasionally shouting at the driver to change the radio station from news to a pop music station as they split sunflower seed shells between unusually white teeth.

The ten-year anniversary of the Camp David Accords had just passed, conspicuous by the lack of celebration in the Arab World with the intifada raging in the Occupied Territories. The 1979 agreement between Israel and Egypt had quickly settled into a cold peace, with one of the few tangible signs that anything had changed being a smattering of Israeli tourists in Egypt.

The Israeli-run bus went as far south as Eilat—a city at the southern tip of the Negev desert where Israel, Egypt, and Jordan intersect with the Red Sea. There we disembarked, walked into Egyptian territory, and boarded a local bus to complete the 265-mile journey to Cairo. To my surprise, there had been only a cursory luggage inspection before boarding the bus in Jerusalem. In Eilat, however, there were more thorough checks, including sniffing dogs, but done randomly. Being somewhat older than the other passengers—who were probably in their teens or early twenties—and with a relatively conservative appearance, American passport, and Jewish last name, I passed by the Israeli security guards in a matter of minutes. Hashish, not carved stones from a Negev prison camp, was what they were looking for.

After several hours lumbering through the dessert, we arrived in the cacophony of car horns, street vendors, and occasionally braying donkeys that is the soundtrack of Cairo. The bus delivered us downtown to Ramsis Square as the most punishing of the day's heat was beginning to fade in the early evening hours.

I jostled my way into a battered taxi and read the address from the paper I had dislodged from my underwear at the last rest stop after we crossed into Egypt. In addition to the actual address, Tawfiq had noted other landmarks that were near the building that was my destination, so I handed the paper to the driver. He read it and looked at me in the rearview mirror. The address was in a northern suburb of Cairo called *Masr al-Jadeeda*, New Egypt, about a twenty-five minute cab ride from central Cairo if the traffic was at all cooperative, an hour and a half if it wasn't. In either case, it certainly was not a tourist destination.

"You want hotel in Cairo? Nice hotel I know," the driver responded. "This far. Not good for tourist," he warned, waving the paper in his hand.

"*Mish mushkeleh.* No problem," I retorted in Arabic.

He turned around and peered at me with the quizzical look I was accustomed to by now.

"*Yalla!* Let's go," I declared, trying to sound like I knew what I was doing and hoping we would still arrive before dark.

He shrugged his shoulders.

"*Yalla,*" he repeated, looking for an opening into the relentless Cairo traffic.

We made decent time, once out of the main throng downtown. Out in the suburbs, the smooth, recently paved road that had been built to entice the population out of the teeming city center gave way to rutted, bumpy back streets. It seemed that there was only so much that was new about *Masr al-Jadeeda.* The taxi bounced and rattled as the driver would occasionally stretch his head out of the window, looking for landmarks or flagging down another driver for a consultation.

After the second or third such stop, I was beginning to get nervous. It was typical for a taxi driver to agree to take you to the requested destination, having only a vague idea where it was. These men had no problem stopping to ask directions; the problem was that direction-giving usually became a collective effort, with other drivers, passersby, and nearby shopkeepers inserting themselves and offering often contradictory advice. After an all-but-toothless ice cream vendor, clicking prayer beads in one hand and gesturing with the other, assured us it was just one more turn, twenty or thirty meters away, I sighed heavily.

We made the left as instructed, and I moved to the middle of the back seat for a better view of the street. The driver slowed, his head pivoting between the paper he grasped in his hand at the top of the steering wheel and the buildings on the street. About twenty feet to my left, I saw two figures emerge from a shop, chatting with each other and walking toward the street.

As the car inched along, I sat up and leaned forward in the opening between the driver's and passenger's seat. The two men came into view and I yelled, "Stop!" The driver's head snapped up as he slammed the brakes. I lunged for the handle, threw open the door and leapt from the car just as the men turned toward it.

"Zayn!" I shouted and waved.

He startled and froze mid-sentence. His slightly opened mouth formed the words "*mish ma'ul* It's not possible." The young man he was with broke into a smile as I jumped into Zayn's arms in the middle of New Egypt.

The happy look of surprise on Zayn's face melted. His eyes shifted from me to the staring passersby. He paid the taxi driver and quickly ushered me and my suitcases into the apartment building entrance where the cab had stopped. The young man he was with—in his early twenties but his swirl of ginger hair already thinning and a paunch pushing out his *jelabiyya*—introduced himself as Alaa.

"Welcome," he said warmly.

He smiled and swept one arm toward the staircase as he took my suitcase with the other. Alaa was Tawfiq's nephew, and he had his uncle's charming smile that revealed the same slight gap between his front top teeth. He was in Egypt studying law at Cairo University.

Alaa and Zayn bounced and heaved my heavy bag up three flights of stairs, knocking empty chip bags and cigarette butts down the stairs in their wake.

"*Shu jibti ma'ak? Kol Gaza?* Did you bring all of Gaza with you?" Zayn quipped.

"*I missed you, too,*" I thought to myself.

But as we waited on the crowded landing for Alaa to open the faded wooden door, Zayn's eyes met mine and he smiled.

The door creaked open onto a living room furnished with a leaf-green couch and a low wooden coffee table that was scattered with papers, cigarette ashes, and glasses bottomed with remnants of tea leaves. The last of the setting sun's rays trickled through a grimy window that opened to a view of rooftop antennas. A tiny kitchen with a refrigerator and a two-burner cooking top was tucked off the living room. To the left of one of the two small bedrooms was a bathroom in desperate need of cleaning.

Alaa hauled my bag into one of the bedrooms and emerged trailed by a chattering Zayn, who was insisting that it wasn't necessary for him to give up his room for me. Alaa ignored Zayn and clicked on the rabbit-eared television, handing me the remote.

"*Ahlan wa sahlan.* Welcome!" Alaa repeated.

He scurried around the apartment cleaning up and eventually disappeared into the kitchen. He reappeared after a short time with a metal tray bearing three tall glasses of overly sweet, orange-colored juice. Zayn followed Alaa around, all the while imploring him, "*Tghalibish halak.* Don't trouble yourself."

"Really it was a shock," Zayn said after we all sat down. "I really didn't think you would be able to find me so quickly."

I raised my glass and toasted my new roommates.

"*Sahtayn.* To your health."

After a dinner of canned mortadella lunch meat, labneh yogurt cheese, olives, chunks of tomatoes, and cucumber slices, I went into the room where my suitcase was and began to prepare for bed. Thus began the battle of the bedrooms in earnest.

Alaa had automatically put my things in his bedroom, a larger room with a double bed. Zayn was insisting that I would sleep in the single bed where he'd been until now—and that he would sleep on the couch.

"*Bidnash nermi halna 'ala rasek.* We don't want to throw ourselves on your head," he protested, sweat beading on his forehead.

"*Ma baseer, ya zalameh.* No way, man," Alaa retorted, his chin thrust forward slightly.

As I brushed my teeth, I could hear their huddled murmurs in the bedroom. I made out the words "your wife" and "together." When I entered the room they both turned to me, suddenly silent.

Zayn lit a cigarette. The wrinkles around his eyes looked deeper. Alaa took the opportunity to hurry out of the room, muttering "*Tisbahu ala' kheir.* Goodnight," as he pulled the door closed.

I turned to Zayn. He sighed a billow of opaque smoke and moved toward me.

"*Alhumdillah 'assalameh.* Thank God for your safe arrival," he whispered as he leaned forward to kiss me.

As we embraced I felt his shoulders slump. Then he pulled away, muttered "goodnight," and slipped out the door. The next thing I heard was the click of the remote and the melodramatic voices of an Egyptian soap opera rising through the next room.

The next morning I awoke to find Zayn on the couch and Alaa in the other bedroom. I went into the small kitchen and began washing the supper dishes. Alaa shuffled into the kitchen and made coffee, and soon Zayn appeared at the doorway. We drank coffee together, and then Zayn boiled eggs and sliced cheese and tomatoes for breakfast.

We ate and chatted about Alaa's studies, his relatives in Gaza, and my last days there. Alaa excused himself to study and prepare for classes, but before he left I asked him if he had an iron I could use. Right before leaving Palestine I had purchased a silk and cotton lavender-color blouse that I thought looked particularly flattering. I wanted to wear it on this first day of my new life with Zayn.

"I have one," he responded, "but it really doesn't work very well. There is a laundry shop a couple of blocks away that does ironing. You could take your clothes there."

"That's okay," I reassured him, "I only have one small thing to iron."

Alaa retrieved the iron and ironing board from his bedroom closet and set them up for me, the board's yellow and pink flowered cover interrupted with the occasional brown singe mark.

"Please be careful—it gets very hot," he warned.

I set the iron on the lowest temperature and retrieved the shirt from my suitcase. The silky fabric slipped easily through my fingers as I unbuttoned the blouse and carefully laid it on the ironing board, hooking the left sleeve over the board's narrow end. As I lifted the iron off the board, a delicate lick of steam curlicued through the morning air. I gently placed the iron on the front of the blouse. Within seconds a bitter smell floated up and I jerked back the iron. With it came a petal-shaped piece of the blouse, its scorched shadow smoldering on the fabric below.

An odd moan echoed off the bedroom walls, startling even me, as Alaa and Zayn rushed into the room. As my vision blurred with tears, Alaa raised his hands to grasp either side of his head.

Zayn turned away and squeezed shut his eyes.

I had never been to *Masr al-Jadeeda*, even though I had made several previous trips to Cairo. About eight miles northeast of downtown, the suburb was connected to the city center by a system of minivans known as *micros.* It took awhile to collect myself after the ironing incident; then Zayn and I boarded one of the *micros* and headed into Cairo together.

The minivan swerved in and out of traffic, taking on new passengers as others got off. The vehicle slowed but didn't actually stop for exiting and entering passengers, unless they were women or elderly. It occurred to me that this was the first time Zayn and I had gone anywhere together outside of Gaza since our trip to visit Galit in Tel Aviv over a year ago.

We were headed to Khan el-Khalili, the historic market situated in Islamic Cairo near the famous mosques of Hussein and Al-Azhar. Our specific destination was the *Souk al-Sagha,* the goldsmiths' bazaar west of the main Khan, where locals bought and sold gold. Given the circumstances of our marriage, buying wedding rings hadn't been a priority. Suddenly it was.

I had been wearing my father's wedding band that, years before, had been sized down to a pinky ring. Zayn had been wearing nothing. When he told me that we were going to the Khan, I was surprised. I had always thought of it as a tourist destination—the place where I bought the mother-of-pearl inlaid boxes and handwoven wall hangings to give as gifts to family members—and Zayn wasn't one for frequenting tourist spots. It was only after we had veered off from the flashy souvenir shops that I asked him where we were going.

"To buy gold," he responded.

The bustle of the touristy part of the Khan faded away as we turned down an alley and entered the *Souk al-Sagha*. Graceful stone arches formed a covering above the street, darkening the small, tidy shops with their glittering merchandise. There were dozens within view and more down the even narrower alleyways that intersected the main street. I could see a flicker of panic in Zayn's eyes. He turned into the first doorway we came to.

"*Ahlan wa sahlan,*" the shopkeeper greeted us.

He rose from behind the back jewelry counter, *misbeh* prayer beads running through his fingers. A young boy appeared almost instantaneously behind us and brought tea.

For most buyers of gold and other high-end items in the souk, these transactions formed over tea or coffee, with the merchant subtly and then slightly more assertively displaying his goods to entice potential buyers. In the process of assessing potential profit from the deal, the most expensive items were offered first—precious gems set in the heaviest white gold with lots of detailed craftsmanship and four- or five-figure price tags. If all went well, a deal was consummated—perhaps not what either party wanted or expected, but a deal nonetheless—and everyone went home satisfied enough.

The merchant offered one of these four-figure items. Zayn lit a cigarette and sipped loudly from his tea glass.

After a few more attempts, the merchant began pulling out plain wedding bands from under the counter. We each slipped our left ring fingers through a metal sizer from a chain of at least a dozen the shopkeeper had hooked on his belt loop. The clank and rattle of the sizers signaled his movement.

We chose thin gold rings. They were placed on a scale, weighed, and paid for. When the merchant offered to wrap them with embossed gift paper in a ring box, Zayn laughed. Instead, he picked up my ring and slid it over my knuckle.

"*Mabrouk*, congratulations," he said softly.

The shopkeeper looked on, mouth slightly agape, prayer beads clicking furiously.

Our next stop was a cloth shop and then a tailor. Earlier in the day, as I sobbed over the ironing board, Zayn had comforted me by assuring me such things could be replaced. So I had collected the remnants of the burned shirt and carefully wrapped them in a plastic bag to take with me. I carried the bag into a fabric shop near the tentmakers' souk. The shopkeeper greeted us, offering tea. I took my blouse from the bag and explained what I wanted.

He led me to a wall of pastels. Huge bolts of cloth were arranged from the floor to the ceiling by colors and patterns: floral, geometric, solids, darks, pastels, shades of white and black. I spent nearly twenty minutes trying to match the blouse's unique color. Zayn and the shopkeeper looked on with increasing impatience. I finally settled on a shade of lavender with matching buttons.

After paying for the material, we asked the shopkeeper to recommend a tailor. He directed us to an ancient sliver of a shop squeezed between two tanneries. Sitting inside was a skinny man with Coke bottle glasses and skin the color and texture of his neighbor's worked leather. When he smiled, his white moustache seemed to wiggle off his lip. I gave him the old blouse and the new material. He unlooped the faded measuring tape from around his neck and delicately took my measurements in the open air of his shop.

A week later when we picked up the shirt, I could tell immediately that it wasn't right. The color was too pale and the cotton material too stiff. In the dressing room I buttoned the last button and gazed at myself in the mirror. What I didn't see was the silky plum-colored blouse that had felt cool against my skin and had flowed slightly with the movement of my body. I stood there alone and told myself, *It's only a piece of clothing—think of what you still have.*

I stepped out of the dressing room and the tailor smiled proudly.

"See! Just like the other one."

I turned to Zayn and forced a smile. His eyes met mine.

"*Yalla!* Let's go," he said.

❦

Um Alaa—Alaa's mother—arrived a couple of weeks after me. It seemed that Alaa had not done well enough in the last academic year to advance to the next grade level, so his mother had come from Kuwait, where the family lived in exile, to take care of household chores and, presumably, to make sure that Alaa focused on his studies. She was large and soft, not unlike her son. Gold bracelets dangled from her pale wrists, and four gold and diamond rings were dispersed among her slightly sausage-like fingers. She was pale with champagne-colored freckles. Her hair, the color of weak tea like Alaa's, was still thick and with enough wave to lend her a youthful appearance. A sweet aroma stirred in her wake when she walked by.

Soon after her arrival, we moved into a slightly larger two-bedroom apartment nearby that was less student-like. Zayn once again engaged Alaa in combat over who would sleep where, although this time Alaa was aided by his mother. The larger bedroom had a queen-size bed and a large wardrobe with matching vanity. The other, smaller room was furnished with two single beds and a chest of drawers. As Alaa and his mother attempted to convince Zayn that the two of them should sleep in the smaller room, I proved a poor ally. At the height of negotiations, Zayn questioned me point blank.

"You don't mind sleeping with Um Alaa in the big bed, do you?"

"Of course not," I responded weakly.

But I offered no further support to my husband. By this time it had been nearly two months since we had slept together. Alaa threw up his hands and wheeled his mother's suitcase into the big room. When later in the day I suggested to Zayn that he reconsider their offer to allow us to sleep together, his terse response told me what I already knew.

"We are already asking too much from them, Rebecca!"

I was well aware of the risk they were taking on our behalf. We were complete strangers when we showed up on their doorstep just a few weeks earlier. But if the Egyptian authorities discovered that they were harboring an illegal Palestinian on the run from the Israelis, Alaa's studies would end in deportation or worse. And Um Alaa and the rest of the family would certainly never be allowed back in the country—a significant loss given that it was the only place they could see their relatives from Gaza. Yet, I couldn't help wanting to be with my husband.

We spent our days making up reasons to go downtown, window shopping and watching television. We were waiting. Somehow Zayn was to get word from political connections of his next move—where to go and how to get there. When the message would come and what it would be we had no idea. In the meantime, we waited. Riding the bus during one of our downtown excursions, I dared to press Zayn to speculate on our future.

"Please don't ask me questions I don't know the answers to," he replied.

I turned toward the window to watch a group of schoolchildren scuttle down the sidewalk, miniature backpacks and pigtails bouncing behind them.

"I wouldn't mind just pitching a tent someplace—as long as it was our own," I half chuckled.

"That's not a joke to someone who grew up in a refugee camp!"

I turned to him, shocked for a moment. Then I offered an apology that elicited no response.

❧

As fall progressed, the summer's heat gradually released its grip on Cairo. In mid-October we got word that two friends from Britain would be arriving soon to show their documentary in the city's international film festival. We had met Francesca and Zaha the previous year when they were making a film about Gaza during the intifada. We quickly became close friends. The prospect of seeing them, seeing anyone, really, from our life before exile buoyed me through the opaque monotony of waiting for what would happen next.

We arranged to meet them at their hotel, and finally the day to do so arrived. We walked into the Semiramis Hotel, which was like landing on another planet. We milled around the lobby waiting for them, trying to avoid the probing gaze of the security guards. Polished crystal glinted in the sunlight that slipped in with the *whoosh* of the lacquered brass and mahogany doors. The tarboosh-attired sons of upper Egyptian peasants whisked the heavy doors open for a steady stream of foreigners and well-coiffed Egyptians, whose high heels and Italian shoes clicked across the marble floors.

We waved at Francesca and Zaha as they emerged from an elevator. Watching them cross the lobby toward us, Zayn's face relaxed into a true smile for the first time in weeks. We embraced and exchanged greetings, all four of us a bit dazed by the surreal context of our reunion. Zayn was a fugitive in the country, while they were honored guests of the Mubarak regime's Ministry of Culture.

Francesca and Zaha had each found her way to Gaza, and now Cairo, via a circuitous route that wound through other parts of the Middle East, and indeed other parts of the world. Francesca was raised in an upper-class British family, her father having served as the U.K.'s ambassador to the U.S. during the late 1950s and early 1960s. His mission was to repair the "special relationship" between the two countries after Britain joined France and Israel in invading Egypt and capturing the newly nationalized Suez Canal. No doubt his young daughter prepared him for delicate repair missions, given Francesca's propensity for doing things like riding her bicycle through the *inside* of the ambassador's residence, and carving "UP THE USSR" on the marble columns of the stately building. Francesca's early film career included documentaries about coal miners in the U.K., apartheid South Africa, and discrimination against Palestinian citizens of Israel. At one point she worked for Amnesty International and visited

Robert Mugabe while he was held as a political prisoner in colonial Rhodesia.

Zaha was the daughter of a long-time Iraqi statesman and former foreign minister who went into exile rather than serve under Saddam Hussein. Her life of exile led to films about Palestinian refugees in Lebanon, an Iranian woman long-distance truck driver, and, after the U.S. invasion of Iraq, a nation picking up the pieces of one historical disaster after another.

We left the hotel under the increasingly long stares from the beefy guards and searched for a place to sit and talk. Weaving through the human and nonhuman traffic of Cairo, we shared snippets of conversation that began to catch them up on our exodus from Gaza and current circumstances. We finally found a café that was emptying out for midday prayers and settled into a quiet table in the back. As the thin, white-shirted waiter leaned a slight bow away from our table after taking our order, we looked at each other across the wobbly wooden table. Outside, the call to prayer was launched from a nearby minaret into air thick with lingering humidity and honking horns.

"*Allah hu Akbar.* God is great," muttered a man's voice in response.

He was sitting close by but was partially obscured by a column, a bubbling *nargeelah* water pipe the only indication of his presence until now. I looked up as his words filled our silence. His skin—a shade or two lighter than the thick coffee he drank—folded into delicate crevices that roamed across his face.

"I can't fucking believe we're sitting here in Cairo with you two!" Francesca's voice burst forth with the perfect accent of the Queen's English. Elbows melting out from underneath us, foreheads bowing down to touch the table, heads arching back, mouths wide open, Zayn and I exploded with the cathartic hysteria of those denied a reason to laugh for too long.

Before their film's screening the next night, we spent the day together at the Great Pyramids in Giza, in the desert just outside

Cairo. As evening approached, we arrived at the downtown theater. The festival director, stuffed into his Ministry of Culture Official Events Suit, nervously introduced himself to Zaha and Francesca, escorted them to their front row seats, and hurriedly excused himself, completely ignoring Zayn and me. We found seats in the back of the theater. The festival director came back and chatted with them for a few minutes, after which our friends began glancing anxiously our way. Francesca suddenly stood and walked to the back of the theater toward us.

"The translator isn't here and no one can find him," she sighed. "There's supposed to be a Q & A afterwards and the festival director is freaking out!"

The director reappeared and motioned toward Francesca to take her seat. She gave us one final eye roll before she turned and walked back. In classical Arabic tinged with the melodic lilt of Egyptian colloquial, the minister welcomed the crowd and briefly introduced Zaha and Francesca. Then the theater darkened.

Images of Gaza floated into view, mirage-like at first and then stretching starker across the screen. The film's opening shot panned across the familiar sandy stretch between our house and the camp that served, at various times, as a soccer field for Shati's youth and as a staging ground for army raids on the camp. Near the end of the scene, our clothesline flickered into view. Then Lutfi appeared on the screen, sitting on the cinderblocks strewn across the roof of the house. He spoke about the uprising and life in Gaza, framed by the glint of the sea in the background and our neighbor Fathi's TV antenna. Trembling slightly, I snuck a glimpse of Zayn sitting next to me. His face was stone-like, his body completely motionless. A chill trembled through me, and I broke into hot tears.

Fifty-one minutes later, as the screen darkened and we blinked against the rising theater lights, I felt I could breathe again. We gathered in a corner of the theater with Zaha and Francesca during the brief intermission.

"So, how did you like it?" Zaha questioned.

Zayn studied his shoes. I could tell he wanted a cigarette.

"Really Zaha," he was looking toward the ceiling, "I was not expecting this."

Francesca and Zaha shifted uncomfortably and glanced quickly at each other.

"You've managed to capture the…the *ruh* of Gaza. How do you say this?" he turned to me.

"The soul of Gaza," I offered.

"Yes! It is the soul of Gaza, its essence…" he trailed off, turning his eyes back to the corner of the ceiling.

For a moment, no one said a word. And then, eyes glistening, Zaha reached out a delicate hand and stroked Zayn's arm.

"Thank God!" Francesca erupted.

We drew in a breath and laughed again.

"Now what are we going to do about this fucking translator?"

"I'll do it."

We all turned and stared at Zayn.

"Zayn…." I started before Francesca cut in.

"Are you out of your bloody mind!?" she hissed, stepping closer to him. "The place is crawling with government officials!"

"I can do it."

"Right. And I suppose I should introduce you as my friend the *fedayee* from Gaza, who's snuck over the border, escaping from the Israelis to be here tonight to translate for the Ministry!"

"Zayn, thank you but…" Zaha offered softly, but with a voice edged with worry.

"I'll do it," he repeated, "Just tell them I am a colleague from Gaza who was involved with the film. *Khallas.* That's it."

The metal doors of the theater began creaking open and banging shut as the audience filtered back in.

"*Yalla,* let's go," Zayn marched toward the front of the theater.

The three of us looked at each other, mouths parted slightly, silent.

"*Yalla,*" we intoned.

Sustained applause accompanied Zaha and Francesca to the microphone. As Zayn stepped in next to Zaha, the minister stiffly stood in the aisle near the first row of seats. During the first question—about the difficulties of filming during the intifada—I could hear him jiggling the change in his pocket without taking his eyes off Zayn. By the third question about the film's reception in the West and the Arab world, the minister stopped jiggling his change, walked to the back of the theater, and took a seat next to a blonde woman wearing pink silk and large diamonds.

Back in Francesca's and Zaha's hotel room after the screening, we emptied the mini bar of Stellas—the local beer—and toasted a truly extraordinary evening.

Zayn raised his glass.

"To my host, Hosni Mubarak!"

"Hosni Mubarak!" we all clinked.

Francesca flipped on the television to the Egyptian equivalent of MTV. Whining violins, tablas, and hand cymbals combined in a quick, sultry rhythm as a woman shimmied and gyrated her ample hips across the screen, shimmering in what was essentially a bikini strung with sequins and scarves. Zayn started beating out a rhythm on a bedside table as Francesca and Zaha started clapping in time. Inspired, I jumped up and hastily tied Zaha's *kuffiyeh* around my hips and launched into a belly dance. Making my way across the room, my hands twirled in gyroscopic circles as my hips did more bumping than grinding. I came to the large curtained balcony window, behind which I could make out the lights of Cairo reflected in the Nile below.

"*Yalla, ya Qahira!*" I shouted to the unsuspecting city as I dramatically flung the curtains back and shook my hips.

There was a howl behind me. I turned back to my small audience and saw Zayn clap the side of his head as he shook with laughter. Without warning he jumped up, bounded across the room, threw his arms around me, and planted a loud kiss on my left cheek. I froze. Looking over his shoulder as he embraced me, I saw Francesca and Zaha look at each other and exchange slow smiles.

"I didn't know you had such talent, Rebecca," Zaha said.

"Neither did I," I laughed in reply.

Saying goodbye at the door, Francesca turned to us and with her eyes focused on Zayn said, "You know, Zaha and I have meetings and interviews most of the day tomorrow." She crossed her arms and leaned against the door jam. "So we could give you one of our keys now and you could come back here and just hang out for a while."

Zayn blinked and my stomach tightened.

"Why would we want to bother you like this?" Zayn replied, a thin muscle rippling almost imperceptibly under his high cheekbone.

"Zayn, don't be such a *hamar*!" Francesca admonished him, with the Arabic word for donkey, her favorite term of endearment. "We really will be gone and you and Rebecca…."

"*La! Shukran*. No, thank you." Zayn insisted, raising his hand in a gesture meant to silence as much as it was meant to bid them goodbye.

"*Tisbahu 'ala kheir*. Good night."

Silence shrouded us in the elevator ride down to the lobby. We exited the hotel's glitter and glass, and walked toward the microbus stop, Zayn smoking and saying nothing. The sounds of horns honking and engines grinding their way through the dusty city traffic rose up like a wall. I struggled to keep up with Zayn's nervous pace.

Zayn stopped and turned suddenly toward me.

"What did you say to them?" he demanded.

During our trip to the pyramids earlier in the day, Francesca and Zaha had asked me about our living arrangements while Zayn had been off buying cold drinks for us.

"They asked about the place where we were staying and I told them about the sleeping arrangements," I confessed.

"*Ya, allah!* Oh, God," he exclaimed, turning away and looking up at the blue-black sky. He lifted both hands upward, then slapped them down on the sides of his thighs, in frustration.

"Giving us the key was their idea," I defended myself. "And besides, there's nothing wrong with it! We haven't been together since we got here, Zayn!"

He turned back to me, shaking his head, and with a half-laugh replied.

"You really don't understand the situation, do you?"

Without waiting for a response, he resumed walking toward the bus stop. I followed. In the distance the Nile flowed silently into the night.

Soon thereafter, a visit from a Gazan relative brought cash—and a plan.

I was to fly to Tunis, where a friend of Zayn's, Nidal—a fellow ex-prisoner who had been deported by the Israelis at the beginning of the intifada—would arrange help. I had never met him but remembered the international outcry that his deportation had caused.

Barely a month after the uprising began, Nidal and three others were arrested, accused of "incitement," and unceremoniously dumped in Israel's then "security zone" in southern Lebanon in another failed attempt to quell the uprising. The U.S. even managed to express its "deep regret" about the Israeli move—a rare if tepid criticism of its staunch ally. With some experience reestablishing himself in exile, Nidal could use personal and political connections to get Zayn out of Egypt. At least that was the hope.

That this trip heralded a move out of the no-man's-land Zayn and I had been enduring in Cairo was invigorating. I left for Tunis hopeful that when I returned we'd have at least some idea of what the future held in store for us.

The plane circled the northern Mediterranean, its tapestry of blues and blue-greens weaving into the Gulf of Tunis, which reached toward the city. From above, the scalloped edge of the coast looked like the top of a Valentine heart. Descending, I caught glimpses of stately French colonial architecture, mosques with minarets that looked like sand castles, and ageless swaying palms.

Nidal met me at the airport and took me to his home in a quiet suburb of the capital. His wife, called Um Ramzi, "mother of Ramzi," after their son was born, emerged from the kitchen after we entered the house. Tall, slender and raven-haired, Um Ramzi greeted us and immediately showed me to my room. She had been an architect in Palestine, but since her arrival in Tunis just a few months ago, Um Ramzi was now a stay-at-home mother of two toddlers in a foreign country. The week I was there she went out of the house once.

She cooked and cleaned fastidiously. So I touched as little as possible, wiped away water splashes from the bathroom sink after I used it, and even made sure the bites of food I took were measured during our mostly silent meals. During one of these, Nidal suggested I visit a museum, and I jumped at the chance to get out of the house.

Late the next morning, he returned to the house to pick me up. Um Ramzi declined to join us. We drove out of the suburb where they lived toward the city center. The museum was housed in a low building the color of light toast. A portico supported by arched-topped columns extended from it. Nidal escorted me in and paid my admission. He waited for me at the ticket counter while I wandered the exhibits: shelves full of ancient relics housed behind Plexiglas and dust; sarcophagus-shaped cases containing shards of pottery and mosaics. A few amputated Roman statues lingered in corners.

I must have been the first visitor in a while—in some rooms I had to wait for a guard to turn on the lights.

I left sadder than when I arrived.

One afternoon the phone rang.

"Allo?" Um Ramzi answered. Instantly her face melted into a smile—the first I'd seen, I realized at that moment.

"Mama! *Keefik?*"

She turned and walked into the hallway. From the living room I could hear murmurs of conversations, her voice lilting again when another relative came on the other end of the phone.

After about twenty minutes, there was silence. She then retreated into the kitchen.

I walked in a few minutes later and found her at the kitchen table, sitting, uncharacteristically, her forehead resting in her palm. She turned to me, eyes rimmed red.

"*Asfah.* I'm sorry," I said, backing out of the kitchen.

Um Ramzi closed her eyes and shook her head slowly.

"You know how we found out they had deported Nidal?"

Um Ramzi's voice was barely a whisper.

"We heard it on the news. Like you hear the football score."

She took a deep breath, lifted her face to the ceiling, and rose from the chair.

"I need to start dinner." Um Ramzi said, sounding like she was trying to convince herself.

Nidal was soft-spoken with a round, boyish face and a shy smile. He moved through this new life with an air suggesting a mixture of determination and resignation. In addition to the trauma of his family being expelled from their home in 1948 when he was six, two other events in his life were what I imagined he drew on in facing exile: being blinded in one eye by shrapnel as his family escaped advancing Israeli soldiers; and being imprisoned for fifteen years after being accused of involvement in a bus bombing, charges he has always denied.

Before his imprisonment he had been a teacher. In Tunis he spent much of his time attending political meetings and writing. His reserved manner and quiet way made an impact in ways that more flamboyant and garrulous men could not. In the house, on the rare occasion when he raised his voice to discipline his children, one had the impression that it was a real effort for him to do so. But the shock of such an uncharacteristic move immediately had the desired effect.

During my week in Tunis, Nidal introduced me to others who knew Zayn from Gaza and from prison. After a few days it was decided that I would fly to Damascus where a larger Palestinian exile community had grown, from the time of the uprising and earlier. They would be in a better position to help. Nidal gave me a letter to deliver to contacts there that summarized the situation.

I had arrived in Tunis hoping to glimpse what our life would be like in exile. Now, on a plane bound for Damascus, I recalled what Nidal had said to me the first day we'd met. "There is no struggle here. Only inside," he'd confided, referring to what was happening in Palestine.

A distressing assessment, but it couldn't be one Zayn shared, could it?

The Mediterranean—shards reflecting the setting sun—which I glimpsed out of the airplane window soon gave way to the dusty outskirts of Damascus. Surely things were better there.

❦

The man sporting the angled military beret peered down at me through his Polaroids. "Welcome to the Syrian Arab Republic," declared the billboard-sized banner. Greeting me was Hafez al-Asad, long-time ruler and strongman of Syria. The clenched, square jaw, thinning hair, and fading moustache conjured up an aging Don Corleone.

The squeal of the luggage carousel had a distinct rhythm to it—a slow waltz in an off-kilter, 5/4 time—but was bereft of any luggage. A bank of plate-glass windows faced the baggage claim area, and I could see people milling about outside.

The *thud* of luggage hitting the side of the carousel from the chute refocused my attention. I moved closer in, jostling for a place near the belt with a surprisingly aggressive sixty-something, who eyed me from under her headscarf. My mother's scuffed Samsonite finally emerged. I hauled it off the belt and turned hopefully toward the windows. Scanning the knots of people I saw him: Abdel Karim from Jebalya Camp—the slight, quick young man in the orange VW Beetle who had shown me around Gaza my first day there. He had gone into exile during the first year of the intifada and here he was. Here we were, peering at one other through a window at the Damascus airport. His tight jaw broke into a smile and he waved. I waved back and moved toward the exit. I noticed then another man standing next to him. Abdel Karim nodded an okay to him, and the man immediately turned and disappeared into the crowd outside.

I stepped into the cool November night, and we shook hands in the glow of the airport's neon lights.

"Ahlan wa sahlan ila Damashk, welcome to Damascus," he said, arms open.

We looked at each other for a moment and laughed.

The man who had been standing next to Abdel Karim pulled up to the curb in an industrial gray Jeep. Khalid hopped out, introduced himself, and slung my suitcase into the back. Another exiled Gazan, Khalid maneuvered out of the tangle of cars, and soon we were speeding down a highway heading north. In the distance I could see houses and apartment buildings, television antennas sprouting from them like exotic flora. A road sign pointed the way toward Beirut, 88 kilometers northwest.

Ten minutes later we exited off the highway onto a two-lane road that wound through a mixture of fields, roadside shops, and simple, rectangular homes. The clusters of buildings began to thicken, as did the traffic. Soon we were driving down a main thoroughfare lined with darkened storefronts and three- or four-story apartment buildings. I could see clotheslines strung over balconies and potted plants peeping over their edges. It was after ten, so most of the stores were closed. One falafel stand, its owner's face illuminated by a kerosene lamp as he stood watch over a metal wok, was the exception.

After a few minutes, the Jeep pulled up in front of an apartment building—a corner, three-story block painted an odd red-brown. Abdel Karim and Khalid got out.

"I thought we were going to Yarmouk camp," I asked, bending forward to peer out the window.

"Yes. We're here," Abdel Karim said, opening the back hatch door to retrieve my suitcase.

"This is the camp?"

It looked nothing like the camps in the Occupied Territories I was used to seeing, with their open sewers and one-room shelters seemingly stitched together with corrugated metal roofs. Yarmouk was established in 1957 to house the thousands of refugees who had been living in neighborhoods on the edges of Damascus since their expulsion from Palestine in 1948. But over the years it had become a lower-middle class suburb of Damascus, also housing Syrians desperate for affordable housing near the capital.

"It's not exactly Jebalya, is it?" Abdel Karim smirked, slamming closed the back door.

I climbed out and looked around. Eddies of dust swirled up from the street with a sudden gust. A patchwork of buildings rose vertically as far as I could see, impromptu balconies jutting out like lips over the sidewalk. I followed Abdel Karim and Khalid into a darkened doorway. Khalid led us up the stairs, flicking his Zippo every few seconds to light the way.

"*Qat'a al kahribah.* The electricity is out," he explained.

I wondered why, but didn't ask.

Khalid rapped on a large wooden door at the top of the second flight. A small woman with short-cropped black hair and kind-looking eyes traced in kohl opened the door. Fida smiled broadly. "*Alhumdillah 'assalameh.* Thank God for your safe arrival," she said, welcoming us in and introducing herself.

She instructed Khalid where to put my suitcase. He and Abdel Karim politely declined Fida's invitation for coffee and left, telling me that they would return in the morning to talk about Zayn.

Fida had grown up in the Tel al-Za'atar refugee camp in Beirut, the sight of a horrific massacre in 1976 by right-wing Phalangist forces backed by Hafez al-Assad. She had made her way to Yarmouk after the

Israeli invasion in 1982 that destroyed much of what hadn't been decimated by the civil war. An activist in progressive Palestinian women's organizations in Lebanon, Fida continued her work here. There was a *joie de vivre* I would come to associate with her that rarely lagged, despite or perhaps because of her personal history.

She settled me into what appeared to be a sitting room, producing a thick foam mattress and plenty of blankets for the cold nights. It took several minutes, but I managed to convince her that I wasn't hungry and there was no need to make me dinner at this late hour and in the dark.

Bright morning light flooded into the room where I lay. My eyes opened to an unfamiliar ceiling. It was one of those mornings where I had to consciously remember where I was. I could hear the unmuffled sounds emitted by the creative transportation options in the camp: three-wheel motorized jitneys generically called Suzukis; circa-1950s banana yellow Chevrolets, and the occasional over-burdened donkey pulling a flat-bed cart. I dressed quickly and emerged from the room to find Khalid and Abdel Karim already drinking coffee with Fida. I joined them, and we made a plan to meet with various political connections they had who might help.

Like the camp itself, this world that I was about to enter was vaguely familiar, but also marked with a foreignness that I hadn't anticipated. The first time I walked outside it was startling to see Palestinian flags fluttering alongside pictures of Yasser Arafat or other Palestinian leaders; in the Territories such gestures would bring a stint in prison, at the very least.

There were offices I visited during the two weeks I was there that were dedicated to working on different aspects of the Palestinian cause: the office of the Occupied Territories; the office of foreign relations; the office of youth programs; the press office. They all had people sitting behind desks, bored-looking guards, and coffee break rooms.

I had come to understand the Palestinian struggle through the lens of the intifada: protests and strikes called by the grassroots leadership and increasing calls to boycott Israeli goods. In the West Bank when schools were closed during the intifada, underground classrooms were established to continue educating the population. To avoid detection by the Israeli army when walking to "school," students and teachers would camouflage their books and teaching materials in grocery bags under loaves of bread and cartons of eggs. Here, resistance and state-building was a nine-to-five job, with a lunch break and health benefits. Why did I register this with a sense of unease?

Once again I met several friends of Zayn's from Palestine—prison and after—and others who had clearly heard of him but who didn't actually know him. Those who knew him would, upon meeting me, pump my arm and exclaim giddily, "*Hathee marat Zayn!* This is Zayn's wife!" The others would extend their arms and ask, "*Hathee marat Zayn?*"

In the end it was decided that I would return to Cairo via Amman, taking with me money and instructions for Zayn, rolled into yet another tiny capsule that I was to give no one but him. Even I did not know what it said.

Standing in a queue at the Cairo airport, every few minutes I heard the dull *thump* of the stamp land on someone's passport. I shuffled closer to the immigration control counter. Behind it, I could see the droopy, raisin eyes of a young man flicker between his desk and the person in front of him. His pressed-crisp uniform, the color and shape of a desert mirage, stood out against the shabby browns and grays of the terminal. A folded red beret was snapped into the shoulder loop, pinned with a shiny brass star.

It was my turn. As I stepped beyond the line separating the queue from the inspector, the shape of the hard little capsule pressed against my rib from its place taped inside my bra strap.

I should have hidden it better, I reprimanded myself. I knew the reputation of Egyptian prisons and that there was little that Mubarak wouldn't do to prove his loyalty to the U.S. Handing over a Palestinian "terrorist" to the Israelis would please his paymasters.

I slid my passport across the counter. The officer's leg jiggled as he flipped through the pages. His eyes darted up at me, then back to my picture, then up again. The jiggling intensified and the aluminum wheels of his chair began to squeak.

I prompted myself, *I'm a tourist. Looking forward to buying lots of Christmas presents for my family.*

He bent over an oversized ledger and began writing, the numbers and words stretching across from right to left. Suddenly he turned to the counter next to him and said something to the officer manning that post. His coworker looked at me and they chortled in unison. The *thud* of his stamp was followed by the *slap* of my passport on the counter. I grabbed it and moved on quickly to claim my luggage.

Back at the apartment, Zayn took the capsule from me and went into the bedroom he shared with Alaa and closed the door. When he emerged, he asked for the money I had been given—about a thousand dollars.

"Was this helpful?" I asked, not sure how to read his expression.

"The money will help," he replied. "I'm not sure of anything else."

By then it was well into November. In the following days, Zayn went several times to the telephone and telegraph office in central Cairo, where you could make international calls from a bank of phones lined up on a wall like slot machines. You prepaid for a certain number of minutes at a dimly lit desk staffed by more men in uniforms, were assigned a phone, and then waited for it to ring. One of these calls finally connected Zayn to his brother Abdullah in Benghazi, whom he hadn't spoken with in over twenty years.

"*Keef halek* How are you?" Zayn's voice, usually discreet and subdued in public since reaching Cairo, boomed when Abdullah came on the line.

I noticed how deep the crow's feet around his eyes had become when he smiled. He waved me over to say hello. After doing so I handed the phone back to Zayn and returned to the waiting area. He leaned in close to the wall and spoke for several minutes, his voice inaudible. The only way I knew he was still talking was by his head nodding every so often. I found an empty orange plastic chair near a group of women doing their best to keep fussy children from becoming wailing ones. Day laborers paced the charcoal-colored linoleum, leaving dusty footprints in their wake. One woman, who had watched me talk to Abdullah, tapped her companion's knee and gestured toward me. They looked at each other and talked in a bent-head whisper. The children—clutching bottles and chip bags—stopped whining and turned to look at me. I rose from the chair and walked back to where Zayn stood talking, hoping his minutes were almost used up and we could leave.

That evening in the apartment, Ayman, his mother, Zayn, and I gathered around the rabbit-eared television to watch the breaking news of November 1989: the fall of the Berlin Wall. Jubilant crowds sang and danced and tore at the structure. Its graffiti-splattered western side gave way, chunk by chunk, to sledgehammers and pick axes, as East German border guards looked on in confusion and amusement. An unspoken foreboding hung in the air. The prospect of unrivaled U.S. power did not bode well for the Palestinians. Nevertheless, the images of long-separated families and friends embracing, as much-hated barriers were forced aside, moved us to tears. Among those expressions of unexpected joy and remembered sorrow, we searched for our own faces.

They were difficult to find.

7
A Man's Home Is His Castle

In early December, I learned that my stepfather had died. The taxi to the airport waited for me, its engine ticking away.

"I will call when I can," Zayn said.

His blue-green eyes had begun to lose their luster.

"Take care." I turned to him. "I love you."

"I know. Me, too."

Back in Ohio, I helped my mother establish her new life after moving out of the house she had shared with her husband. Being there turned out to be a welcome break. Zayn, too, was no doubt relieved.

My mother bought a two-bedroom condo in the same suburb where I grew up, and I took pleasure in lining her kitchen cabinets with contact paper and helping her pick out new dishes. For months I had been living as a guest of strangers, not knowing where or when I would again have a home.

She allowed me to deflect questions about what Zayn and I were doing in Cairo. I suspected she was just glad we were out of Gaza. When Zayn called, she would smile and chat with him first, telling him about the new place and asking how he liked Cairo. I cringed when I heard that question, although I never knew how he answered it.

After the New Year, Zayn told me to apply for a Syrian visa. He also gave me a number to call if he wasn't in Cairo when I returned.

"Are you going to Syria?" I asked him.

I was puzzled how he could make such a journey that required crossing several countries on a nonexistent passport.

Silence on the other end.

And then, "Of course not. I'm going to visit my brother."

As soon as I hung up, I searched the country codes listing in the phone book for the number he had given me: 218. It wasn't there. It took a call to the operator and an innocent-sounding inquiry to find out that he was going to Libya.

In January 1990, the U.S. travel embargo against Libya was still in effect. If Zayn was going there and I was getting a Syrian visa, how were we going to end up together? The wall-to-wall carpet in my mother's living room floated around me, and I felt adrift in a sea of beige.

I procured the visa and a week later, the last day of January, I was standing in the Cairo airport. The *thump* of visa stamps and the stern gaze of Hosni Mubarak once again welcomed me. A friend from college had recently moved to Cairo to teach at American University. Staying with Christina saved me from having to return to the same apartment with Alaa and his mother and relive those excruciating months with Zayn.

The day after my arrival I went to the same telephone center downtown where Zayn had first called his brother. Egyptians and foreigners streamed into the French colonial building, but once inside, they separated into small clusters. Calls to Middle East countries were put through to phones banked along one wall, where locals and other Arabs sat. Calls to Europe and the U.S. happened on the opposite side. After a few minutes, a young man wearing tight jeans and too much aftershave approached.

"Excuse me, miss," he said.

With an exaggerated smile, he pointed toward the other side of the room, where Europeans wearing shorts and floppy hats were calling home.

"I think you're meant to be in that section."

At that moment, the phone I had been directed to, rang. I darted toward it and greeted Zayn in Arabic. Glancing back, I saw the smile on the young man's face fade into confusion. A few of the waiting women suppressed giggles. A janitor sweeping the floor said something to the young man, prompting laughter from those seated. The young man turned quickly and disappeared.

"*Keefak?* How are you?"

Zayn and I chatted briefly. Then he put on Abdullah, who put on his wife, who then brought three of their children to talk to me. Throughout all of the essentially identical conversations, I could hear Zayn laughing and chattering in the background. I smiled into the phone.

When he came back on the line, his voice shifted.

"*Isma'ee,* listen."

I nestled the phone in the crook of my neck and pulled a notepad and pen from my purse. Someone was to meet me at the airport. The plan was, they'd get me through immigration without having to stamp my passport. I asked Zayn if he would be at the airport, too.

"I will try."

His answer lingered in my ear for a moment. I said nothing in response. I was learning not to ask questions he couldn't answer. Then I walked directly from the telephone office to the travel agent near Tahrir Square I had used before.

Three days later I was on a plane bound for Benghazi.

My window seat offered a view of the yellow desert that stretched out in undulating layers, like cake batter before the baking. Lunch was served, and when I covered up the uneaten contents of my aluminum tray, my seatmate—an older woman squeezed in the seat next to me, her round face framed in a white headscarf—pointed to the roll and butter still sitting on the little plastic plate. I looked at her and nodded. She smiled and quickly wrapped up my leftovers in her napkin and wedged it in a plastic bag, along with the unopened cup of water from her tray.

We deplaned on the tarmac and were met by ancient buses that bounced to a halt in front of the terminal. The buses' doors squeaked open, and the passengers streamed out. Those who could, ran for the terminal entrance. Children and the elderly, including the woman with my roll safely tucked into her carry-on, fell behind. I was among the laggards.

Entering the squat, dusty-white concrete building, I scanned the scene before me for a face I might recognize. My fellow passengers jostled past—even the roll lady overtook me. When I heard that familiar sound of the passport stamper echoing in the mostly empty space, I swallowed hard. The signs for immigration control came into view, and I had no choice but to join the queue. I had no Plan B if I reached the counter where the immigration official would expect me to offer up my passport. To my right, a large man approached, the burgundy color of his suit jacket and tie surprising me. He stopped in front of me, his bulk obscuring my view of anyone behind him.

"Ribeekah?" he said, looking down at a piece of paper in his hand. His thinning comb-over glistened unexpectedly under the fluorescent lighting.

"Yes?"

Without another word, he turned and started walking toward the far corner of the arrival hall. I hesitated. Then, a movement at the edge of my vision. I turned slightly toward it and saw Zayn waving and smiling just beyond passport control. When I smiled and waved back, a panicked look spread across his face as he gestured for me to follow the man. I rushed after him, catching up just as he approached the very last passport counter, ignoring the hostile stares from those in the queue. His knuckles rapped the formica counter, eliciting from the officer seated behind it an acknowledging smile and sidelong glance. The officer finished recording and stamping the passport of the passenger standing there, who was taking in the burgundy suit and tie with a mixture of disdain and caution. The officer handed him back his passport and he scuttled away.

"*Bassbort.*"

The large man turned to me and opened the palm of his paw-like hand. I rummaged in my purse for the document. He mumbled, "*Istukfor allah,* oh, God," and slid a cigarette from the pocket of his jacket.

I fished my passport from the bottom of my purse and offered it to my escort. He reached for the document, still holding the burning cigarette between his index and middle fingers. As he snatched it out of my hand, the quick movement sent ashes fluttering down onto my knuckles like dirty, burning snow.

He stepped halfway behind the counter and gave my passport to the officer, who began registering the document. My companion leaned in closer to look over his shoulder at the information being registered, his pot belly pushing against the back of the chair so that it rolled the officer flush against the counter. When he tried to move back, my escort and his heft were impervious to the officer's efforts. Trapped, he quickly finished jotting down my information, stamped the piece of paper handed him by my escort, and handed both documents back. My companion turned and walked out of the cubicle and toward the main terminal. Before following him, I glanced at the officer behind the counter. He was rubbing his temples with the thumb and middle finger of one hand.

I caught his eye.

"*Shukran,* thank you" I said.

His head nodded slightly, the look on his face more a grimace than a smile.

By now Zayn was down at our end of the terminal, behind the opaque wall of windows separating passport control from the rest of the airport. He paced a small circuit, smoking and stealing glimpses at us. When we emerged, Zayn approached the escort, who still had my passport. He handed it to Zayn, who stretched out his hand as if to greet him. Something small and white flashed between their outstretched hands, and the escort was gone.

Zayn turned to me with a quick smile.

"*Yalla,* let's go!" he said.

He came toward me, planted a furtive kiss on each cheek, took my hand luggage, and headed for baggage claim.

Out in this larger space, the emptiness of the airport came to life like a ghost: shuttered shops meant to cater to passengers not there or who couldn't afford anything if they were; a newspaper stand selling the official state newspaper, local chocolate and soda; and one cafeteria whose white-capped workers slouched against empty food stalls but who could be coaxed into selling muddy black coffee and tea, their only offering save some Chinese biscuits packaged in shiny foil and dust. Looming over the main entrance was a massive picture of Colonel Gaddafi in full military regalia, a constellation of stars pinned to his chest, hand raised in greeting.

Welcome to the Great Socialist People's Libyan Arab Republic.

A small car, the make of which I did not recognize and that bore no clues to its identity, waited outside. Zayn tossed my suitcases into the trunk, which took the combined effort of Zayn and our young driver Younis to close. The coast receded as we drove toward Zayn's brother's house to the east. Startlingly lush steppes rose farther east and north. In the distance, *Jebal al-Akhdar,* Green Mountain, rose like hips from the body of the surrounding landscape.

We turned off the highway onto a mostly dirt road, the mystery car rattling. Trees I recognized as olive dotted the road. Occasional blooms of jasmine bore testament to the winter rains. We pulled up to a low brick house, modest and well kept. Potted herbs and a skinny chicken stood in the yard; behind the house I caught sight of a small vegetable garden. Before the engine was off, three women and a man emerged from the house's open door. Zayn's older brother Abdullah looked like the younger one Lutfi would in twenty years: his tight fuzz of hair thinning and graying along with his moustache; his coffee-with-cream-colored skin smooth and taut when he smiled. He, his wife Basima, and two of their daughters, Nisreen and Nermin, greeted me with customary cheek kisses and warm embraces.

My suitcases were wrestled out of the trunk and ushered into their home. The door to the tiled entrance—freshly-washed, judging from the still drying squeegee marks—stood open to the relative warmth of the late winter sun. We were shown into the sitting room where mattresses sheathed in bright floral patterns lined the concrete walls. A television propped on a low table stood at one end. Nisreen opened the shuttered windows and pulled back the curtains, welcoming in the breeze.

"*Ahlan wa sahlan, ahlan wa sahlan,* welcome," she repeated, like the others, smiling.

Cold, sweet colas were followed by tea and nuts. By then, the oldest son Nabil had arrived. He had just returned from studying engineering in the Soviet Union, the lightning-quick changes that were happening having left his studies in question. His two younger sisters were getting engaged to two brothers, so he was back in Libya with his family. We all gathered around a huge metal tray filled with couscous and lamb, pungent and sweet. We spent hours eating, talking, drinking tea, and watching television.

Evening brought air cold enough to warrant blankets, which were pulled from a tall wooden armoire in the girls' bedroom. Abdullah tried to give up his and Basima's bed for Zayn and me, which got as far as Ayman's offer in Cairo. Instead, we pushed two of the sitting room mattresses together and spread one large sheet across them. It didn't matter. When the television finally went off and the rest of the family said goodnight, the door was closed and we were alone for the first time in months.

It almost felt like a honeymoon.

Over the next several days, the house buzzed with the preparations for Nisreen's and Nermin's engagement party. Hours were spent preparing party favors—little squares of lace filled with pastel-colored Jordan almonds and tied with pink ribbon—baking sweets, shopping, and arguing with their father over the cost of it all. It felt like a home.

In between shopping trips, the family would take me to see downtown Benghazi—a city sleepy in the way second largest cities are: active enough to attract attention, but not too much attention. The main commercial area was dominated by Italian colonial-era architecture, baked white by the Mediterranean sun. Date palms waved in the sea breeze like giant feather dusters. Life-size portraits and statues of Colonel Gaddafi—portraying him as benevolent overlord, Arab nationalist, or African king would appear unexpectedly in different parts of the city: in the courtyard of a mosque, in the middle of an exhaust-choked roundabout, or on the side of a taller Benghazi building. Our shopping expeditions in government-run stores were short, since most of the shelves were empty. Most goods were procured in the local markets clustered in back alleys of the city. It must have taken months of strategic planning to acquire everything needed for the party, which explained the stacks of boxes, neatly sorted and labeled, in every corner of Abdullah's house.

The celebration was held at one of the few seaside hotels in the city. The garden surrounding Hotel Faradis—Paradise Hotel—had seen better days. Parched shrubs and scrawny rosebushes welcomed visitors to the reception hall. Everything was painted white, creating a sharp contrast to the red velvet upholstered chairs that surrounded small tables set up for the guests. One wall of the hall was all plate glass, the outside of which appeared smoky from years of dried, salty spray, offering a sea view of sorts. We seemed to have the place to ourselves, as there were no signs of actual hotel guests anywhere.

A few musicians arrived, along with the prebaked sweets, cans of soda, and arrangements of plastic flowers I had seen boxed up in the room where we slept. Guests started trickling in, and the pastel pouches dotted the tables where they sat. The band started warming up: an over-synthesized keyboard, drums, and a singer whose patterned shirt colors matched the almonds.

The two brothers, Adel and Marwan, entered the room first. Immaculately groomed in navy blue suits and ties, they were accompanied by their older brother, Bashir, who was married to Najwah, the older sister of the brides-to-be. Bashir stood in for their parents, who lived in Yarmouk Camp in Syria and could not travel.

Then the fiancées arrived—one a shimmer of pink, the other of red, in strapless dresses studded with sequins and rhinestones, each with a strategically placed spray of chiffon lace emerging from the top of one breast. Their jet black hair was shellacked into up-dos, and their eyes were made-up with elaborate layers of color. The girls' stiletto heels clicked their way toward their betrothed, and the room erupted into a wave of ululating women, clapping, and the keyboard's synthesizers blasting at full volume. It was a party.

Guests linked hands and encircled the two couples, each taking a turn to dance. At such gatherings, a modified belly dance—raised hands, rotating wrists and moderately shaking hips—was the only move one needed. Soon virtually all the guests joined in—children and teenagers, middle-aged women in tight dresses with their paunch-bellied husbands, and even an extremely reluctant Zayn, who was dragged laughing to the dance floor and placed in front of me, his red-faced wife.

A few days after the party, we prepared to leave. Arrangements had been made for us to go to Syria, where we would make our new life, thus my need for a Syrian visa. Once again, things had been organized so the Libyan authorities would not stamp my passport. We bade goodbye to Abdullah and his family, who plied us with Arabic sweets, homemade pickles and jams from the bounty of their garden, and many, many kisses. Our luggage was packed into a Land Rover borrowed from a family friend and it was time to leave for the airport.

Zayn laughed and joked with his nieces and nephew as he bade them farewell. Abdullah, I noticed, lingered on the edges. The driver started up the car and turned to look at us. Abdullah moved toward Zayn, whose laughter slid away with the morning mist.

"*Shukran kteir, ya akhuyee.* Thank you very much, my brother," Zayn said, moving to embrace him. The edges of his mouth twitched.

"*Insha' allah, bil gareeb.* Soon, God willing," was Abdullah's only response.

Twenty years had passed since they had last said goodbye,

At the airport some Libyan official met us to facilitate getting us out of the country—the Palestinian without a passport and the passport-laden American without evidence that she was there.

We checked in and got boarding passes. So far so good. I even started to get excited about flying together for the first time. Our escort told us to take our luggage and led us down a hallway next to passport control, where two officials in gray-green uniforms waited. They instructed us to open our luggage on a low table in front of them. One proceeded to poke and prod at Zayn's things, lifting the jars of jams and pickles and looking at Zayn, who smiled.

"*Marat akhuyee.* My sister-in-law," he said and shrugged.

Meanwhile, the other man, about my height, with a narrow face and midnight-black moustache that gleamed in the unnatural light, took me in with a glance. Without a word he gestured toward my bag. I hesitated, then realized he wanted me to open it. I unzipped the large bag and opened the top. Without moving, his eyes swept over the contents and then flickered up at me for an instant. Then he went to work.

He started in the middle, first lifting out some clothes and then rooting through others. He proceeded to the edges of the suitcase, taking out the socks I had stuffed into shoes, unrolling a belt, and unzipping my cosmetic case. From the last item he pulled a white envelope that bulged slightly. It contained pictures I had brought with me when I left Gaza. The officer opened the flap and slid out the photos.

One-by-one he began viewing them, his body perfectly still except for the motion of his right hand moving the front photo behind the others, and then looping to the front to grasp the next one. I hadn't looked at the photos in months. All I could remember was that they were pictures of friends and family.

Then the hand motion stopped and his eyes darted up to me. I didn't move. His eyes moved back to the photo in his hand, then he turned to the guy searching Zayn's luggage and stuck the photo in front of his face.

Zayn looked over at me. I shook my head as my mind raced.

The other officer straightened up from where he'd been leaning over Zayn's suitcase and joined in the viewing with his colleague, heads bowed together like schoolboys on the playground. Finally, the one who had found the photos looked up.

"*Shu hatha?* What's this?" he asked, thrusting the photo at me.

There I was, not-quite-submerged in a bubble bath I was taking while visiting my friend Ellen, the woman with whom I first went to Gaza. She had snapped it as a joke. The humor clearly wasn't translating.

It was bad enough that photos of me half naked were being shared among a couple of bored Libyan bureaucrats. What made the situation potentially catastrophic was that Zayn and I were completely at their mercy—he as a stateless exile and me as someone who wasn't technically supposed to be there at all. If they decided that the photos offended their moral sensibilities or were evidence of other indecent activities, or if they just wanted to show us who was boss, our plan to get to Syria could implode.

My mouth opened, as if to speak, but nothing came out. A flash of heat started behind my eyes and traveled downwards, leaving me slightly dizzy.

"*Sahibti sawaratni beedun ma 'arefet.* My friend took the picture without my knowing." I mumbled. "*Nukta,* a joke."

The men gave no indication that they were listening.

Then Zayn stepped next to me and whispered, "What are they looking at?"

When I explained, a groan escaped him and he turned away.

I turned to the officers again to continue with my explanation, but instead a sob came out. They paused a moment, but then continued shuffling through the photos.

By then, our escort had approached Zayn to ask what was happening. Zayn took him aside, and they whispered together for a few moments. Zayn came back and approached the man who had found the pictures. In a low tone, I heard him apologize and make an off-hand remark about "how foreigners are." He then slipped something out of his pocket and into the officer's free hand. The officer quickly pocketed the contents of his hand, gave Zayn a withering look, and approached me.

"*Irmee hum.* Get rid of them," he snarled, shoving the pictures at me.

I spotted a garbage can near the door where we entered. I grabbed the photos, ran over to it, and tore them into confetti.

I was allowed to close the suitcase, and we proceeded through customs and our version of passport control. Finally seated in the departure lounge waiting for our flight, I tried to speak to Zayn.

"Don't say anything else to me about this," he retorted. "Ever."

We didn't speak until reaching Syria.

❧

Familes are forged in the crucible of revealing who we are to those we love, sometimes in unexpected ways. Long after my father's death, I learned from my mother about the beginning of their marriage. It was a story about my father unlike any I had heard before. But it gave me as much insight into the person I had become, as it did into the person he had been.

Eloping for my parents wasn't difficult. Finding a place to honey-moon proved more so. From their hometown of Cincinnati, they crossed the Ohio River to Kentucky, the state of bluegrass, thoroughbreds, and lax marriage-age laws. My mother wore a tea-length dress of white chiffon, patterned with the faintest pink roses. My father wore his Marine uniform, newly pinned with a Purple Heart from the battle of Iwo Jima, grenade shrapnel still in his leg. His sister Shirley was their witness. The reality of 1940s America disabused them of the desire to honeymoon in Florida, where finding a nice hotel room that far south would have been impossible with a Jewish last name. Instead, they spent a few days in Berea, Kentucky, near the college my mother had left to marry.

Their first meal as a married couple was at a truck stop somewhere in southeastern Kentucky. My father always preferred the front counter to a booth. He would sit with one foot on the metal foot rest that ran the length of the counter, the other bending and straightening, accordion-like, when he swung around to eye the restaurant's comings and goings.

Growing up in our Cincinnati suburb, after Friday night football games I would always check for him at the local coffee shop by looking through the front window from the parking lot before going in. If he was there, he was always on the same stool near the entrance, chatting up the waitresses assembling carry-out orders or schmoozing with customers paying their bills. He never seemed to eat, but always had a cup of coffee growing cold in front of him as he swung from conversation to conversation on his swivel seat.

On that warm June evening in 1945, a Black man wandered unnoticed into the busy truck stop. Tentatively he approached the counter, still invisible to the manager who was yelling orders back to the kitchen, in between refilling coffee cups. Finally he was noticed.

"Whadda you doing here?" sneered the man behind the counter.

My father's leg straightened as he swiveled his seat around to look.

"I just want a glass of water," the Black man said. "Please."

The thunk of the coffee pot the manager had been holding was followed by a loud sizzle as the sloshed coffee hit the burner. His mouth contorted and for a moment he could say nothing.

Then, "Get out of here, n…"

The Black man looked away and turned to go.

"Wait."

My father rose from his chair, wrapping his large, weathered hand around his water glass.

The man behind the counter started to protest.

"Whadda you think you're…"

"Shut up," my father said in his deep voice, still gripping the water glass.

The waitress cutting pie from the sliding-door refrigerator case turned around. The cook in the kitchen peered through the little square window where orders were placed, squinting against the glare of the heat lamp. The other customers at the counter set down their forks and stopped their chit-chat and turned to take in the scene.

My father silently handed the Black man his glass. He gulped the water and hurried out the door. The white man swallowed hard and began chewing the inside of his cheek. My father looked at him and set down the empty glass.

"More water, please."

❧

The cold damp of February greeted us in Damascus. We drove north from the airport through the same countryside off the main highway I had passed through the previous November. Potholes that had become massive puddles with the winter rains slowed us, but the camp's concrete jumble of buildings soon appeared through the fogged car windows.

"It doesn't look like the camps in Gaza, does it?" I observed to Zayn.

He shrugged and lit a cigarette. I couldn't tell if his silent reply was lingering anger from the airport scene, or resignation from coming face-to-face with what would likely be his home-in-exile.

We arrived at Fida's, where we would stay while we looked for an apartment of our own in the camp. As news of our arrival spread, friends of Zayn's from Gaza and from prison began visiting—Abu Hafez, Khalil, Samih, Abu Ahmad, mostly middle-aged men, now with wives and children, who had shared another life with Zayn. They had been young revolutionaries together, full of hope and the just certainty of their cause—one centered not only by the struggle against a common enemy, but by the community they had created among themselves, even though it was bound by iron bars and razor wire. This struggle—exile—was altogether different and showed itself in the hard edges of their mouths and the dullness of their eyes.

But when they saw Zayn, that difference between now and then momentarily slipped away. Huge grins would break across their faces. They would grasp his hand and pull him close, multiple kisses alternating one after the other on each cheek.

"*Alhumdillah 'assalameh.* Thank God for your safe arrival," was the first thing they'd say. Then, sitting back in the plush, overstuffed chairs in Fida's sitting room, they would exhale. For the briefest moment, before anything else was said, I could see them take in Zayn with their breath. And remember. The pause, like the silence of the wind changing direction, filled the room. In an instant it was gone.

"*Keef halek, Abu Omar.* How are you, Abu Omar?" referring to Zayn as "the father of Omar."

Tradition would dictate that if we had a son, he would be named Omar, after Zayn's father. Even though we had no children yet, it was a sign of respect for someone to refer to Zayn this way.

They introduced their wives and children, exchanged family news—the death of parents, the marriage of siblings, the whereabouts of other friends—and inevitably extended invitations to lunch.

It took about a week to find an apartment—*beit ardee,* a ground floor flat looking out onto a large empty lot that reminded me of the sandy stretch between our house in Gaza and Shati camp. But a ground floor apartment was the least desirable kind because it drew more mosquitos and got less natural light. I could feel the dark and cold of the place when we first walked in. What little light that wasn't blocked by the apartment buildings in front of ours mostly escaped the high, small windows that seemed to have been built into the walls as an afterthought. I urged Zayn to keep looking, but he was more concerned with unburdening Fida and her husband Basel. We moved in by the first week of March.

As the month progressed, I waited for a warmth that was slow to arrive. We set about furnishing the apartment, but the gap between my aesthetic sense and Zayn's brought more challenges. My tastes leaned toward the simple. Those represented in Yarmouk Camp furniture stores decidedly did not: crushed velvet sofas, faux Louis XIV tables and chairs, and needlepoint upholstery in bright floral patterns. After visiting three or four stores, Zayn's irritation level rose after each store we left without my agreeing to buy anything. We were sleeping on foam mattresses on the living room floor, so he would have purchased the first bed we saw.

I returned to the house one day and found that, indeed, he had bought an entire bedroom set on his own and had it delivered. I walked into the bedroom to find a massive bedframe the color of melting vanilla ice cream, with an elaborate headboard upholstered in tufted red velvet, accented with shiny gold-colored tacks. The matching armoire and vanity were etched in gold-leaf. The drawers were covered in the same blood-red fabric.

"*'Ajabik?* Do you like it?" Zayn asked, his hands slipping into his front pockets.

I felt like I had walked into a brothel.

"Where did it come from?"

"*Min al shaari'* From the street!" Zayn responded, pulling his hands out of his pockets again. "Where do you think it came from? A friend of mine has a store nearby. He gave us a very good deal."

I bet, I thought but didn't say.

"It's very…bright," I offered.

"*Mish 'ajebha* She doesn't like it," Zayn exclaimed to the ceiling.

"Zayn, I'm sorry," I tried to explain, "it's just that I like a plainer, simpler look."

"Simpler. Plainer," he repeated, eyes rolling.

"Why did you buy it without asking me first?" I retorted.

"Rebecca, *habibti,*" he started in. "We are not in the American suburbs. We are not even in the Gazan suburbs. We are in Yarmouk Camp and this is what we have. This is what I can do."

I looked at him in the vanity's mirror. The slump of his shoulders seemed sharper in reflection.

"I know where we are, Zayn," I sighed.

The afternoon call to prayer broke in, filling the space. Lingering.

He let out a deep breath.

"*Yalla*. I'll go tell him to take it back."

He walked toward the bedroom door.

"I'm sorry. I'm not trying to be difficult. It's just that it's the first time we're making a house together.

"*Mazbut*, that's right," he said.

Within a few hours the bedroom set was gone.

The next day we managed to find a neutral brown, velvet-free replacement. Both of us thought it wasn't bad.

❧

I began freelancing. I wrote pieces about the intifada, mining work I had done as a human rights researcher. Zayn sat for hours at a formica dining table in our apartment, writing about the situation in the Occupied Territories—the intifada, the political dynamic, tactics and strategies that had succeeded and failed, and the people involved in it all. He was putting to paper the life he had left behind.

I would come home from work for a mid-afternoon lunch, and we would eat together. After lunch I would bring him cups of tea as he continued to write, hunched over the gray table as he filled page after page of a notebook with his graceful, neat handwriting. When I set down the cup, he would glance up and thank me, his eyes quickly returning to the words spilling out on the page. Every so often he would use White-Out to change a word, blowing on the milky liquid before writing the more considered replacement. Finally, in the evening or sometimes late into the night, I would hear him moan and stretch. The screeching sound of the metal-legged chair against the hard tiled floor would follow. He would come into our room, face drawn, and flop into bed. Then he would get up the next day and do it all again.

One night as I lay there next to him, I thought of Zayn's reputation as a writer, earned during his decade and a half as a political prisoner. I could still remember sitting with his brother Lutfi on our patio in Gaza as he told me about the smuggled *capsulat* —the tiny pieces of paper folded into pill shapes and wrapped tightly in plastic—that came out of the prisons written by Zayn and others. Over the years, Zayn's intelligence and political education had emerged and blossomed on those pages, nurtured by the focused subculture unique to political prisoners. Rather than deterring his creativity, being behind bars as part of the nascent Palestinian movement allowed him to harness the potential and hope it offered, despite the hardships of hunger strikes, punishing stints in solitary confinement, and torture.

But no matter how difficult life was back then, Zayn was still in Palestine. Now he was in exile. This changed everything. Indeed, it seemed to unmoor him, and he had begun to float away. What I didn't know was how far would he go? Or what, if anything, would bring him back?

Zayn finished his report and began working in an office that analyzed events in the Occupied Territories. We started socializing, mostly with friends from his past but also meeting new people from his work and mine. We would be invited for lunch—the main meal of the day—if the woman in the house didn't work outside the home. In other households we would visit in the evening, after eight, when the afternoon shift ended, and eat a late *mezza* dinner of small appetizers—hummus, olives, spicy stewed tomatoes, fried eggs, and *labneh.* Sitting on mattresses covered in colorful cloth, the conversation would revolve around politics and personalities, mostly on the personalities after the *'araq* was brought out.

When we acquired living room furniture, we began hosting people. One day while I was at work, it appeared in the house—I came home and found a burnt-orange color sofa and two matching chairs, one with the plastic still covering it. Zayn walked in from the bedroom. I sat down on the fuzzy crushed velvet sofa and thought *this will be itchy and hot in the summer.*

I looked at Zayn and smiled.

"*Helu,* nice."

"*Mabrouk.* Congratulations," he responded, marking the official end of our house furnishing efforts.

❦

One of the first guests we hosted was a revered Palestinian leader whom Zayn had long admired and respected for his secular thought and dedication to Arab nationalism. *Al-Hakeem*, as he was commonly known, Arabic for doctor but also meaning wise man, wished to meet Zayn personally as someone who had recently come from Palestine and who had sacrificed many years of his life in prison for their cause.

We decided that I would make *maqloubeh*, upside down, so called because the cooking pot was turned upside down on a platter to reveal, if all went well, a perfectly molded mound of fragrant chicken, spiced rice, and eggplant. It was the one Palestinian dish I made successfully on a consistent basis. The *maqloubeh* would be accompanied by yogurt, salad, and a mix of olives and pickled vegetable sides.

Al-Hakeem was coming on a Friday, our day off. Zayn spent the two days before shopping for the perfect eggplant and buying more olives, bread, and rice than we could eat in a month. We cleaned the house the night before, and I began cooking late morning. Zayn hovered in the kitchen, instructing me not to burn the eggplant or to make sure the rice was rinsed well. He fluttered out of the room, and I heard the living room door slam. He returned a half hour later with more fruit for dessert. Then he disappeared again and came back toting new pictures to decorate the walls and at least two pounds of Arabic sweets. Zayn was like the mother of the bride—*zay um al 'arus.*

Known as "the conscience of the revolution," al-Hakeem was born into a Christian family in Lydd in the central coastal plains of Palestine. Coming of age, he was influenced by the values of pluralism, secularism, and nationalism that were being developed and championed throughout the Arab world. In 1948, his family was driven from their city, now best known as the site of Israel's international airport, during a major attack on it and the neighboring town of Ramla. Israeli forces imposed a curfew, trapping townspeople, and then killed hundreds of men, women and children. Working at a hospital during the curfew, he saw his own sister die. Once the curfew was lifted, he dug a grave and buried her in the yard of her home before being expelled with her six children.

We were told by al-Hakeem's secretary that he would arrive at two. A little before three, there was a knock on the door. Al-Hakeem entered with his driver-bodyguard. His large frame filled the door, but he teetered slightly as he walked into the room, likely due to the stroke he'd suffered years before. His graying hair and moustache were neatly combed. He wore a simple dark blue suit and a sweater vest with a red tie. Zayn buzzed with excitement as he introduced me. Al-Hakeem leaned slightly forward to shake my hand, and when I did the same a trace of his cologne drifted between us. His hand, warm and soft, completely covered mine.

"*Marhaba*," he smiled. "It's a pleasure to meet you."

"*Marhaba,*" I replied. "Welcome."

He asked about my work and my family. Zayn offered beer and soda, which we drank sitting on the new sofa. Soon the *maqloubeh* was ready. We set the formica dining-writing table with the salad and sides. I turned out the *maqloubeh* on a round, metal platter, sautéed a handful of pine nuts and sprinkled them over the perfect birthday cake-shaped mound of rice and chicken. I brought the steaming platter into the room and set it on the table. Al-Hakeem looked from the dish to me.

"*Maqloubeh?"* he said, his right eyebrow arching slightly. "Do they make *maqloubeh* in Amreeka?"

We laughed, and I thought of my Grandma Loretta's chicken and rice.

"Not exactly," I replied.

He smiled.

"It's beautiful."

I smiled back.

Most of the evening's talk was, of course, about the situation in Palestine, and Zayn's experiences and observations. I spoke about my work with the women's committee and the negative impact on women of Hamas's increasing popularity, particularly in Gaza. Al-Hakeem's response—not uncommon among Palestinian nationalists—highlighted the importance of the women's committees' activities, but emphasized that national liberation should come first, after which women's rights could be addressed.

"How can we talk about rights for half the population when our entire people suffer under occupation?" he asked.

When we finished eating, I began clearing the plates for coffee and dessert. Zayn prepared a dish of food and took it out to the driver, who had retreated to the car parked outside our door.

We ate dessert, and soon after al-Hakeem rose to go.

"How did you like the *maqloubeh*?" I ventured to ask him.

"*Yislam yadeeki,* bless your hands, it was good!...But it could have used a little more eggplant."

Spring finally arrived, but the relief of warmer days was overshadowed by Zayn's increasing agitation at the unfamiliar world around him. At work he argued with colleagues, disparaging the routinization of office-based political work in this new environment. It was nothing like the frontline political activity he had come to know in Palestine.

"It's like working in the Egyptian archives!" Zayn declared.

He seemed to feel at risk of becoming a modern-day Bartleby the Scrivener of the Palestinian national movement. He moved from the office researching events in the Occupied Territories to an aborted assignment in a political communications office. At one point, there was talk of his going to Cuba to work in the PLO office there. For a brief time he even worked with the magazine where I was—that was the shortest stint of all.

As Zayn bounced from one job to another, leaving in his wake broken friendships and bad blood, at home he became increasingly demanding of my time. One day after work, he complained of not having a hot lunch waiting for him when he returned from the office. When I pointed out that I, too, had a job to go to, his reply came.

"A man's home is his castle. It's where he goes to relax and be in control."

I stared at him, not sure I'd heard him right.

He turned and walked out of the room.

By summer, arguments between us were almost daily occurrences. What seemed to bother him most was coming home and finding an empty house. When this happened—which it did regularly when I was up against a deadline—he would leave again. When I got home, I would have no idea where he was. Increasingly, he came home late at night, long after I had gone to bed.

In Gaza, our life together had room for my own work and friends, alongside our shared social life. And the eight o'clock nightly curfew ensured that we had time alone. That "big tent" way of being together was what I wanted with Zayn: both of us working for a cause that had significantly shaped our lives—although, in such different ways, for different reasons—while having our own interests, and sharing others. This vision of our life together seemed to be shrinking day by day under the dusty Damascus sun.

In July, a friend of Zayn's from his time at Bir Zeit came to visit, along with her mother. Even though I didn't know her, I looked forward to the visit with the same sense of expectation as when Francesca and Zaha visited us in Cairo. Perhaps the presence of an old friend from our former life would bring some much-needed levity and relief.

Amal was a young but seasoned activist from a town outside of Jerusalem. She was thin and kinetic, flashing through the house in a simple T-shirt and baggy pants as she hurried to clear the breakfast dishes or make the beds before leaving for her appointments. There was an unassuming warmth that drew people to her, me included. The combination of her kindness and sense of emotional groundedness gave her a maternal air that belied her twenty-something years.

But it didn't take long to realize that her presence wouldn't moderate the dynamic between Zayn and me. If anything, the tension intensified with Zayn's expectation that I would cook and entertain our guests. One evening, after an argument over something long since faded from memory, I sat in our bed reading, while Zayn was in the living room with Amal and her mother. Zayn came into the bedroom and asked if I was going to join them.

"*La*," was my stubborn reply.

He left the room without a word.

Less than a minute later, the bedroom door banged open and Zayn charged through—his face taut, mask-like.

I looked up from my book. But before I could take in what was happening, a hand slammed down across my thigh. Stunned still for a moment, I yelled out and pushed him away as I jumped off of the bed. Inside me something clicked and fired.

"How dare you!" I shrieked.

My fist lashed out and caught him. I don't know where the blow landed, but I remember the sensation of my hand striking someone I love.

My throat suddenly felt parched.

Amal came running into the room and grabbed Zayn.

"*La, Zayn. La!*" she yelled, grabbing his arm and then throwing her body in front of him. He muttered something laced with curses.

"Get him out of here," I screamed.

Amal backed him out of the room and I slammed the door and locked it.

I walked toward the bed and sat down, catching a glimpse of myself in the vanity mirror. My face was blotchy, and there were deep creases that formed a parenthesis around my mouth. I closed my eyes. When I opened them again, I looked down and saw Zayn's handprint outlined on my thigh, rising red as the blood rushed to it.

The next day, the staff from the magazine where I worked had an appointment to meet with al-Hakeem. It was an interview, months in the planning. Sleepless, I made my way across the camp in the morning and arrived at the office just as the rest of the staff was getting into a cab.

"I'm not feeling well," I told Miriam, another writer with whom I had become good friends over the past several months.

She looked at me, and I could tell she sensed what was wrong.

"I'm really sorry you're going to miss this," she said.

The look of concern on her face grew as tears welled in my eyes.

"Me too," I said.

I turned quickly and began to walk away.

"Come over later, if you want," she called after me.

I looked back a moment later and saw them pulling away,

Miriam's face turned to the back window. She waved. I wiped my eyes and managed a weak smile.

I drifted through Yarmouk, trying to clear my head and think of what to do next. The decision to leave Gaza was meant, at least in part, to preserve not only Zayn's life but our life together. But at what cost? I thought that the strain in our relationship that began to manifest itself in Cairo would subside when were finally able to settle somewhere. Now that we had, the opposite was happening as the distance between us was beginning to harden.

I took a taxi into Damascus and wandered into the Cham Palace, one of the city's newer five-star hotels whose carefully crafted oriental glamour and inlaid mother-of-pearl charm we could never afford. I sat in the lobby. When the waiter approached, I moved my feet under the Damascene silk table cloth to hide my shoes, thick with camp dust. I ordered tea that cost more than my fifteen-minute taxi ride.

I thought of leaving Syria. I imagined calling my mother and having her buy me a ticket back to Ohio. But then what? Eight years of studying about and living in the Middle East so I could be back in a place where most people couldn't even locate on a map where I'd been, let alone understand what I'd experienced?

Unwilling to admit the failure of my marriage, and dazed by the situation I found myself in, I took a taxi back to the camp. I spent a few nights with Miriam, not quite knowing what to do or even what to think or feel—humiliation, anger, confusion, fear of getting stuck in a country I hardly knew, with a man I used to know, but suddenly did not.

I stopped by the house to pack a few things when I knew Zayn would still be at work. From underneath a pile of winter blankets stored in the wardrobe, I pulled out my duffle, which I hadn't used since arriving from Libya. I opened it on the bed and began tossing into it things I thought I would need—pajamas, underwear, a few changes of clothes.

Noticing the inside pocket in which I'd hidden the two stone charms for safe keeping, I paused and sat down on the bed. Slowly unzipping the pocket, I carefully pulled out the tiny bundle, peeled away the tissue in which the tiny heart and map were wrapped, gently picked them up, and placed them in the open palm of my hand. Marveling—for at least the hundredth time—at our initials so finely etched into each one, I sat there, turning them over and over again in my hands.

On my third day at Miriam's, Zayn appeared after lunch. He wanted to talk.

Miriam made the excuse of having work to do at the office.

Zayn and I sat across from each other on the pillow-strewn mattresses that were her sofa. We both lit a cigarette and said nothing. The sounds of the subdued siesta-hour traffic floated past the curtains drawn against the afternoon sun.

Zayn sighed a long gray stream of smoke.

"Rebecca, you know I love you. But we can't continue like this."

I reached forward and flicked my cigarette into the ashtray between us.

"That's true," I responded.

I looked directly at him for the first time since he arrived. His eyes were bloodshot, and it looked like he had been sleeping in his clothes.

"I'm sorry about what happened," he continued. "But I feel we live like graduate students."

"Graduate students?" A laugh escaped me. "Zayn, I work, too, so what do you expect?"

I crushed out my cigarette too hard, sending a cascade of ashes over the edge.

"If you wanted a *sitt beit*," I said using the Arabic word for housewife, "you should have married your cousin."

He looked at me, then quickly looked away. I could tell he wanted to say something but was reconsidering.

"You know," he turned toward me, his mouth trembling slightly,

"I called your mother."

"You what?" was all I could manage.

"I called your mother," he repeated.

An unexpected breeze billowed the curtains noiselessly into the room.

"Why in the world would you call my mother?"

"I wanted to get her opinion."

My mother knew that we were in Damascus. But I hadn't shared any of the difficulties we were experiencing, playing my role in that sure-to-fail dynamic of not wanting to worry her.

Zayn was vague about what they had discussed. Years later, my mother told me that he had called to complain to her about my shortcomings as a cook and housekeeper. She had listened sympathetically, but then observed that this was who I was, and had always been. She told him that the family had joked for years that I could burn water. Finally, she ventured gently that he must have known this about me before he married me.

Sitting there with him in Miriam's living room, it was hard to say what either one of us knew about the other. Or what we knew about ourselves.

A few days later, Zayn and I sat together in the office of Talal, the head of the political magazine where Zayn was working—at least for the moment. Others had heard about the problems we were having and were staging an intervention, of sorts.

Called a *sulha,* or reconciliation, this was a twentieth-century version of how village elders in earlier times dealt with social and personal disputes that came to their attention. The goal was preserving social stability in the interest of the greater community, and in a manner that acknowledged individuals' dignity. Despite the tumult that had followed him from office to office, Zayn's years of work and sacrifice accorded him the respect of this community—one of exiles who shared political values. And while under no illusion that I occupied a similar position, I had earned the respect and even affection of those who knew me through my work in both Palestine and Yarmouk.

We were served tea while Talal exchanged awkward chit-chat with a couple of others who had joined us—Abu Tarek, the head of the Occupied Territories office, and Abu Bashir, the father of the two young men Zayn's nieces had married in Libya.

After a few minutes, Talal asked Zayn to explain the problems, from his point of view.

Zayn excoriated our "graduate student" lifestyle, as—once again—my cooking and housekeeping, or lack thereof, took center stage. I observed what was happening as if I were watching a play. It was hard to believe I was sitting there with a group of men I hardly knew, talking about my marital problems. A poster mounted on the wall above Talal's head caught my gaze. "*Lan narqa'!* We will not kneel!" These iconic words of the Palestinain poet Tawfiq Ziyad formed a calligraphic block alongside a black-and-white image of a mother cradling her child.

Zayn abruptly stopped talking.

The sudden quiet caught my attention, and I looked at him once again. His lips trembled slightly. A flush of pink rimmed his eyes. Then he began to weep.

A stillness washed over the room. Abu Tarek rested his head in his hands. Talal looked down at his desk.

"*Mish mushkeleh, ya rafeek.* It's okay, comrade," Talal said quietly to Zayn.

Abu Bashir offered him a cigarette. I took one as well.

I can't remember what was said after that. I must have given my perspective on things. Maybe there was an apology, promises to try again. Mostly what I remember is the watery blue of Zayn's eyes, and those three Palestinian exiles quietly absorbing the pain of another.

8
Our Amira

Gradually, things did improve between us. If I had to work late, Zayn would either go to a friend's house for lunch, or pick up a roasted chicken from one of the restaurants along Palestine Street that had rows of them turning over a charcoal fire. Five or six birds would be lined up on long blackened spits, the ends of each one's legs tied together around the skewer as if in prayer. Teardrops of liquefied fat would slide off the chickens onto the coals, igniting a sizzle of flame. Without the pressure of Zayn's demands, I attempted to cook extra and freeze the leftovers when I didn't work in the afternoon, or on my day off. He would do the same.

But that summer of 1990 brought bigger changes in the world, which shifted the focus of everyone's attention. In August, the Iraqi invasion of Kuwait scrambled traditional alliances in the region in ways that few anticipated. The U.S.'s reaction to Saddam Hussein's calculated move threw into stark relief the lengths it would go to protect its economic interests anywhere. The American-led coalition prepared for war to liberate Kuwaiti oil fields and to ensure that those in Saudi Arabia would remain "free."

As a U.S. invasion loomed, the Palestinian political leadership threw their support behind Saddam. In retaliation, tens of thousands of Palestinians in Kuwait—many of whom had lived there for decades and who formed the professional backbone of the country—would be expelled from the country after the war.

What few foresaw was Syrian president Hafez al-Assad joining the coalition against Saddam. With Assad's army poorly prepared to do much actual fighting, the joke circulating in the camp asked what would Syrian soldiers' job be on the front lines? *Lucky! Marlboro!* went the punch line, imitating the cry of cigarette hawkers on the streets of Damascus, poking fun at Syria's moneymaking motivation for joining the coalition.

In October, I returned to Palestine on a reporting trip, first crossing into Jordan and then into Palestine over the Allenby Bridge. From the bridge I went to Ramallah, where I worked for a few days while staying with expat friends. As soon as I could, I took a *serveece* to Gaza. Lutfi and Sawsan had moved back to their house in Shati, leaving our house on the edge of the camp empty. Before letting anyone know I had arrived, I took a taxi from the Erez crossing into Gaza to our neighborhood. I had kept my key, so I let myself in.

I entered the house excited just by the thought of being back in a place that actually held memories. I wandered through the garden, brushing past the lemon tree. I was startled by the citrusy smell of the ripe fruit that prickled my nose, as if it were signaling indignation at my ignoring its accomplishments of the past year.

Once inside, I peered into the kitchen. It stood bereft of the smells that had always lingered there—garlic and onions, warming bread and olive oil, the pot of Arabic coffee that should have been simmering on the stove.

Our bedroom door was ajar. I entered to reclaim some clothes I had left behind. Stepping into the room, I had the dizzying realization that the same sheets were on the bed as the day I left. The pattern of pale green flowers peeked over the sky-blue wool blanket that had been hastily thrown over the bed. My throat tightened.

I went into the bathroom, where the economy-size bottle of Jhirmack shampoo I had schlepped from the States still stood guard on the edge of the tub. I leaned over the wash basin and burst into tears as I was accosted by the sweet scent of the hand-milled soap given me by the French journalist for whom I had arranged the interview with the Islamic political leader.

Standing in that hushed house, I understood that it wasn't the Palestine Street chickens or leftovers that shifted the course of our relationship. It was the realization that despite all we had lost—friends, family, our home, our work—there was still more left to lose.

By the time I was back in Damascus in late October, American forces were massed in Saudi Arabia. Meanwhile, the summer détente between Zayn and me grew into a period of real happiness and affection. We had rekindled our ability to enjoy friends, work, and each other. We talked about starting a family, an idea that until now was so practically or emotionally impossible in our two-year-old marriage as to not even warrant serious discussion. So, when I learned soon after the new year that I was pregnant, the news brought more than the usual happiness and excitement—although there was plenty of that, with Zayn passing out celebratory sweets in every office where he had ever worked. For me, it was an affirmation that we had made it through the gauntlet of exile: We would not only survive but would now thrive.

Yet, the joy and anticipation of a baby on the way was tempered by the proximity of war. The U.S. air force attacked Baghdad in mid-January, and ground troops entered Iraq and Kuwait a few weeks later. The overwhelming military superiority of the U.S. and its European allies soon made an Iraqi retreat inevitable. In late February, I lay on our orange sofa after lunch, listening to the BBC. "It was like shooting fish in a barrel," was how one U.S. air force pilot described the slaughter of retreating Iraqi troops along what became known as "the Highway of Death," the road between Kuwait City and Basra where ten thousand Iraqi soldiers died in less than twenty-four hours.

Fish in a barrel.

People had been talking in hushed but excited tones in the camp since late summer, buoyed by the hope that the reactionary oil regimes might be undermined. But the inevitability of another Western-led military victory drastically altered the atmosphere. Fear descended like nightfall as the Syrian regime began to reap its spoils of war. Black Suburbans full of Syrian intelligence *mukhabarat* all but occupied Yarmouk. We began hearing reports of middle-of-the-night arrests. As the weather warmed, those of us in ground-floor apartments kept our windows shuttered when conversations turned to the war, or even when listening to a television station other than Syrian TV.

In the spring, we were able to move to a second-floor apartment in another part of the camp. Even among the fear and uncertainty, or perhaps because of it, Zayn and I grew closer. We began discussing names for the baby. For a girl, I initially suggested Salma as it was an Arabic name and the name of my father's cousin, to whom he'd been particularly close. Zayn thought it was too "old fashioned," and he suggested Yara—an Arabic name with pre-Islamic roots.

Deciding on a boy's name was harder. I assumed that Zayn would want to name a boy Omar after his father, but he was not interested in that tradition. I suggested Ramsey, an Arabic name but also with Ramsey Clark in mind, Jimmy Carter's former attorney general who had taken a principled stand against the U.S. war in Iraq. So it seemed that we would have a Yara or a Ramsey.

But then one day in April, Zayn came home after work, bounding through the door.

"If it's a girl, I want to name her Amira," he announced.

That time in Tawfiq's office—when Amira had shared her observations about Gaza and her gratitude toward Zayn—flashed in my mind as clear as the spring day. I needed no explanation for the decision and was only sorry that I hadn't thought of honoring the woman who had spent so many years defending the rights of Palestinian prisoners, Zayn being just one of many.

"Amira it is," I replied.

We sat down for lunch.

❦

In May, I flew to Ohio, five and a half months pregnant. Our plan was for me to be with my family for the birth and return to Damascus a couple of months later. I spent those warm spring and summer months pampered by my mother in Cincinnati, swimming, napping, and shopping for baby things. My routine included reading "how-to" books on childrearing and breastfeeding and checkups with a midwife who would be assisting the birth.

I managed to keep busy, but I missed Zayn—his playful humor and his take on the postwar news, those delicately tapered fingers and the way people listened to him when he talked, the softness of his lips and the random questions he'd ask me about the meaning of an English word or an event in U.S. history. My longing became particularly intense when I started taking birthing classes and was the only woman attending without a partner.

Nevertheless, looking back on this time of rest and hope, it seems almost surreal, magical. After all we had gone through—living underground, enduring separation, and weathering marital discord—we had come out this other side. Pregnancy for me was a time of healing, catching my breath, rejuvenating—not only to give birth to our child but to prepare for a new chapter in our life together. It would certainly be fraught not only with the difficulties and problems faced by new parents everywhere, but by the unique challenges the world was constantly imposing on us—war, political instability, insecurity. There were many things about our life in Syria that I was not happy with. It was not Palestine, where we both had built a life of meaningful work and close friends—a place where we felt we belonged. But Zayn and I were finally happy together, so I was determined to set aside those misgivings in order to build a future with him and our beautiful baby.

❧

My pregnancy was problem-free, and toward the end, apart from finding it difficult to sleep, I'd never felt better. I still think of it as the only time in my life when I could eat as much as I wanted, sleep as much as I wanted, and buy new clothes without getting disapproving looks from anyone.

But soon after my September 25th due date passed, I noticed that the baby was moving less. When I called the midwife to report this, she told me to come into her office immediately. An ultrasound later, I was admitted to the maternity ward of University Hospital and labor was induced. The placenta was getting old, so ready or not—and it soon became clear that she was not—this Amira needed to make her appearance in the world.

I had planned a drug-free delivery. Several hours of excruciatingly slow progress in labor and difficulties in the final stages changed those plans. After receiving Pitocin to induce labor and a sedative meant to relax me (it just made me hallucinate), an epidural was administered. It had been over twelve hours since I was admitted. When I was finally able to begin pushing, Amira's head would crown. But when I stopped pushing to breathe, it would recede—the umbilical cord was looped over her shoulder and would pull her back into my womb, bungee-cord-style, without the force of being pushed. Her heartbeat was becoming irregular, so the midwife called in an obstetrician for a consultation.

A tall man in green scrubs and a surgical mask entered the room. He had parchment-colored hair that had just begun to recede from the forehead he rubbed habitually between his thumb and index finger.

"This is Dr. Levy," Karen, my midwife, introduced us. "I need him to examine you to help us make a decision about a Cesarean."

I was desperately trying to avoid one—I had no health insurance, and I objected to the procedure for philosophical reasons.

"How are you doing?" he asked, his voice tinged with a gravelly accent I immediately recognized .

"I've been better," I replied. Then almost without thinking, I asked him, "You're Israeli, aren't you?"

He looked up from the clipboard he was paging through and blinked. He nodded, then went back to his clipboard.

Dr. Levy examined me and conferred with the midwife. Another set of contractions came and went, with Amira no closer to being born. The epidural was wearing off after so many hours of fruitless labor. The pain was dizzying.

After catching my breath, I looked over at the doctor slumped silently in a chair next to the bed, kneading his forehead.

"Please help me," I gasped, tears mixed with sweat streaming down my face.

Soon, another set of contractions seized my body. He rose from the chair and began issuing instructions to the nurses. There was a flurry of activity at the foot of the bed. I heard the sound of bags ripping open and metal instruments clanging on trays. I had no idea what was happening. I pushed when the midwife told me to and focused on not passing out.

"Yes!" I heard someone say.

Karen looked up and told me to stop pushing and just breathe.

"You did it!" she said.

"Oh, God!" I cried. "Oh, God!"

Amira was quickly weighed and swaddled and put in my arms. She looked exactly like her father.

"How did it happen?" I asked.

I had resigned myself to a Cesarean section, so was unsure how I had managed to give birth.

"Dr. Levy used forceps and pulled her out," Karen explained. "He did a really good job. Look."

Karen gently folded back the tiny knit cap keeping Amira's head warm. Her pink face was perfect, but a slight red mark grazed her scalp.

"What's that?" I asked.

"Nothing that won't heal with the proper care," she replied.

I already had someone waiting to visit me. My friend from Ramallah, the human rights advocate Joel Rosenberg, had arrived from North Carolina the day before. He had returned to the U.S. at the start of the Gulf War. Joel and I had planned for him to visit me at my mother's, anticipating that by now Amira would be about a week old. Instead, he appeared at the hospital just a few hours after I was checked into a room. My sister had updated him about the change in plans.

The maternity ward of University Hospital was unusually full, so I was upgraded to a private room, which included a "celebratory dinner for two," replete with steak and sparkling cider. Aides came and went, checking my blood pressure and temperature, and helping me nurse Amira. While I took what may have been the longest shower of my life, Joel held Amira. An orderly brought our steak dinner and congratulated Joel when she saw him cooing at Amira.

"Oh, I'm not the father," he replied.

She threw him a contemptuous look and left the room.

"*Mabrouk! Mazel Tov!*" We lifted our glasses and toasted with our sparkling cider. After sharing our "celebratory dinner for two," we said goodbye.

Less than twenty-four hours later I was back in my mother's apartment. The next several days were a blur. I slept, and my mother brought me Amira to nurse every few hours. We would fall asleep together until my mother returned to retrieve Amira, change her diaper, or bathe her. She brought me food. Days—I'm not sure how many—passed this way. It was early October.

Eventually I was able to stay awake and take meals at my mother's oak dining table. Amira had developed a mild jaundice, the remedy for which was exposure to the sun. Since I was still too tired and shaky to feel safe doing it myself, my sister Carol took Amira outside. Morning sun filtered through gold-tinged leaves, past aunt and niece, and filled my mother's living room. I watched through the patio door as Carol cradled the bundle of my daughter in both hands as they bathed together in the sun.

October progressed, with more friends visiting, all of whom were former expats from my time living in Ramallah.

Soon I started preparing to return to Syria. I took Amira for well-baby check-ups and learned to do things like function on four hours of broken sleep and give my daughter a bath without drowning her. A few days after Thanksgiving 1991, we said a tearful goodbye to my mother and boarded a plane for Damascus.

I emerged from the crowd in the airport arrival hall with Amira facing me, snug in the baby carrier. I saw Zayn's head bobbing through the crowd as he made his way toward us. Even at a distance I could sense his body's buzz. He reached us, leaned over Amira to kiss me and then slowly lifted her. As she rose, her eyes widened, and she kept them on me.

"*Habibti, ya binti.* My love, my daughter."

At the sound of Zayn's voice, her tiny mouth formed a pea-size "O." Zayn turned Amira around and held her out before him.

"*Ya, ayuni,* you are my eyes!" he declared to his daughter.

She was motionless. Then she blinked once, twice, three times.

Zayn pulled her into him and gently kissed her cheeks. She emitted a sound somewhere between a squeak and a whimper. Zayn laughed. The music of his laughter set her legs and arms in motion, like a wind-up doll lifted off the floor in mid-trip.

I came around to stand next to Zayn. We stood illuminated under the harsh fluorescent lights of the Damascus airport, Zayn and I next to each other, Amira hovering just above us.

❧

Soon after we arrived, Damascus experienced one of the worst snowstorms on record. Nearly two feet shrouded the camp in less than a day. The excitement that initially greeted such an unusual event soon morphed into panic, as the already unstable electricity grid buckled under the weight of the snow. The blackouts became longer and more frequent than usual. From the balcony of our second-floor apartment, the sagging electricity lines looked like row after row of thick, taunting lips. The camp's narrow streets and alleys became largely unpassable to cars. Our only source of warmth was a kerosene heater in the living room. Fortunately, the kerosene was delivered by a man driving a horse-drawn wooden cart that could be pushed from behind to maneuver over the flattened snow. We dragged our mattress into the living room and slept close together under thick blankets, Amira snuggled between us.

I had planned to put Amira in daycare when I returned to work. But now that the time for me to do so was here, I was shocked to discover that I simply couldn't bear the thought of leaving her with strangers who had several other babies to care for. I insisted on bringing a crib mattress and a few stuffed animals into my office, where Amira spent the day napping, nursing and being whisked away by the young women who worked on my floor. Our friends and my coworkers politely tolerated the crazy American who brought her baby to work.

"You are obsessed with her," Zayn observed, shaking his head.

I couldn't say that he was wrong.

During the six months I was away, the postwar political situation in the camp had continued to deteriorate. Several of our friends—Palestinians from the West Bank—were able to acquire Jordanian passports, since Jordan had ruled over the West Bank before the Israeli occupation. They had left for Jordan, or were preparing to do so. Gazans had no access to such documents, since Egyptian rule over Gaza hadn't produced this benefit.

The added responsibilities of parenting—dirty diapers, bathing and feeding Amira, checkups and immunizations—reignited conflict between Zayn and me around managing the house. The frequent electricity and water cuts didn't help matters. Neither did my insistence on having Amira sleep in bed with us. Tensions in the street, in the house, and among our colleagues and friends only hardened the edges of the already steely winter. After work I would often spend hours alone in the house with Amira, afternoons turning prematurely into nighttime in the darkened apartment. Sometimes Zayn returned to the apartment before I went to bed, sometimes he did not. We would go days without speaking to each other.

Spring finally came, but I hardly noticed. More friends left for Jordan, or other countries if a family connection allowed. One bright spot was Miriam introducing me to two Fulbright scholars from the U.S. who were doing research in Syria. Greg and Don shared an apartment in Abu Rumaneh near the city center. Through their invitations, I saw more of Damascus in a few months than I had the previous year and a half. The country's postwar relationship with the U.S. brought a spate of State Department-sponsored cultural events to the capital.

One evening a bluegrass band called the Red Clay Ramblers were performing in an auditorium near the main square downtown. Zayn declined most invitations from Greg and Don, and this one was no exception. He did agree to babysit Amira so I could go.

Expats filtered in first—a smattering of Arabic students with backpacks, suntanned diplomats in opened-collared shirts and khakis, accompanied by women in tight jeans and high heels. As the start time of the concert drew nearer, knots of locals began arriving. Stopping briefly in the doorway as if making sure they were in the right place, they made their way in: couples, some carrying children, dressed for the evening with the men in jackets and ties and the women in floor-length skirts, wrists and necks wreathed in gold. Smoke from the men's cigarettes curled around their wives' headscarves in a bluish haze.

The tinny sounds of a lone banjo began to rise. Four plucked notes reverberated throughout the hall and then a voice called out.

"*One, two, three, four.*"

A wave of music rolled out from the stage toward the audience. Children quieted and sat up. Those still smoking quickly took a last drag and crushed the remnants under their heels. With the fully raised curtain swaying in the rafters, the six-man band of banjos, bass, fiddle, guitar, and mandolin was revealed. The band acknowledged the audience's applause with a collective nod but remained focused on their instruments, fingers flying and wrists sawing.

The Westerners in the audience were soon nodding their heads in time. The Syrians sat very still, taking it all in, the notes of the banjos and fiddles tumbling and turning over one another like boys wrestling in a schoolyard. The tempo quickened. The musicians now looked at one another, a sense of daring in their eyes. Then there was a sudden crescendo, one final down beat. Then silence.

Applause filled the auditorium and when the lead musician let out a loud "Whoop!," the trancelike state of the Syrians seemed to break, and they erupted in whistles and ululation. All six musicians broke into smiles, raised their hands, and bowed.

After the concert, we had pastries and coffee at a café near Marjeh Square. Then Miriam and I shared a taxi back to the camp. I unlocked the door to the apartment and Zayn was standing there waiting for me, balancing a red-eyed Amira on his hip.

"She's still awake?" I said.

It was after eleven. Zayn said nothing. Amira let out a thin whine and reached for me to nurse. Zayn handed her over, turned and walked out onto the balcony. I followed him.

"What's wrong? Was Amira cranky? Did I not leave enough milk?"

She seemed tired but not overly distressed. He was clearly worse off than she was.

"Amira is fine. It is her mother who is the problem."

He looked up at me as he lit a cigarette. The glow from his lighter reflected the anger in his eyes.

"What the hell are you talking about, Zayn?" I demanded, "You were invited to go too, but you didn't want to. We could have gotten a babysitter, but you said it wasn't necessary!"

"That's not the issue!" he hissed through teeth clenched around his cigarette and around his rage. "It's after eleven o'clock at night!"

I was stunned into silence. Confused, almost.

"Of course it's after eleven. The concert wasn't until eight, and we had coffee afterwards."

We had come home from visiting friends much later than this on many occasions.

"Miriam and I shared a taxi, and it brought me right to the corner of the house."

I thought for a moment that he was concerned that I had walked from the main street down the dark side street to our building.

"I know where the taxi dropped you. I was standing here on the balcony watching for you."

He wouldn't look at me.

"Zayn, what is the problem? Why are you so angry?"

"How long is it going to take you to understand where you live!" he shouted. "How many women do you know who come home at eleven o'clock at night by themselves? You're not in Manhattan! What will neighbors think?"

"Neighbors?" I had to suppress a laugh. "Which neighbors? The one across the hall who beats his wife? The others in the rest of the building whose names we don't even know?"

A familiar dull pain seeped in behind my eyes. On one side of the balcony, light from the house stretched out and fell just short of where Zayn and I were standing. I suddenly felt the darkness that came from the other side.

"You honestly believe that the neighbors are going to think I'm some kind of a tramp because one night I come home late? This is how you think?"

"It doesn't matter what I think, Rebecca. It's how these people think!"

"That's bullshit, Zayn. You seem bothered that you had to actually take care of Amira for a few hours, and the longer I was out, the angrier you got."

I brushed past him and went to put Amira to bed. She fell asleep almost immediately. I went back out on the veranda, where Zayn still stood, smoking. I wasn't ready to let this go.

"You come and go as you please, without explanation, at all hours of the night," I fumed. "The *one* time you have to take care of your own daughter, it's a problem."

He was leaning over the rail of the veranda, staring out at the TV antennas and laundry that had been forgotten on the clotheslines, averting my glare. I waited for him to say something. When I couldn't wait any longer, I retreated back into the house. About halfway to the bedroom I turned and stomped back out to the veranda.

"You don't *deserve* Amira!" I spat out.

This turned him around. Behind Zayn, the night ran liquid above the camp's rooftops. I could see his chest moving up and down as his breath quickened. He flicked his cigarette away between his thumb and forefinger. It arced into the street, trailing a miniature plume. Without a word, he walked off the veranda. A moment later I heard the door slam.

❦

Spring passed into summer. The precariousness of the future stretched on, taut and unyielding. More friends and colleagues departed, shifting the delicate balance defining the rest of us from those who stayed to those who were left behind. My freelance work was falling apart amid the uncertainty surrounding us, and while Zayn had managed to settle into a writing job, the future was bleak—for us as a couple and for our daughter. We didn't talk much about leaving Syria, both of us knowing our options were limited with Zayn's background and lack of a meaningful travel document. By then, I had lived in the Middle East for over six years.

"We've got to get out of here," I blurted out one day after putting Amira down for her nap.

We were sitting on the sofa, drinking mint tea and waiting for the day's heat to break. Zayn didn't even flinch, his gaze fixed on the sugar melting in his glass of tea.

"*Ya*, Rebecca," he replied, his voice inflected with the tone of someone who had anticipated having to say what he was now saying. "Where are we going to go?"

"*Amreeka,*" I replied.

Despite the periods of hardship, instability, and even fear, I hadn't ever seriously considered returning to the U.S.—until now.

A little laugh escaped him. Then he got up to get a cigarette from his jacket pocket, sat back down, and lit it. Stretching his legs out in front of him and raising his arms above his head, he tilted his face up and blew the smoke at the ceiling.

"And what am I going to do in *Amreeka?*" he asked the ceiling.

"I don't know, Zayn," I replied.

Exhaustion suddenly swelled in me. I wanted nothing more than to crawl in bed with Amira.

"You're smart and your English is good. You could go back to school and finish your degree. You could keep writing. There are lots of things you could do," I assured him.

"*Amreeka.*" His laugh was more pronounced this time. "I have nothing to do there."

"Zayn, soon you will have nothing to do *here.*"

A crackling noise suddenly broke the afternoon haze, as the *muezzin* of the neighborhood mosque prepared the loudspeaker for the call to prayer.

"And what will Amira's future be here?"

He took another drag from his cigarette.

"*Allah hu akbar*. God is great," he murmured, echoing the *muezzin's* call.

"Zayn, *habibi*, we have no choice."

9
Unpacking

My days became filled with preparing to leave. Our plan was for Amira and me to return to Ohio, where we could stay temporarily with my mom until I could find a job, a place for us to live, and apply for Zayn's visa.

When I called my mother to tell her, there was silence.

"Hello? Mom?" I thought the line had been cut as often happened.

"I'm here," she sniffed. Giving up her attempt to hold back tears, her voice burst over the line, "Thank God!"

Longtime friends of Zayn's, those he knew from prison, would take in our news and pause. Looking at Zayn they would ask, "*Amreeka*?" The tone wasn't accusatory; it was confused. In response Zayn would shrug, sometimes laugh, not quite meeting their eyes.

"*Yalla*," they would respond to his discomfort. "*B'ayn allah.* We're in the eyes of God."

"*B'ayn allah*," he would reply.

❧

We decided that before I left I should take Amira to Palestine to meet her family there. Once we left for the U.S., we didn't know when we'd return to the Middle East or have the opportunity to see them again.

In September, Amira and I took a shared taxi from Damascus to Dera'a in southern Syria, where we crossed into Jordan. We boarded another taxi for Amman, where we stayed with friends while I applied for a pass to cross the Allenby Bridge into Palestine. A few days later, we exited a bus that had taken us through the no-man's land between Jordan and the Occupied West Bank. The passengers—Western tourists and Palestinians returning from visiting relatives —were separated for processing according to ethnicity: "Non-Arab passport holders" were directed one way; the rest were directed by a sign that read "Others." I was, of course, "non-Arab," but in my arms I held an Arab—a child whose father was one. The non-Arabs were being processed in the main hall where we entered; the Arabs were being led out of a side door into a different section of the building. I took Amira and, with the privilege afforded by our U.S. passports, queued with the foreigners on vacation.

The Israeli soldiers behind the desks looked to be barely out of their teens, laughing with each other and flirting with the blonde Europeans whose passports they stamped. The desk soldiers had black felt berets snapped into a strap on the shoulder of their dull green uniforms. Those standing guard near the door where the Arabs were exiting wore scarlet berets and no expression, Uzis gripped with both hands. We were instructed to complete a form that asked our religion, our fathers' names, and their places of birth. No interest was shown in my father, Marvin Max Klein, born in Cincinnati, Ohio. Zayn Omar Majdalawi, born in Shati Camp, Gaza, prompted a look up from the young man behind the desk.

"Where is her father?" he asked.

"I don't know," I lied.

Explaining Zayn's presence in Damascus was not a conversation I wanted to have with him. Playing the naïve Western woman who'd had a misguided romance with an Arab was easier, and no doubt aligned more comfortably with their stereotypes.

"Do you have relatives in Israel?" he asked me, looking down again at my passport.

"Yes," I replied.

He looked back and forth between Amira's form and mine. He finally said something in Hebrew to the soldier at the desk next to him, who glanced at me and nodded. The soldier with our passports stood and said to me, "Just a minute," and disappeared behind a door at the back of the hall. I turned around to see the tourists in line behind me slouching under the weight of their backpacks, sunburned faces tilted and taking us in.

The soldier soon reappeared, handed me back our passports and directed us to the "Others." I readjusted the diaper bag on my shoulder, secured Amira in the baby carrier strapped to my front, and wheeled our suitcase toward the door. Behind it was another large room with metal benches running along stark white walls. Palestinian women in embroidered black *thobes* sat on the benches clutching babies and plastic bags of food. Older children leaned against them or sat together eating snacks from the bags. Old men wearing suit jackets over *deish-dashas* paced nearby, strings of *musbaha* prayer beads running through their brown calloused fingers.

A soldier near the door looked at Amira and me. After a moment he reached out his hand.

"Passport."

He examined our documents and pointed me to a low table where a few suitcases were opened, their rumpled contents spread out like wayward blossoms before a female soldier. I sat on one of the benches near the table and unhooked Amira from the baby carrier. She was desperate to nurse, so I stood and faced the nearest corner, draping a small blanket over her. I laid her on the bench and quickly changed her diaper.

From the bench I watched the female soldier slowly paw through the clothes spread out in front of her. A young male soldier behind her kept up a steady chatter in Hebrew. Occasionally she would stop what she was doing and turn to him to laugh or respond. A Palestinian woman in a long black *abiyah* and white headscarf circled nearby, trying to console a crying baby. She kept her eyes on the soldiers, bouncing the baby whose cries only crescendoed. I clutched Amira tighter. A metallic, bitter taste rose in my mouth.

After a few minutes the Palestinian woman slowly approached the table, mumbling something to the soldier, still chatting with her friend, who turned and snarled in Hebrew, "*Lo! Shvi!* No! Sit!"

The woman turned quickly with the baby in her arms and walked away. She looked at the ceiling and muttered something. After a few more minutes of the baby's intensifying cries, she made another pass at her suitcase. "*Bambers.* Pampers," I heard her say, holding up her index finger to the soldier to indicate she wanted only one diaper from her luggage. The soldier turned sharply and glowered. The woman retreated and the soldier turned back to her companion.

I stood again and walked with Amira toward the corner where I had nursed her, unzipping the diaper bag as I went. As I passed the woman and crying baby, I slipped some diapers from my bag, thrust them into her hand and kept walking. I stood in the corner for a few minutes, Amira looking up at me, clearly wondering about seconds.

Our turn at the table came. I opened our bags as instructed. The soldier—more attentive to us if slightly confused by why we were there—half-heartedly groped our belongings. She asked me to open a shampoo bottle, which she then sniffed. After a few more questions about where we were staying ("With an American friend on a Fulbright in Jerusalem") and for how long ("Two weeks"), we were told to go. I zipped up our bags and secured Amira back into the baby carrier. I looked around for the Palestinian woman and her baby, but they were gone. The soldier retreated to a chair at the end of the search table and opened a Coke. The bitter taste in my mouth returned. I forced myself to look away and leave.

❧

The taxi ride from the bridge took us out of the Jordan Valley, with its lush green expanses attesting to its prized fertility, and then south to Jerusalem. Here the landscape undulated in a familiar pattern of dusty brown hills dotted with groves of ancient olive trees and other vegetation less recognizable. The smell, though, I knew. I rolled down the window and drank it in. It was the smell of this land: dust and baking bread, thistles softened with purple blooms; sun and stones, both relentless and welcoming. I wondered if Amira could smell it too.

We arrived at the Erez checkpoint at the northern entrance to the Gaza Strip. In the short time since my previous visit in 1990, the changes at the border were startling. The checkpoint already presaged the bulwark of Israeli control that was to come: the single gate, which once stood like an iron arm raised and lowered to let cars pass after the soldiers' ID inspections, had been replaced by a menacing guard tower and machine gun turret; a maze of three-feet high cement blocks stood across the road; and a line of handcuffed and blindfolded Palestinian men knelt baking in the sun on the side of the road.

Most vehicles were now prohibited from entering the Strip, requiring us to disembark from the taxi at the checkpoint to be searched and questioned by Israeli soldiers. Then, if all went as hoped, we could walk into Gaza.

Finessing the search and questions, I walked through the barricades. After crossing over, I searched the line of cars at the side of the road for the face of my brother-in-law, Lutfi. Over staticky, abruptly aborted phone calls in Jordan, I had arranged for him to be waiting for us on the Gaza side of the checkpoint. It was during those calls that I had learned of my father-in-law's failing health. *Ta'aban*—literally, tired—was the word Lutfi used to describe his father, one of those vague, could-mean-nothing-but-really-*means*-something words that I'd come to admire in the Arabic language. It was a word that at first blush suggested inscrutability, but over time revealed great precision, if one listened to the breath behind it. Was the word pushed out with a sigh (this is serious) or a rising lilt (not so bad)?

A warm wind suddenly whipped dust and sand into a small funnel cloud that danced at my feet. A bubble of panic rose in my ribs. Nearly identical circa-1960 Peugot 404s lined the road with horns honking and drivers waving at those who trickled through the checkpoint. You could tell those who were merely cabbies hoping to pick up a fare—seeking shade in their opened-door cars with radios fanning the voices of Fairuz and Um Kulthoum into the scratch of sandy road—from those waiting for relatives and loved ones. The latter stood hopping foot-to-foot, craning their necks so tightly that the veins strained against their bronze skin.

Plunging ahead, I shifted Amira to my other hip and rearranged the diaper bag on my shoulder to get a better look at the waiting cars. Suddenly, I saw a tall man leaning against one of the Peugots push away from it, raising his hand and waving. Lutfi caught sight of Amira and waved even harder, the key chain hooked around his fingers rattling like chimes.

We moved toward each other, grinning broadly. Tears singed my eyes in the hot dusty air, and before I knew it they were spilling over into his shirt. He enveloped Amira and me in a bear hug and whispered in greeting, "*Alhumdillah 'asalamitkoum.* Thank God for your safe arrival." Emerging from the hug, Lutfi and I exchanged kisses on both cheeks before he turned his attention to Amira. He scooped her out of my arms and planted loud, smacking kisses on both cheeks, arms, legs and forehead. He held her slightly away from him as she blinked repeatedly in recovery from the torrent of kisses. They slowly took each other in. His already enormous grin somehow managed to grow bigger. With his honey-brown eyes flashing, Lutfi lifted Amira high above his head as if offering her to the Gaza sun.

"*Btishbahee abouki.* You look like your father," he murmured, to her squealing delight.

We loaded our luggage into the car and headed south. Past downtown Gaza City, Lutfi turned off the main paved road into the lane of sand that served as the street for smaller neighborhoods like ours. We pulled up in front of the tall metal door that opened onto the small driveway leading to the house. Lutfi hopped out to open the gate; I held my breath. The rusty metal scrapped the cement driveway with that familiar sound.

There was our former home.

The garden that Zayn had carefully tended—I once complained that he spent more time in it than with me—was overgrown and in desperate need of weeding, but still producing late summer vegetables and fragrant bushes of basil. Remnants of the coral pink roses Zayn had fussed over stood with heads drooping on their stems, like sentinels that had fallen asleep at their posts.

Lutfi's family lived there now, and the sound of the gate opening brought my sister-in-law rushing to the front door. I ascended the porch steps, and Sawsan, carrying baby Omar (the newest member of the family and named after his grandfather), wrapped one slender arm around my shoulder while nestling her son in the crook of the other. A warm, moist smell of milk and onions wafted up from the mother-son bundle. Their two daughters rushed to the door, anxious to meet their baby cousin.

Behind me Lutfi grunted and lugged our things into the house, plopping them onto the bed Zayn and I had shared. I asked Lutfi if we could go to my in-laws. A shadow grazed his face and he nodded wordlessly.

I held Amira as we bounced over the roads and alleys into Shati camp, stopping at the familiar weathered door.

Lutfi knocked and said, "*Ana, ya ma.* It's me, Mama."

The door clicked and groaned open. Lutfi stepped in front of me, stooping down to kiss his mother. Her head scarf fluttered down around her shoulders in his embrace, and as she looked up from rearranging it she saw us. I stepped over the threshold and embraced her as tightly as I could, balancing Amira between us.

"*Alhumdillah 'assalameh, ya binti.* Thank God for your safe arrival, my daughter," she whispered in my ear.

"*Mishtaklik kthir.* I've missed you a lot," I choked through tears.

"*Ya Allah! Meen al bint il hilweh?* Oh my God! Who is this beautiful girl?" she said, gesturing at Amira.

She clutched Amira to her embroidered Palestinian *thobe* and burbled a stream-of-consciousness string of Arabic sweet nothings into my startled daughter's ear. We crossed the tiny cement courtyard to the door of my in-laws' sleeping room. Lutfi slowly cracked the door open, craning his head around it into the darkened room. Looking past him I could see the lower part of my father-in-law's body swaddled in thick wool blankets. Then Lutfi noiselessly pushed open the door revealing Omar's face—the only part of him that wasn't blanketed. Seeing him I realized I now knew what death looked like. His russet skin had an ashen pallor; although his eyes had been sealed by blindness decades earlier, sunken hollows announced themselves atop prominent cheekbones that stubbornly refused to give way.

We knelt down beside the mattress and Asma gently prodded him awake.

"*Ya, sheikh. Bint Zayn hun.* Zayn's daughter is here."

"*Bint Zayn?*" he rasped, the muscles around his eye sockets barely twitching.

He struggled under the covers, trying to free his hands. I moved closer, sitting Amira on my lap, then gently peeled back the blanket and gingerly lifted his hand. I took Amira's tiny hand in one of mine, turning her palm upwards, and with my other guided Omar's fingers along hers. His labored breathing seemed to relax into the soothing, circular pattern I traced with his fingers along his granddaughter's.

❧

After a few more days in Gaza, I left for Jerusalem and Ramallah to visit friends. My second day there, I received word that Sheikh Omar had died. I immediately returned to Gaza for the wake. By the time I arrived, he had already been buried, as dictated by Muslim tradition. The *'azza* was hosted by Zayn's cousin Shadi, who lived in a large flat near the entrance to the camp. White plastic chairs were arranged in a semicircle in what was normally the garage, its large metal door opened to the street that edged Shati. Salty air occasionally wafted in from the sea. Warbly recordings of Quranic verses played on a battered boom box.

Visitors streamed in and greeted Shadi and Lutfi, who sat in the garage with the men. The women relayed their sympathies and went upstairs to the living room to sit with Zayn's mother and sisters. In the garage, Shadi's son Mahmoud served the coffee of mourning—a thin, unsweetened liquid whose bitterness is meant to reflect the bitterness of loss. Mahmoud approached each arriving mourner and offered him a handleless cup with lips that flattened and extended outward like pudgy tulips. I first observed this ritual during one of my early trips to Gaza, at the wake of a young man who had been killed by the army at the beginning of the intifada. This coffee isn't lingered over and savored; it is drained in one quick gulp followed by traditional phrases of condolence: "May you find peace" or "May the remainder of his life be yours." Words meant to comfort, as much as any can, the mother of a sixteen-year-old shot by a sniper, or the father of a schoolgirl who is, regrettably, collateral damage.

The mourning of an old man in this community felt different. His death was felt less as a shock and outrage but even more as the loss of an elder with historical memory: one who could still remember life not just in the camp but in Palestine before the Nakba; one whose own memories still inhabited the place that belonged to him and could be unlocked by the key he still wore around his neck.

Later I learned that in Yarmouk Abu Bashir, the father of the men Zayn's nieces had married in Benghazi, had hosted a wake for Sheikh Omar. I called Zayn from Jordan on our way back to Damascus, telling him about the people from all over Gaza who came to the wake.

"People whose families were neighbors in Simsim came," I said. "They told the story of his jumping over the well."

A legendary story from Sheikh Omar's youth in Simsim that I'd heard was how, after he'd gone blind, he accepted the challenge of jumping over the village well. It was a feat of daring and physical prowess that still made the rounds in Shati camp many decades later.

Zayn was silent. Of all the goodbyes he was unable to say, I knew this one was the hardest. I grasped the receiver to steady my voice.

"I'm really sorry, *habibi.*"

Exiles are faced immediately with missing the lives of those they love. But in Zayn's silence, I could hear the helplessness and pain of missing their deaths.

"Allah yerhamu. May God have mercy on him," Zayn whispered.

❦

Soon after Sheikh Omar's death, Amira and I returned to Damascus via Jordan. It was an uneventful departure, as Palestinians exiting the country face no Israeli obstacles at the border. At the end of September, we celebrated Amira's first birthday at our apartment with Abu Bashir, his wife, and a small group of friends. I returned from Palestine to find the exodus of friends and colleagues continuing. Political, financial and moral support for Palestinians was at an historical ebb.

The beginning of October marked our fourth wedding anniversary, so I suggested we ask a friend to babysit and go out to dinner in Damascus to celebrate, something we had never done. It took some convincing, but Zayn finally agreed.

We had lived in Damascus for nearly three years but had no idea where to go. We took the suggestion of a friend and chose a restaurant in the city, but not too far from the camp. Zayn was quiet and stiff in the taxi on the way there. I chose to ignore this and made small talk instead, excited by the novelty of dinner out. We arrived at the restaurant and were greeted by a host who asked if we wanted to sit inside or on the patio outside. Zayn responded "Inside," but I said I'd like to sit outside to enjoy what was left of the warm weather. His mouth clenched slightly, and he looked at me. The host looked at

Zayn; he unclenched his mouth and said, "After you," sweeping his arm toward the patio door.

The host led us outside to a table. A smiling young man soon arrived to pour us water. We perused the menu of standard Arabic fare. Zayn muttered something about being able to buy three kilos of eggplant for the price of the *babaganoush*. The waiter returned and took our order —a variety of *mezza* and two bottles of *Barada*, the local beer. He brought the sweating bottles and began ceremoniously pouring the golden liquid into glasses. He poured one for me but Zayn waved him off, telling him he didn't need a glass. I looked out at *Jabal Qasiyoum*, the mountain that dominates the Damascus skyline, and took a deep breath.

"Happy anniversary," I raised my glass in Zayn's direction.

He glanced at me, grasped his bottle and said, "Happy anniversary," before taking a swig.

The food came, and we ate in silence except for when I tried to start a conversation.

"How do you like the food?"

"On the menu it says this place is five stars," he responded, holding up his palm with fingers spread wide to emphasize the rating. "But if that is so, then I know a hundred others in Yarmouk alone whose food is ten stars!"

I put down the piece of pita I was using to scoop up some *hummus* and looked toward the decaying mountain.

A few minutes passed. Sensing he had crossed a line, Zayn ventured, "*Shu malik?* What's wrong?"

I kept my eyes on the barren, dust-colored *Qasiyoum*. Nearly shaking with the effort to hold them back, I finally felt hot tears slowly leak down my cheeks.

"*Lesh tibki*? Why are you crying?" Zayn asked in the way one does when you already know the answer.

"I should have known better!" I blurted out, my voice thick and watery. "Is it so hard to have dinner with your wife on our anniversary?"

Now he stared at the mountain.

"Rebecca, how can I 'celebrate' anything? I'm to sit here and drink beer and eat like a king and think what about the situation in Gaza?"

The waiter appeared with a water pitcher but assessed the situation and abruptly turned away.

I wiped my face with a napkin and got up from the table. "Get the check," I said to him, walking toward the door.

❧

Toward the end of November, Amira and I left Syria. After checking our luggage at the airport, Zayn and I milled about the terminal, the patches of silence growing, the closer it came to our departure. Whenever Zayn held Amira I had to turn away.

Finally, inevitably, it was time to part. An escalator would take Amira and me up to immigration and security. I stood at the bottom of it, a rhythmic creak whining in the background whenever one of the moving steps would unfold itself and begin its ascent. Zayn folded Amira into his arms and bent his lips close to her ears, his mouth quivering as he spoke. Then he kissed her on both cheeks and rocked her from side to side in one final hug. He handed her back to me and we embraced, one or both of us trembling.

I stepped on the escalator with Amira. Zayn's eyes grew rounder, the whites seeming to overwhelm the blue-green irises; his forehead didn't so much wrinkle as buckle. As we ascended his mouth opened in a frozen "O." I shifted Amira to my other hip and held her against me to get a better view of Zayn. I peered over her shoulder just in time to see him turn and leave.

We flew back to Ohio by way of London, stopping to visit Francesca and Zaha, our filmmaker friends. It was the first time they had seen Amira. At the breakfast table our first morning there, Francesca spent the entire meal teaching my daughter how to blow raspberries. Zaha arrived with tiny gold earrings for Amira's recently pierced ears. A cultural difference battle that I surrendered to about six months earlier after my control-freak sister Carol said to me, "Oh, just do it," when I complained to her about Zayn's request.

Our third day there we all piled into Francesca's white Honda Civic and drove out to Oxford to visit a friend of hers, Margaret. The clear, crisp air and the lush verdancy of the village was slightly disorienting. After years of living surrounded by concrete and arid landscapes, I could physically feel my eyes relax with the onslaught of green. We had tea with Margaret in her very English garden and then strolled along the river.

Years later Francesca would tell me that when she spoke to Margaret after we left, she had said to Francesca, "That woman has left her husband, but she doesn't yet know it."

We arrived in Ohio in early December. At my mother's apartment, preparations for the holidays were soon underway. While my mother may have dubbed herself the "Jewish hillbilly," Christmas was still very much part of our family tradition, and she was determined to make sure Amira experienced her first full-blown Klein Christmas. She succeeded.

Amira was outfitted in a red velvet dress, white stockings and black patent leather Mary Janes. We decorated a miniature fake evergreen, stuffed stockings, and baked cookies for Santa, who rewarded Amira with enough toys and clothes to fill her own toy store.

The new year arrived, and I began focusing on two things: getting a job and getting a visa for Zayn. I consulted with a lawyer, and since it seemed that the process consisted mainly of completing forms and supplying documents, I decided not to retain one for the application. After all, I had arrived at my mother's with three hundred dollars, two suitcases and Amira.

I started working for a temp agency while I looked for a full-time job. My mom watched Amira, while I headed off to a nine-to-five shift in some nondescript office in the Cincinnati suburbs. In an attempt to keep up with what was going on in the Middle East, I subscribed to *The New York Times*, watched CNN international every minute I could, and listened to National Public Radio as soon as I walked in the door after work. Whenever Amira heard the *All Things Considered* theme song come on the radio in the late afternoon, she would run to the front door and brightly declare, "Mommy home!"

In the meantime, I collected documents and completed questionnaires, the answers to which ultimately would determine our future as a family. I thought of somehow trying to hide Zayn's past, but I was sure the Israeli and U.S. intelligence services cooperated on immigration matters. I sought Zayn's input and we discussed things, but in the end he acknowledged he had no experience maneuvering through U.S. government bureaucracy. He left the final decision about what to do to me. I had no interest in yet another bunch of armed men banging on our doors in the middle of the night and answered accordingly.

Check the box Y or N:

Was your spouse a member of a terrorist organization seeking to overthrow the U.S. Government?

My husband was a member of an organization seeking to liberate his country from an illegal military occupation, as provided for under international law. Yes, arms were used against the soldiers, one of whom was killed.

Answer: No

Was your spouse ever arrested, jailed or convicted of a crime?

My husband was arrested at age seventeen by the Israeli military in Gaza, tried in an Israeli military court, and convicted of fighting the same army who stood in judgment of him and sentenced him to life in prison.

Answer: Yes.

My husband was convicted of resisting the Israeli occupation.

I submitted the visa application in March and waited.

In September, I finally found a full-time job as an international student advisor at the University of Dayton. My sister Carol lived near

Dayton and had offered to take care of Amira if I found a job in the area. We moved to a two-bedroom apartment within walking distance of my sister in West Carrollton, a nearby suburb. I bought my first car—a 1989 Oldsmobile—took out a life insurance policy and started my professional career in the U.S. I was thirty-one.

After work I would sometimes take Amira, now two years old, for a walk in the neighborhood. The neat lawns of the nearly identical houses were bordered by sidewalks startling in their geometric uniformity and emptiness. Accustomed to the teeming streets of Yarmouk, Damascus, Cairo, and Gaza, I felt like I was living on a movie set after the last cut. The four years I lived in Dayton, I knew the name of one neighbor.

Working entailed not just learning a new job, but understanding how the work world functioned in the U.S. For the first time, there were human resource policies to learn, tax withholding calculations to make, and vacation time to track. Selecting mutual fund investments for my 401(k) was like contemplating which lottery numbers I wanted to bet on.

I became friendly with the international students I advised, but given the age difference and my position they weren't going to become close friends. It was the first time since leaving college that I had to find a social community in the U.S., and I soon realized how different doing so was with a kid in my early thirties, compared to being single in my early twenties. What distinguished now from then was less the passing of nearly a decade and more what I had experienced during it. In college, my peers and I were interested in the same things, sought out similar experiences, and shared many values. Now, as an adult, those I met as peers and potential friends—at the university or through my sister—had mostly passed the decade going to graduate school, establishing a career, maybe starting a family. What they weren't doing was crossing into another culture, living underground, and moving from country to country to escape the aftermath of war and occupation.

When we first moved into our West Carrollton apartment, I met a woman in the parking lot one evening when Amira was riding her tricycle in circles and figure eights on the soft, licorice-color asphalt. I had seen the woman and her daughter, who was about Amira's age, coming and going in the building. They emerged from their sliding patio door, the little girl pulling her own tricycle behind her to the edge of the lot. Amira stopped her bike and smiled; the little girl joined her loop-di-loops and soon they were chattering away. The mother and I stood watching them, exchanging basic demographic information about our daughters. Soon the conversation turned to our lives.

"Where did you move here from?" she asked, smiling.

"Most recently, Cincinnati," I began, excited to be talking to someone my age *and* with a kid Amira's age. "But before that we were living in Damascus, in a refugee camp. My husband is a Palestinian from Gaza. He was forced into exile from Gaza during the intifada, and then the situation became untenable for us in Damascus after the war…"

I paused, expecting that she would ask a question, express surprise or concern or something. There was silence. I turned my attention from the girls circling around each other to look at the mother. Her arms were crossed in front of her pastel polyester blouse. Her tight mouth almost looked drawn on. In her eyes, glass-like, I could see the reflection of the setting sun.

❦

In September of 1993—the same month I started my job at the university—PLO Chairman Yasser Arafat and Israeli Prime Minister Yitzhak Rabin had their famous handshake on the White House lawn, officially launching the Oslo Accords. Heralded as ushering in an era of hope in the region, the agreement was doomed from the start as evidenced by its main results—shifting the occupation's day-to-day administration to the Palestinian Authority, while Israel further entrenched its control over Palestinian land and lives.

Amira and I stayed in touch with Zayn via weekly phone calls and letters. I had email access, but the internet hadn't yet come to Syria. In March 1994, Amira and I visited Zayn. It had been nearly a year and a half since we left Syria and a year since I had submitted the visa application. A visit was long overdue.

Zayn was still in the same apartment. Amira was two and a half, old enough now to play with the young girls who lived next door. This visit formed her earliest childhood memories: playing with the neighbors on the flat rooftop of our apartment building, where laundry hung, children gathered, and people sometimes slept to escape the summer heat; and first riding on a bus.

Zayn immersed himself in Amira's presence and, of course, completely indulged her. In the afternoons, he would take her for a *mishwar,* a walk or errand, which usually meant taking her to visit his friends' offices while they were doing their afternoon shift. She inevitably returned to the house laden with presents—either a toy bought by her father or a gift from his friends—and her face smeared with chocolate or clutching a bag of chips.

We took day trips as a family—something we had never done before. On one memorable trip to Aleppo, the last of the winter rains brought a sight I had never seen before: a double rainbow arcing a stream of pastels across a slate-colored afternoon sky.

We visited old friends and new ones Zayn had made in my absence. When he introduced us, I could hear his words stiffen when he explained that Amira and I were here for a visit, but he smiled and made no other comment. I enjoyed being in Damascus as a tourist, visiting the ancient souk and Omayyad Mosque in the Old City. We kept talk about future plans to a minimum; waiting for the visa was excruciating, but at least we still had hope.

After our return to the U.S., Zayn called me at work one afternoon in May. He had received a reply from the embassy in Damascus. The letter read:

> Under the Immigration and Nationality Act, Section 212 (a) (2) (A) (i) (I) prohibits the issuance of a visa to anyone convicted of a crime involving moral turpitude (other than a purely political offense) and Section 212 (a) (3) (B) prohibits visa issuance to those involved in terrorist activities.

I held the phone closer to my ear. An echoing silence filled my office.

"Allo?" Zayn's voice reached me through the descending fog.

I don't know what I intended to say, but what came out was a kind of yelp.

A tide of fear, disbelief and powerlessness rose up and washed over me. Attempting to choke back sobs, all I could manage was, "I don't know what to do. I don't know what to do."

The low lull of Zayn's voice only heightened my alarm.

"I don't know what to say, *habibti*. I'm sorry."

I looked out of the window at the parking lot full of modest sedans and minivans, the white-striped spaces gripping the cars like arms. "Sorry?" I replied.

I was unable to say much more, so we agreed to talk later when I was home.

My head sank down onto my desk. Outside my office door, I could hear the click of the secretary's fingernails on her keyboard, and then the ring of the office phone. Marta's voice answered the call. Marta was a student worker in the office from Bosnia with whom I had grown close. She had been an exchange student at a local high school before her country disintegrated. At the beginning of the civil war, Marta returned to Dayton to live again with her host family and attend UD. Her family, including a sister from whom she had been separated at the Sarajevo airport amid the melee of Bosnians trying to get out, was in a refugee camp in Denmark.

I opened my office door and peered into the reception area. The secretary looked up from her typing and lowered her eyeglasses-on-a-chain onto her tabletop bosom, taking in my tear-stained face.

"Marta," I said in as normal a voice as possible, "can you come here a minute?"

She looked up from her filing. Her mouth parted slightly and then hinged closed. She stood and followed me back into my office. Eventually I would have to tell the news to my family, whose primary concern I knew would be that I might return to Syria with Amira. But at that moment, I was desperate to tell someone who wouldn't need reassurance, someone who would understand without my having to explain.

I turned and looked at her. I said nothing but slowly shook my head. Tears filled both of our eyes and I closed the door.

❦

The initial shock evolved into a maze of problem solving: there had to be a way to fix this and I needed to find it. I began by contacting my congressman's office. His local aide, Diane, seemed genuinely sympathetic and had made inquiries on my behalf with the immigration authorities during the long wait for an answer. Throughout the summer of 1994, she helped me devise a strategy to appeal the decision.

Zayn would need to request a reconsideration of the denial through the embassy in Damascus. It would be supported by expert legal opinions challenging the assertion that Zayn had been involved in "terrorist activity" and identifying the "offense" which Zayn had been convicted of as, indeed, political.

We enlisted "big Amira"—our daughter's namesake—in this task, along with Tawfiq Salem, who had been awarded the Robert F. Kennedy Human Rights award in 1991. I talked to several attorneys from organizations like the ACLU and the Center for Constitutional Rights, as well as immigration attorneys and academics.

Zayn's request to reconsider the visa denial read:

> When I was arrested in 1970, there was massive resistance to this occupation and had the Israelis applied the Geneva Conventions to my case as international law requires, I would have been held as a political prisoner of war and not tried as a criminal.
>
> Under international law, it is permissible to resist a foreign occupier…I have always opposed any use of violence against civilians anywhere and anytime, and it should be clear that I was convicted of an offense that should be considered as legitimate resistance against a military occupier and not a criminal act of violence. A French citizen would not be denied entry into the US because he was convicted of being a member of the French underground during World War II.
>
> Even though I was convicted, my trial was conducted in an Israeli military court, not a normal court of law. These courts were not established to determine guilt or innocence, but rather were set up to punish any opposition or resistance to the occupation…It has been well documented by Amnesty International and other Israeli and international human rights organizations that the Israeli military courts rely almost exclusively on confessions obtained by the use of torture for convictions, which was the case with me…
>
> My wife finds it ironic that her relatives, Russian Jews who fled their home to escape repression, went to the

> U.S. to build a life for themselves…and that now we are attempting to do the same…Even though I served 15 years in prison, I feel like I am being punished twice by being denied the right to be with my family, which is one of the most basic human rights…
>
> At this point I have missed half of my daughter Amira's life. I only hope that the day will soon come when she knows me as the baba who teaches her to throw a ball, upon whose shoulders she views the world, and who tucks her into bed at night, instead of the "baba" in the picture on the wall.
>
> …Although I understand your need to ensure the security of United States citizens, I pose no risk to anyone. In this era of reconciliation and renewal of hope, I am asking you to please reconsider your decision and allow me to enter the U.S. to be with my family.

A professor at The Ohio State University and a specialist in international law analyzed the case and wrote in support:

> If Mr. Majdalawi's act was undertaken as part of an effort by a group of Gazans to resist Israel's occupation, there is a strong argument that the act would not qualify as terrorism.
>
> Terrorism, as generally understood, involves an act of violence outside a military context, undertaken in order to cause fear in a population. The act apparently undertaken by Mr. Majdalawi was directed against the military forces of a state, and the manner of execution of the act, namely the use of grenades by an organized group, bespeaks a military-type assault. This is far different from such typical acts of terrorism as the hijacking of an airliner.
>
> The concept as developed in British and U.S. case law

> includes an act of violence undertaken in order to bring about a change in the political order of a society…the act apparently undertaken by Mr. Majdalawi would fall under the definition of a political offense…

We also asked Israeli friends and prominent Palestinians to write character references. I enlisted the aid of the spokesperson for the Palestinian delegation to the Washington peace talks, Dr. Hanan Ashrawi. She had been Zayn's professor at Bir Zeit University, and in her official capacity had developed high-level contacts with the State Department and other members of the U.S. government. Arab-American civil rights organizations that I contacted were willing to inquire on our behalf with the government.

Two women who were part of the Israeli group we met in Gaza in the early days of our relationship, Edit and Ilana, wrote how they had met Zayn while involved in the Israeli peace movement at the beginning of the intifada:

> Zayn never concealed from us the fact that he had in his youth participated in the armed struggle against the Israeli occupation forces, and that he had served a long jail sentence as a consequence. Having been soldiers ourselves, we were always aware of the mutual violence in the Israeli-Palestinian conflict. What we found that we shared with Zayn was the conviction that it was time to consciously give up the road of violence and find out a way for peaceful coexistence between Israelis and Palestinians. Zayn, committed as ever to the fate of his people, was now putting his energy into building a new kind of relation with the Israelis.

Since the signing of the Oslo Accords, the Israeli authorities were allowing former fighters back into the Palestinian Territories. "This turning of a new page should, we feel, influence a similar leniency on the part of the American government," they wrote.

In October a cable was sent by the State Department to the embassy in Damascus in response to our request to reconsider the denial: No waiver of the denial would be granted. No consideration would be given to his age at the time of his actions, the circumstances under which they took place, or anything else that had ensued in the intervening two decades.

Our increasing desperation seeped into the faxes I sent out. "The State Dept. denied the appeal to reconsider the visa denial," I wrote Dr. Ashrawi. "Did you have the chance to talk to anyone in the State Dept? I'm trying to figure out if they made the decision in spite of your appeal, or if it was not part of the equation...What do we do now?"

I spent that winter of 1995 contacting people who I felt might be able to intervene on our behalf. I had already written to President Clinton, whose response duplicated the language of the original denial. Hanan contacted former President Jimmy Carter requesting "urgent humanitarian assistance." Her office also suggested that Zayn consider applying for political asylum in Norway, or contacting the UN High Commissioner for Refugees and pleading ours as a special case for family reunion. The aide at my congressman's office proposed some kind of media campaign.

I heard National Public Radio commentator Andrei Codrescu speak at a conference and asked him if he thought anyone at NPR would be interested in our story. In June of 1995, right before we left for another visit with Zayn, a producer from NPR contacted me after hearing about the story from Codrescu and asked for a summary of our situation. I sent him a letter describing the basic details of our predicament but waited in vain for a reply.

10
A New Page

Much of my life the preceding seven years I had spent waiting.

Waiting for Zayn to get out of prison. Waiting to know if he had made it out of Gaza alive. Waiting with him in Cairo for something to happen. Waiting for the visa.

Now it was interspersed with bursts of activity meant to bring the waiting to an end—activity that produced both hope and anxiety. In my hopeful moments, I envisioned the three of us together again as a family. Zayn—with his intelligence and hunger to learn—would be able to take advantage of the good this country had to offer: educational opportunities and the possibility to start anew.

During sleepless nights, I feared that the gnawing existence of a Palestinian political exile living in America's heartland would be too much. In getting to know international students, I observed how some of them, far from home and the familiarity of their society, would react to being "foreigners" by clinging to the most conservative elements of their culture and closing off the dominant culture around them. I had felt this at work during our lowest moments in Yarmouk. What would it be like in America?

Amira was nearly four. She grew close to my sister, her husband Bob, and my niece and nephew, who became the sister and brother she never had. One day pulling into Carol's driveway after work, making sure to park close enough to one side to leave room for Bob, who often arrived soon after me, I saw Amira sitting on the front stoop. She sat straight-backed, hands folded in her lap, her head of curls swiveling from side to side as she looked up and down the street.

"Hi, sweetie," I greeted her, expecting her to come down to the car.

When she didn't move from her lookout post, I was curious.

"What are you doing?"

"Waiting for my dad to come home," she replied.

❦

That summer we spent three weeks in Syria. A friend of Zayn's invited us to spend a weekend in Latakia on the northern coast, a welcome escape from dry, dusty Damascus. On the bus trip north, I told Zayn about the latest plan to try and overturn the visa decision through a media campaign. He shrugged. I noticed that the little hair he did have left was graying.

We disembarked from the bus into a bustling station-cum-market. Zayn's friend Ra'ed was waiting for us. I gathered up Amira and her little backpack of toys and snacks. Zayn and Ra'ed took our luggage and we set off for his apartment.

We made our way slowly through the crowd of shoppers preparing for the weekend and workers going home. The two of them walked ahead of us, snaking a path along the narrow sidewalk, but I struggled to keep up. The late afternoon heat rose from the asphalt and cement in shimmering waves. The sunhat I had packed for Amira was still in the suitcase, so I tried to shield her head and face as we walked. I was more cautious crossing the street with her and at one point I had to yell for Zayn to wait when they made it across a busy intersection, leaving us on the other side.

When we caught up with them, Zayn admonished me.

"*Yalla, ya Rebecca!* Come on, we've bothered Ra'ed enough."

He was in his someone-is-doing-something-for-us-so-we-must-not-ask-for-more mindset, which apparently precluded walking at a pace I could manage.

I looked at him but said nothing. It was just the beginning of our vacation together.

"*'Ateeni Amira wa a-shanta.* Give me Amira and the bag," he said. He slung the backpack over his shoulder and took Amira in his arms. "*Yalla!*" he vowed, turning back to Ra'ed. On we went.

I watched him walk away, chatting and joking with Ra'ed as the bright pink knapsack bounced against his hip. Amira buried her face in his shoulder to escape the relentless sun. I started out after them. My pace quickened for a while but the humid seaside heat soon wore me down again. Falling farther behind I called out to Zayn a couple of times, but between the swirl of street noise and his banter with Ra'ed, he didn't hear me.

I wiped away the sting in my eyes, but the tightness in my chest only grew. I could make out the bouncing backpack for a few more yards. But then all I could see was a jostle of bodies, unrecognizable to me. I stopped trying to find him.

My pace slowed and then I stopped. I looked around to find some place to sit—a café or park bench—but there was none. I wandered down the sidewalk, retracing our steps for a while, and then turned back toward where we had been. After a few more minutes, I came across a bus stop that had part of a plastic bench still intact. I sat down and stared into the street, besieged by the honking of horns that were used instead of turn signals.

I could sense long looks from passersby. I looked around but everyone seemed to be going about their business. Then I heard a voice rise above the street din: Zayn calling my name. I turned to the right and saw him half running down the street, his face reflecting sweat and anger.

"*Wein kountee?* Where were you?" he started before even reaching me. "What are you doing here?" his voice rose until people nearby turned to stare.

I just turned my face away.

"Rebecca, what's wrong with you?" he repeated.

I turned to look at him.

"I told you I couldn't keep up. So I stopped trying."

An overloaded city bus roared by and its phantasmagoric cloud of exhaust rose and wove into nothingness behind Zayn.

He stared back, squinting against the sun in his eyes.

"Ra'ed is up the street with Amira and all of our luggage. We need to go."

He turned and walked back up the street. I got up and followed one more time.

❧

We got through the weekend and returned to Damascus. The rest of the visit was spent like the last one—visiting friends and showing off Amira.

Our last night there, I tucked in Amira and made tea for Zayn and me. After the nine o'clock news, I turned off the television while Zayn was smoking on the veranda. He came back into the living room and I filled our cups. I began talking in more detail about my efforts to contact the media and Hanan's suggestion about political asylum in Norway.

"Rebecca," he interrupted after a short while, "this will do nothing."

I topped off my teacup, even though I had barely drunk any.

"What do you mean?" I ventured.

"Rebecca, it is no use. It's been three years since you left with Amira," his voice trailed off as he reached for his cigarette pack.

I had stopped smoking before I got pregnant, but suddenly felt the urge for a cigarette.

"I realize that, Zayn," I said, my voice coming out unexpectedly shrill. "But we haven't tried contacting the press yet. That's something my congressman's office advised holding off on doing until we tried other things first."

He closed his eyes and slowly shook his head while I talked. I stopped talking. We sat there in silence for a few minutes, the neighbor's television broadcasting the latest Arabic soap opera through the open windows.

"What else can we do?" I continued. "Do you have other ideas?"

He tapped his cigarette ash onto the tray holding the teapot and sugar bowl. He took another sip of tea and turned to face me.

"I know you've tried very hard to get the visa," he started, his voice low and steady. "I understand you've been working hard doing this along with your job and taking care of Amira. But it's enough. It's time to face reality."

Facing reality. Isn't that what we had been doing for the past seven years?

I looked out of the open window into the night of Yarmouk.

"Rebecca." Zayn waited until I looked at him before continuing. "You need to come back here or we need to end this."

I was unable to reply.

The next day I distracted myself packing and saying goodbye to friends. A cold took hold of me, and by the time I boarded the plane my head throbbed with congestion.

With each passing hour, my voice trailed off into a coughing fit whenever I tried to speak. My ears gradually closed up, and as we descended, the pain pulsed and ricocheted in my head. I could do nothing but weep.

Amira reacted by being out of control. She refused to sit down and kept unbuckling her seatbelt and standing in her seat, clapping and babbling, despite several warnings from the flight attendants. When the captain instructed them to take their seats for landing, they gave up on us and watched reproachfully as I sobbed while holding onto Amira. But we made it back to Ohio.

When I got out of bed the next morning, the room listed sharply, sending me lurching toward the bathroom, where I threw up. The vertigo and nausea were a result of a bruised and infected eardrum. After a day in bed and a course of antibiotics, I began to recover.

In late July I faxed Hanan.

> I recently returned from visiting Zayn and need to ask you a pointed question. Do you feel there is any real hope that he will get the visa? I know when we talked last spring you were intimating that there wasn't, and that perhaps he should consider alternatives, as you were getting nowhere with your efforts. If you honestly believe this is so, please tell me frankly now. He is insisting on making final plans for our future *now*, and is no longer willing to wait in limbo as he has been for the past three years.
>
> In any case, as always, we are grateful for all that you've done.

The reply came that the best thing was for Zayn to consider returning to Palestine, what many of our exile friends from Yarmouk (and elsewhere) were doing post-Oslo. Hanan informed us that returning required advance permission from the Palestinian authorities, who then must ask the Israelis. So he would know beforehand what awaited him.

Indeed, Zayn did know what would await him if he returned to Gaza, were we to live under the Palestinian Authority. During our last visit to Syria, he had adamantly refused to consider it when I raised the possibility.

"I will never ask Arafat to allow me to return to Gaza. I will not be beholden to this corrupt PA," he'd said.

End of discussion.

❦

My boss at the university, who was director of international services, planned to leave his position and proposed appointing me interim director of the office. After three years back in the States, a career was beginning to take shape from the odd patchwork of skills and experiences on my resume.

That September, I traveled to Southeast Asia on an international student recruiting trip, representing the university as part of my new duties. The three weeks I was away provided more of an excuse to not reply to Zayn.

It was also the first time in four years that I had no "mommy" duties for an extended period, and the first opportunity to forge relationships with peers and colleagues since leaving Syria. I traveled with a group of international educators representing different universities across the U.S. While my experience in the Middle East was unusual, even in this collection of ex-Peace Corps volunteers and experienced global travelers, their eyes did not glaze over when I told them what I had done before working at U.D., and they knew that the West Bank was not in Paris.

We worked hard during the day, talking for hours to prospective students at high schools and college fairs. But we also went out at night, which was key to surviving a seven-country, ten-city trip in less than three weeks. Professional and personal bonds formed. I dined and laughed and stayed out late for the first time in years. Not surprisingly, I experienced much of what I saw through the filter of what I had seen in the Middle East. But I also began to see that life could be informed and inspired by the nearly seven years I had spent in that part of the world, and not just mired in it.

My conversations with Zayn after returning from Syria tiptoed around our tea-and-soap-opera discussion my last night there. Instead, we talked about Amira, my family, and his work, which increasingly consumed him. At times I sensed that he regretted what he had said, that his words were, perhaps, more an expression of frustration and powerlessness than how he truly felt. It was tempting to pretend that the conversation hadn't happened, that I hadn't been asked to choose. But continuing on as we had the preceding three years—living apart while trying to find a way to be together—would require Zayn to go forward with me into unchartered territory yet again.

Our options were narrowing and we needed to pursue alternatives. But the years had taken their toll, particularly the last ones separated from Amira. Zayn was now in his forties, and his health was beginning to bear the physical signs of what fifteen years in prison can do: chronic headaches, back and neck pain, serious dental problems, contracting the flu several times when I had never known him to be sick beyond a mild cold.

I also saw depression descending; he was dark and brooding in a way I had not seen or felt before. Finding and forging yet another life in another place would require a mental and physical energy that had been sapped. Was *Come back here* more an appeal for me to be with him in the emotional space that he was inhabiting, than the physical one?

❧

When I returned from Asia in October, I knew the time had come to give Zayn an answer; indeed, to give myself one, too. I tried to broach the subject a couple of times during phone calls with him but lost my nerve. I kept telling myself that I had not planned on single motherhood, even if Zayn and I had struggled with parenting together.

Finally, during a call just before Thanksgiving, Zayn asked if I had any news "on the visa front." I knew what he was asking.

Sitting at my little fake wood table in the kitchen of my apartment, I looked out of the patio door across the asphalt parking lot. The neighborhood's bare trees scraped at the sky portending winter.

"Sort of," I responded, closing my eyes.

There was silence on the line.

"Zayn, I cannot go back there."

It felt like the words were tumbling down and into the phone from somewhere else, that someone else had broken into the conversation and was speaking.

"I love you and I want us to be together. I want Amira to be with her father." My voice broke at the mention of her name. "But I can't go back to the way things were in Syria. I was miserable there. We were miserable there."

I opened my eyes. The naked trees swayed a bit in the wind.

"That is no way to live," I said.

The silence returned. I felt compelled to fill it.

"I can still pursue the media contacts. And you can contact the Norwegian embassy in Damascus." I paused to breathe. "Do you want to do that?"

Zayn's voice was tight and low.

"Rebecca, I've told you what I feel is possible. Nothing has changed."

My gaze shifted to the blank wall in front of me. The silence between us spun and hummed.

"I don't know what else to say," I offered.

"Me too," was his reply.

The winter holidays passed and I heard nothing from Zayn. I knew, of course, that he would be upset, but I wasn't sure how that would manifest itself. Nevertheless, the complete radio silence threw me. I suppose I was expecting more sound and fury from him. I tried calling him but could only leave a message at his office. He had thrown himself into work, writing and translating into Arabic articles from Israeli newspapers. Finally, in February of 1996 he called.

"*Keefak,* how are you?" I asked, honestly not knowing.

"*'Aish,* alive," he responded.

I flinched a bit, and then just dove into what I wanted to say.

"Zayn, I know how hard our last conversation was. Believe me, it was hard for me too. I just don't know what else to do, but I had to be honest with you."

I paused, not sure he was still on the line.

"Hello?"

"*Allo.*"

"What are you thinking?"

"Rebecca, I do not want to be alone, and I do not want to be *ab murasalee,* a father by correspondence."

His voice wavered and then rose with an angry flash.

"*Bidi ansaki, ansaha, wa aftah safha jadeeda bhiatee.* I want to forget you, forget her and open a new page in my life."

Ansa? Forget?

"I don't understand what you mean, Zayn."

"I mean exactly what I said," he retorted. "Let me know if you need any money. But don't expect to hear more from me."

I opened my mouth to speak, but couldn't. My eyes darted around the room.

"*Allo?*" he said.

"Yes, I'm here."

"Am I clear? I have to go now. I'm very busy with work."

"Zayn," I managed.

"Goodbye, Rebecca."

What does a new page look like when opened? How blank is it, really?

Aftah safha jadeeda.

After the sting of Zayn's pronouncement subsided, his words bobbed in and out of my life, connected to me like a balloon on a string. Life's daily exigencies—working, caring for Amira—would push the words away for a while. Then something would thrust them back in: Amira asking about her father, a dream of a scene in Palestine.

I understood that his words came from a place of pain, despair, from a world of fear and powerlessness. He had lost his family, his country, the political struggle he had all but given his life for, and now he was losing us. I also understood that I was the real target of his anger. But the way he lashed out reflected the reality that Amira's immediate future was inseparable from mine. She was collateral damage wrought by a relationship that failed amid dispossession, injustice, and the inability of two persons to navigate the treacherous waters those things create.

The way I dealt with Zayn's "new page" was to keep Amira's open to the old one. I continued Amira's relationship with her father on his behalf—signing his name to cards I sent her, buying her birthday presents from him, and making sure there were gifts under the Christmas tree with his name attached. I did so in part because I understood his anguish and wanted not to add to it, but also because I simply couldn't tell Amira anything else.

This decision was eventually validated by Francesca, our British filmmaker friend. She visited Zayn in Damascus that spring. He told her of his intention to "forget" and start anew, to which she'd replied, "That's what you think." Sharing her own story of her son's estranged father, who moved to America and cut off relations after their divorce, Francesca told Zayn, "Amira will come after you, just like Edward showed up on my ex's doorstep in America."

Zayn's reaction to Francesca's warning was muted at the time, eliciting only nervous, dismissive laughter. But it was enough to keep me going back to the "from Dad" section of the greeting card display for the next couple of years.

❧

After nearly four years in Dayton, I was ready to find a way back to the East Coast. My college experience in Philly had taught me how much that part of the country had to offer someone with my interests. I got a job at Rutgers University in New Jersey, and in August of 1997, Amira and I decamped for the Garden State. I soon realized, though, that I had traded the Dayton suburbs for a bedroom community of commuters whose lives were lived largely on the New Jersey Turnpike or in their homes recovering from it. Now, without even the social interaction my family provided, I was lonelier and more miserable than ever.

Early in 1998, I found a job as a paralegal with an immigration law practice in Philadelphia. The caseload included political asylum work, which reconnected me with the human rights world I left behind in Palestine. Equally appealing was the prospect of living again in Philly—a city large enough to be cosmopolitan but small enough for a single mother to manage. It was also the first but not last place I lived where the government bombed neighborhoods, as the City of Brotherly Love had done in the spring of my junior year at Temple during the police standoff with MOVE—a Black liberation group.

I rented an apartment in Mt. Airy in Northwest Philly. Dubbed "The People's Republic of Mt. Airy" for its progressive reputation, Mt. Airy is a neighborhood of old hippies, yuppies, and Black families who had integrated the neighborhood starting in the 1950s. Unlike many such neighborhoods at that time, Mt. Airy didn't resegregate with white families fleeing to the suburbs when African Americans began moving in. There was an organized effort, boosted by the neighborhood's liberal Germantown Jewish Center, to keep "white flight" from happening.

The parents of Amira's kindergarten classmates became my friends, and I had a regular social life with non-family members for the first time in years. I found a community who shared my values and interest in the world, even if not my experience abroad. I felt at home for the first time since leaving Gaza.

In November, my phone at work rang and caller ID showed a number I didn't recognize. I hit the speaker phone button and continued typing on my computer.

"Is this Rebecca Klein?" a man's voice asked. He sounded serious.

"Yes. Who's calling?"

"Officer Edward Carver from the Federal Bureau of Investigation."

I turned away from my computer screen and picked up the receiver.

"Yes," I responded, not knowing what else to say. I noticed that the phone cord was twisted so tight, its two halves had almost bound into one.

"I'm with the FBI terrorist investigation division. I'd like to ask you a few questions," he continued.

I held the cord in my right hand and started trying to unwind it with my index finger.

"Why? What kind of questions?" I responded.

I looked at the caller ID again and wrote down the seven black numbers displayed on the screen.

"Someone associated with Islamic Jihad has been using your social security number, and I need to ask you some questions."

His words pounced and skidded to a landing in my head. I took them in, silent.

"Miss Klein?"

"What? Islamic Jihad? What are you talking about?" My mouth was dry. The words caught and tumbled out.

"Yes. I'd like to ask you some questions," he repeated.

I wrote "Islamic Jihad, social security #" on the note pad. My upper teeth began pulling back my lower lip, letting it go, and then doing it again.

"I can't talk right now. I'm expected at a meeting," I lied. What did he want? "Is there a number where I can call you back?"

He gave me the number I had already written down. I hung up the phone and looked down at my hand. The cord, wrapped tighter than ever, had imprinted salmon- and flesh-colored rings around my finger.

I needed advice and called an attorney I knew from my student activist days in Philadelphia. Judy Beinart was a labor and human rights lawyer. She had stayed with me in Ramallah when she was part of a National Lawyers Guild delegation to the Occupied Territories during the intifada.

"What do you think they want?" she asked.

"I have no idea," I blurted out. "How could someone use my social security number without my knowing?"

"Easily," she responded, her voice both matter-of-fact and sardonic. "Has anyone who wouldn't normally do so ever asked you for it? Or has your card been stolen?"

Other than doing things like opening a bank account and enrolling Amira in school when we moved, I could think of no other times when I used the number. I remembered that my purse was stolen my last year at Temple. My social security card was in it and I had to apply for a replacement.

"But that was over thirteen years ago," I said. "They want to ask me questions. What should I do?"

She suggested that I go to my boss, tell him what was happening, and ask if he would be present at a meeting with the FBI agent at the office.

Judy didn't think her presence was necessary at this point.

"They seem to be playing this low key," she said. "Sniffing, as it were. I think you should do the same."

David, the lead partner of the immigration group, was understandably shocked by my request. This was a business immigration practice and part of a large corporate firm—not the kind of place where you'd expect the FBI to be questioning employees about Islamic Jihad. I was fully expecting David to say no. To my surprise he said yes, and a meeting was arranged for a few days later.

A man and a woman entered the conference room; I was only expecting him. They introduced themselves—Carver and another agent named Barbara Emerson—and showed us their FBI badges. Both wore dark jackets. He looked slightly nerdy, with black rim glasses and a bad haircut. She had aviator sunglasses pushed on top of her hair and a walk that suggested the stiff-legged swagger of a cowboy in chaps. It soon became clear who would play good cop and who would play bad.

They sat across from me and began by asking me questions about where I had lived.

"Have you ever been to Ohio, Minnesota, New Jersey, or Kentucky?" Agent Emerson asked, her back ramrod straight and her hands clasped in front of her on the table.

"Well, I grew up in Ohio and moved here from New Jersey," I replied.

Agent Carver looked down at a small notebook he had pulled out of his breast pocket and made a note.

"And what did you do there?" Emerson pressed on, her head cocked slightly.

I explained my job at U.D. and Rutgers.

"And what do you do here?" she asked, her knuckles barely rapping the table indicating the law firm.

"I'm an immigration paralegal."

"So what does an immigration paralegal do?" her upper body inclined slightly when she said *do*.

"I prepare documents, research cases—generally assist the attorneys in filing different kinds of immigration petitions," I said.

"So you help people get in to the United States," she responded immediately.

I looked at her, and then at David. The chair that I was sitting in emitted a surprising *squeak* when I turned to him.

"David, do I help people get in to the United States?"

A ripple made its way down his jawline.

"We're an immigration law firm," he told her. "That's what we do."

Carver had stopped taking notes. Emerson turned and looked at him, and he once again hunched over his notebook.

They asked a few more questions about where I lived in Philadelphia, and then they got up to leave. Finally, Carver spoke.

"I have some photos of people I'd like you to take a look at."

He reached into his pocket again and handed me his business card. "Give me a call to arrange a time to do so."

They left the conference room and David walked them to the elevator. He came back in the conference room to get his jacket.

"Thanks, David," I said, "I appreciate you doing this."

He lifted his jacket off the back of the chair where he'd been sitting.

"You're welcome," he said as he turned to go.

He never mentioned the incident to me again.

I sat alone in the conference room and made notes to myself about what they asked. It then struck me: they hadn't asked a single question about Zayn or my life in the Middle East. I was immediately suspicious.

I got up, turned off the conference room light and went back to my office to make a call.

I'd slept very little in the days leading up to that meeting, and did so even less afterward. The maximum dose of Ambien the doctor could prescribe didn't help. I had nothing to do with Islamic Jihad, so what was this all about? They certainly knew that I lived in the Middle East, so why would they pretend not to? But what really kept me up at night was thinking of Amira. She was seven. What would happen to her if they arrested me?

Finally, I agreed to meet with Carver to look at the photos.

"Meet him in a public place and have someone else you know there observing at a distance," Judy suggested.

I agreed to meet him at a café in the lobby of my office building during my lunch break a few days later. Carver was already there when I arrived. There was another man sitting with him. I approached them, and he quickly introduced the second man, whose name I didn't quite get. The last name sounded like Stein or Stern, but I was too nervous to ask. He looked vaguely familiar—young, black jeans, leather jacket, and wrap-around Raybans pushed up to shade his closely shaved hair—but he said nothing the entire time.

My friend Lynn came in soon after I did, but we made no eye contact. She sat at a table not far away.

Carver produced a thick envelope and began showing me photos, the edges snapping against the table each time I shook my head. Photo after photo were of men clad in *jelabeyah*, a few of whom may have been Arab but most of whom looked African.

"*They* are Islamic Jihad?" I asked.

Carver nodded.

I continued shuffling through the photos. I could feel the guy in black leather looking at me.

"I don't know any of these people," I told him after examining the last photo.

The man in leather leaned back in his chair.

"You're sure?" Carver responded.

"I'm sure," I looked up from the pile of photos. "But I do have a question for you."

Judy had suggested that I look at the pictures but also go a bit on the offensive.

I looked at him and asked, "If Islamic Jihad is using my social security number, what are you going to do to protect me?"

He gathered up the photos and slipped the bulging envelope back into his briefcase.

"Obviously I'm going to need to contact Social Security and get a new number. But what else should I do to deal with this?"

"No! There's no need to contact Social Security."

Carver snapped the briefcase closed and leaned over the table. The guy in black leather ran his hand from the top of his forehead down the back of his head.

"So I'm supposed to do nothing?" I asked.

"We'll let you know if any further action is needed," he responded, smiling.

I went back to my office and called Judy.

"They tell you Islamic Jihad is using your Social Security number and they want you to do nothing. Interesting," she observed.

"Should I do anything?" I asked.

"Not for now," she responded. "I don't think you're going to hear from them again. But let me know if you do."

I finished the day at work and took the train home. I got off at my usual stop and walked up Greene Street towards Amira's after-school center, mulling over the day's events. As I crested the first hill, I froze in my tracks.

"Oh, my God," I said to no one, "Of course that's who it was." A mumbled name, no identification badge, that look of black leather and power. He had said nothing so I wouldn't notice an accent. I suddenly knew who the other man was: Mossad—Israel's equivalent to the CIA.

11
On His Shoulders

That spring, Zayn started calling again. His first call was to let me know that his mother Asma had died in Gaza. Standing in my bedroom and hearing Zayn's voice for the first time in months give me this news seemed to suck the air out of the room. The bottled-up anxiety and fear of the past several weeks spun out in a hot stream of tears. I couldn't talk, but Zayn consoled me. He sounded tired, his voice tinged with the hollowness of grief.

"I'm so sorry, Zayn," I managed after a few minutes. "You know how much I loved her."

"I know," he replied. "Thank you. *Allah yerhamha.* May God have mercy on her."

Zayn began calling more regularly to talk to Amira. He had left Damascus and moved to Beirut, where he was working for a daily newspaper. He would talk to me to ask if I needed money or to ensure that Amira had gifts from him for her birthday and Christmas. I never told him that I had continued buying gifts for her in his name.

"Don't worry," I said, "I'll take care of it."

A few months later, after one of his chats with Amira, she handed the phone to me.

"Baba wants to ask you something," she said.

Surprised, I took the phone from her. The call usually ended after they were done speaking.

"*Marhaba. Keefak?*" I greeted him.

"*Marhaba, ya hajee,*" he responded with a word used to address an old lady—a tongue-in-cheek term of endearment he had often used with me.

He asked the usual questions about work and money. I could tell there was something else on his mind.

"What do you think, Rebecca, about bringing Amira to visit me in Beirut?"

Beirut? With Amira? The civil war had been over for nearly a decade, but I had never been and knew no one there other than Zayn.

"Rebecca?" He interrupted the silence on the line.

"Yes, I'm here," I said. "I don't know what to say, Zayn. I've never been there. Are there flights from the U.S?"

"Many Lebanese living in America come here to visit," he assured me. "Of course I will pay."

He heard my hesitancy in my silence.

"*Bitfakree fee almawdu'a,* think about it," he said. Then he said goodbye.

I hung up the phone on the kitchen wall and turned to see Amira standing there with a big smile on her face. I had overheard her conversation with her father, so I knew he hadn't said anything to her about the visit. Nevertheless, she understood something was up.

Amira had grown independent and responsible beyond her nine years. I'd once overheard her lecturing a friend who had forgotten to tell her mother about a play date they had made, informing her, "You have to communicate, Molly!" By middle school, her friends would refer to her as the "mom" of the group. She became fascinated first with mysteries and detective stories, then obsessed with witches. Our Friday night ritual was pizza and "Sabrina, the Teenaged Witch." Her vacation dream was going to Salem.

I knew her adolescence might not be so bad when, around age ten, she announced from the back seat as we sat at a red light, "You know, Mom, I'm nothing like you."

The light turned green. She continued musing.

"Yeah…except for being really smart and caring about other people, we really aren't much alike…"

I smiled and thought to myself, *I'll take that.*

After he broached the topic of a visit, Zayn called fairly regularly to talk to Amira. We eventually got a webcam so that they could see each other and speak. Zayn clearly had second thoughts about his decision to "open a new page," which I could only be happy about. Despite the tumult in our marriage and his anger-induced declaration, there was more to him than that. I wanted Amira to know this intelligent, complex, essentially good-hearted person whose life had been buffeted by history and politics. He was doing what he could to survive, and like all of us he suffered from his own shortcomings and mistakes. Zayn Majdalawi was Amira's father and a man I had not only loved and married but continued to respect. When I felt angry or resentful at his distancing himself from us, I would remember the day in Gaza under curfew when he nodded agreement with the Israeli woman on the radio talking about ending the killing of each other's children. Or the risk he took to visit Galit and Shai in Tel Aviv. Or his infectious and often ill-timed laughter. Amira deserved to know all of this. Our daughter deserved to know her father.

Still, I hesitated to travel to Beirut with her. I would be venturing into an entirely unknown place with her after not having seen Zayn since 1995.

Over the next couple of years, he was patient but persistent with his invitation. In the interim, I left the law firm to manage an in-house immigration program for a consulting firm and bought a house in the Mt. Airy neighborhood, around the corner from where we'd been living. Amira attended the local public school through third grade. She transferred to a Quaker school in fourth grade, in September 2001.

My hesitancy ended that fall. On September 11, I was sitting at my kitchen table in my pajamas with a laptop propped in front of me and NPR on the radio, working from home. Bob Edwards's voice broke into the broadcast tentatively announcing the news, his words tripping over the first sketchy details. I remember thinking to myself, *Some idiot with too much disposable income and a new pilot license has done it again.* I went back to answering my morning email.

As the minutes passed, the tentativeness in his voice gave way to the edge of controlled fear. I got up and turned on the television. Black smoke, thickening by the moment, floated out of a gaping hole in the tower and lifted above the Manhattan skyline. I stood in my living room taking the scene in, trying to understand how someone could not see they were flying into a giant building. A strange buzz came from somewhere outside of the camera's eye. Then the second plane slammed into the other tower.

"Oh, God."

I stood in the middle of the living room, desperately wanting but unable to look away. I felt nauseous and cold, although I had begun to sweat. I went back to the kitchen and turned up the radio. News reports started filtering in of another plane, then two, headed for D.C. I called the school, but the line was busy. I returned to the television. After a few more minutes the tower seemed to vibrate. Then the missile-like cell tower on top leaned back into the billowing white smoke and the building sank into the ground. Debris and dust swirled with the force of the collapse for a few minutes. Then there was just bright blue sky where the building had been.

I ran upstairs, threw on clothes, and barreled out of the front door toward my car. As I fumbled with my keys, I saw my neighbor two doors down sitting on her front steps, sobbing. Passing the corner where Amira caught the bus with her classmate Anna, I called her mom and asked if she wanted me to pick up Anna also.

"I don't really think that's necessary," was her reply. "I haven't heard from the school, and I've got a meeting later."

"Pam, do you understand that this country may very well be under attack!"

I was practically yelling at her, this kind, soft-spoken woman whose family we had been paired with as our "buddy" to help us transition to the new school. In the silence that followed I could hear myself breathing heavily.

"Well, okay," she hazarded. "If the school is letting kids go, you can get Anna."

I hung up the phone and turned up the radio. Pundits were already speculating about who they thought was responsible. "Middle East terrorism" was the unsifted phrase immediately in the ether. At the school my car joined a line of others parked illegally on the street, hazard lights flashing. It reminded me of the scene in front of Ramallah Friends School when we tried to open the school during the intifada and the army showed up, except now I was one of the frantic parents.

I went straight to the lower school building and asked to see the principal, Mary Pearson. Her assistant asked me my child's name and told me that Amira could be picked up directly from her classroom. She then began directing me to the room.

"I know where Amira's classroom is," I interrupted. "I want to talk to Mary." The assistant gave me a look that clearly said *now is not the time for a parent meeting*, but knocked on the principal's door when she saw I was going nowhere. An ashen-faced Mary emerged from her office, eyeglasses pushed up over her mousey brown hair, her mouth forming a tight smile when she saw me.

"How can I help you?" she sighed.

"I'm Rebecca Klein, the mother of Amira Majdalawi," I introduced myself. The assistant observed me from behind her desk. "I think you know that my daughter is Arab-American."

Mary blinked. I continued.

"While she's here, no matter what happens, I expect this school to protect my daughter." My voice trembled over the last three words.

Mary crossed her arms in front of her and exhaled, "Of course we will."

I turned and headed out of the door toward Amira's classroom.

❧

What distinguishes the days following that one in my memory is the silence: The absence of sound falling from the September sky while flights were grounded. The radio muted and the television darkened, kept off in my futile attempt to protect Amira from the discussion of "Arab terrorists" and the horrific images that were rebroadcast endlessly. School and my office were closed September twelfth. Both resumed the next day. I knew the school had not told the students much on 9/11, leaving it up to parents what to tell their children. I had told Amira appropriately accurate information: everyone was upset that a lot of people had been hurt in "some other cities," but we weren't sure yet who was responsible. When I picked up Amira, I asked her about her day in as normal a voice as I could muster.

"Fine," came her answer from the back seat.

"What did you do?" I pressed.

"We had meeting," she replied, referring to the Quaker tradition of silent reflection, with participants speaking only when so moved. "Some people were crying."

When we got home Amira went to her room. I busied myself in the kitchen. When I went to get her for dinner I found her lying on her bed, quietly staring at the ceiling.

"Are you OK, sweetie?" I asked, kneeling beside the bed and slipping two fingers into her palm.

"Yeah," she responded, her eyes still fixed on the ceiling, compelling me to look up to see what she saw. Just the same old ceiling.

"Time for dinner," I said in that mommy-cheerful voice.

Her eyes shifted over to me and she slid off of the bed. I

started walking down the stairs, then Amira's voice came from the top landing.

"Mommy, I want to wear a scarf."

I put both feet on one step and turned, looking up to her.

"A scarf?" I cocked my head slightly.

"Yes. A scarf. On my head. Like the women in Syria."

So much for shielding her from the effects of the news.

She stood looking at me, waiting for a response. For a moment I contemplated the steps that separated us. Then I retraced my path and joined her on the landing. I slid open the closet door along the hallway that led from the stairs to her room. On the shelf above where the winter coats hung was a pile of scarves folded into squares of various sizes. There were thick wool ones, an old *kuffiyeh* of mine from Palestine, and some colorful silk pieces my mother had given me. I dug through them and pulled out one that had been Amira's favorite when she was a toddler. It was a swirl of purples and blues that she would tie around her waist as her pretend ice-skating outfit. During our holiday visits to my mother's, she loved turning on figure skating shows and "skating" her performance in Grandma Jean's living room.

I shook loose the folds and gathered two diagonal corners between the fingers of one hand, while I stretched the triangle shape flat. I placed the longest edge at the top of Amira's forehead and let the ends drape over the front of her shoulders. I had her hold the top piece while I crossed the ends under her chin, looped around the back of her neck, and gently tied the scarf into place.

I tucked some of her unruly curls into a blue edge. She looked at me and smiled warily.

"*Helwa,* pretty," I said.

Framed that way, she looked more like her father than ever, her startling green eyes staring straight out under his thick lashes and brow.

Amira was two weeks from her tenth birthday. This is the day I mark as the beginning of her search for her Arab identity.

The scarf didn't last long. The next morning it lay on her bed when she came down for breakfast. Preparing to leave for the bus stop, I asked her if she wanted it.

"I'll get it later," was her response.

I recoiled from the tide of unthinking "patriotism" that quickly swelled from the initial shock and sorrow in the weeks that followed the attacks. What I saw when I looked at the ubiquitous yellow ribbons stuck to cars and shop windows was a noose. My thoughts and feelings reached in a different direction. One night after Amira was in bed, a friend and I were watching a news show featuring pundits discussing 9/11. One of them, a historian who had also worked in the intelligence service, noted that the U.S. had trained and armed the Afghani fighters who became the Taliban. The U.S. clearly bore much responsibility for the regime that had been harboring Osama Bin Laden.

"You'll never see him on the talking head circuit again," I quipped. Indeed, that narrative was one effectively buried by the bombs that rained down on Helmand Province, Kandahar, and Tora Bora.

Throughout the fall I watched events unfold, first with an increasing sense of foreboding and isolation. The more radio and television I listened to, the more I felt like I had slipped down the rabbit hole. But then something shifted. I started more regularly calling friends from the Middle East—other expats who were back in the U.S. or who still lived abroad, and Palestinian friends I had stayed in contact with over the years. I eagerly reconnected with the ones with whom I had lost touch. The common denominator was that they were people to whom I didn't have to explain blowback and who knew 9/11 had nothing to do with enemy loathing "our way of life."

By winter I was talking to Zayn on an almost weekly basis, and Amira conversed with him even more. He had become the editor of the Israeli affairs section of the newspaper in Beirut and published translations from the Hebrew press—both activities being exceptional in the media of the Arab world. Zayn was becoming a sought-after pundit throughout the region, with views informed by the unique combination of his fluency in Hebrew, time in prison, and political experience. Often our conversations were interrupted by calls from other Lebanese news outlets or ones from Syria or the Gulf wanting to interview him on the latest developments.

He also had become the center of a firestorm among journalists and intellectuals in Beirut. The U.S. embassy had invited a number of writers and newspaper publishers to a meeting to "discuss" the situation with Iraq. In other words, in the run-up to the war, the Americans were hoping to enlist them in selling the invasion to the Arab public. Zayn was among the invitees.

Some of his colleagues and counterparts were interested in attending the meeting, if only out of curiosity, as it wasn't often that the embassy opened its doors to locals. But Zayn steadfastly refused to attend. And the political dynamic was such that Zayn's absence from the meeting would be an indictment of those from his newspaper who did attend—if he didn't go, no one would. Of course, he didn't budge from his position, so no one went. No doubt his stance didn't endear him to some of his colleagues. But I could not have been prouder.

With the spring's thaw it was clear to me what I had to do: take Amira to visit Zayn. In July 2002, I took three weeks off from work and we packed our bags for Beirut. But preparing for the trip meant renewing Amira's passport, which had expired in the intervening years since our last trip to visit Zayn in Syria.

One afternoon, while I was looking through my dresser drawers for the old document to submit with the application, Amira stuck her head around the door to check on my progress. She came into the room eyeing a small leather box I had pulled out during the search.

Preoccupied, I explained that it contained some of her Grandma's old jewelry and mine.

The box creaked open, the leather stiff with time, and Amira examined its contents.

"Mom, what is this?!"

Her astonishment caught me off-guard. She had uncovered the stone heart and map of Palestine her father had carved for me in prison.

The midsummer sun pushed in light, filling and warming the room. I knew then that the time had come for those stones to be in her hands.

Amira took to calling them her good luck charms.

❦

The cerulean expanse that opened up as we descended from the clouds was disorienting. Suddenly, glints of light dotted the Mediterranean; I thought for a moment someone was signaling from below. Craning my neck and expecting to see at least a ship, I realized it was the sun's last rays sparking off of the waves. The plane's shadow stretched itself over the sea that I hadn't seen for seven years, its blueness never ceasing to startle and amaze. The runway appeared, squeezed by a south Beirut neighborhood whose concrete apartment buildings edged so close I could see laundry flapping dry on rooftops. Beyond, pink, sunbaked hills stretched up toward Mt. Lebanon.

Inside the terminal, I stood hypnotized by the endlessly revolving baggage carrousel. I looked over at my ten-year-old daughter, her eyes sweeping across faces that for once looked like hers. A big yellow smiley face sticker plastered on the luggage chute urged, "Smile! You're in Beirut."

We loaded our bags onto a metal cart and headed for the exit. Amira carried her backpack in one hand and held onto the cart handlebar with the other. Ahead of us people disappeared behind an automatic door that swished open and closed. With each opening I could glimpse the crowds of families and friends waiting to welcome home loved ones. Men leaned their middle-aged bellies against the peeling-paint metal rail separating the passengers from the receiving crowd; children stood on the rail's lower bar, waving and calling out, "*Khalto! Jiddo!* Auntie! Grandpa!" Women stood behind the children, talking and laughing.

Steps away from the door, I looked down at Amira. She glanced up and smiled, her hand tightening next to mine around the handlebar. Then the door opened for us. The din from the reception area surged forward. In the Middle East, meeting someone at the airport is a family event that often entails a caravan of cars stuffed with relatives. The process of double- or triple- cheek kissing each family member at the end of the metal barrier was backing up the line of those exiting the baggage claim. I began searching the faces for Zayn's. I noticed the puzzled expressions of people who looked at me, then at Amira, and back to me. I scanned the crowd twice. A sudden flitter of panic rose in my chest. Then I saw a hand shoot up from amid the throng.

"Rebecca!"

Zayn's beaming face parted the crowd. Suddenly there was a flash from a camera as he took the first of over a hundred pictures of Amira during the next three weeks.

She froze.

"Give me your bag, honey," I instructed her.

She slipped the backpack off of her shoulder and handed it to me.

"Go!" I nodded toward him.

She raced to the end of the railing; Zayn did the same on his side. She flung herself into him, burying her head into his chest. He kissed the top of her head and I could see his lips form the words "I love you, *baba,*" an Arab father's term of endearment for his children.

I stopped walking, on the pretense of rearranging the luggage on the cart. I took a deep breath and wiped my eyes. *Yes*, I thought to myself, *this was the right thing to do*.

Zayn smiled as I approached.

"*Alhumdillah 'assalameh.*"

We exchanged a cheek kiss. He took our luggage in hand and started for the door.

"*Yalla!*" he said.

I looked at Amira. Her eyes and Zayn's looked even more alike when wet with tears.

"*Yalla!*" I replied.

Beirut greeted us with a wave of oven-hot air as we exited the airport. Men with button-down shirts, opened to a "V" of sweat, stood in pairs fingering prayer beads. "Taxi?" they asked as I walked by. We crossed through a line of vehicles crawling past the arrival doors and made our way to the crowded parking lot. Dusty SUVs and ancient Toyotas reflected the last of the day's heat. Our luggage loaded in the trunk, Zayn started the car and looked in the rearview mirror. He caught sight of Amira and paused.

"Really, *baba*, you are very beautiful," he said.

I looked back and took in Amira's radiant smile. Her eyes shifted to the city that loomed in the distance.

"Thank you, Baba," she replied.

Zayn shifted into reverse, eased his car into the melee of Beirut traffic, and headed toward his home.

❧

Beirut is like a once-beautiful woman whose attempts to restore her looks have gone awry. The summer of 2002 marked twenty years since the siege of Beirut by Israeli forces and twelve years since the end of the civil war. But scars were everywhere. In the swankier parts of Beirut—once dubbed the "Paris of the Middle East"—the controversial post-war reconstruction effort embarked upon by then-Prime Minister Rafik Hariri had done much to erase many of the physical reminders of the wars waged from within and from without. However, the southern slums, not to mention the Palestinian refugee camps, still evidenced money's limitations in papering over the forces of history. Even within the middle-class areas of the city, jarring reminders of the devastation pushed their way through the shiny façade of prosperity. Amid Starbucks and McDonald's were occasional building shells, their shorn exteriors exposing dangling metal bars protruding from crumbling concrete like spider legs. Among the buildings still standing, it was hard to find one not pockmarked with bullet holes.

A few hours after our arrival, something streaked the evening sky. Then a massive wave of sound reverberated throughout the city, as if Beirut itself was a bell that had been rung. With precision honed over years of terrifying the city, Israeli fighter jets had flown low enough to create a deafening sonic boom, but high enough to escape anti-aircraft fire. I rushed onto the balcony of Zayn's apartment, not knowing what to expect. Women in nightgowns emerged onto balconies across the street, clutching children and scanning the horizon and the street below. Young men peered from car windows, slowing uncharacteristically to examine the sky. After a period of time, the calculus of which was indiscernible to me, the city seemed to let out its collective breath. An old man with three days' stubble, sitting in his undershirt and smoking on the roof of the building in front of me threw his head back and laughed.

Amira and I unpacked and settled into the bedroom Zayn had given up for our visit. She had taken the shock of the sonic boom in stride, and although I could tell she was tired, she went out with Zayn to pick up *shwarma* sandwiches for a late dinner. I went to bed soon after eating. Amira and Zayn stayed up to watch the World Wrestling Federation (WWF) spectacle, which became their nightly ritual.

Jet lag woke me in the middle of the night, a sleeping Amira cuddled beside me. It had been years since we slept in the same bed, so I turned on my side to take in the unguarded ten-year-old face of my daughter. Asleep, Amira's features relaxed into a broader, slightly more masculine visage: her eyebrows flattened, her lips blossomed into a fullness twice their normal size. She turned onto her back and I observed a gesture I never noticed before: Still sleeping, she opened her right hand, raised it to her mouth and licked it, starting from the base of her palm and moving her hand down her tongue until it flicked off of the tip of her middle finger. It was a sight that still bewilders me.

The next morning Zayn took us to the newspaper where he worked. For Palestinians, obtaining residency and work permits in Lebanon was all but impossible, since they were prohibited from working in most professions. The newspaper he worked for no doubt assisted him with the extraordinary *wasta* connections—and most likely substantial sum of money—it must have taken to get permission to work there.

We made our way through all four floors of the office. Zayn didn't hesitate to knock on closed doors, interrupting phone calls and meetings to introduce Amira. He would step into the room with a ringing *Marhaba*, and she would enter the room after him. The women would let out a "*Ya, allah!* Oh my God!" and move in for multiple cheek kisses. The older men would shake her hand and offer perhaps one kiss on each side; the younger men smiled broadly and shook her hand. When conversation revealed that Amira didn't understand Arabic, Zayn's friends who couldn't speak English would often substitute what they wanted to say to her with fistfuls of sweets dug out of their desks. The first comment uttered often to Zayn after seeing Amira was "She looks like you," said in a tone unable to conceal surprise. By the evening, Zayn had taken control of the remark. Upon hearing the puzzled observation that his daughter's looks resembled his own, he would reply: "*Lema kunt bint sagheera, kunt zeeha bzupt!* When I was a little girl, I looked exactly like her!"

He was in rare form.

Our first weekend in Lebanon, we headed to the south with friends of Zayn's. Nabil was a fellow journalist and his wife, Jamila, a teacher. Theirs was the first home Zayn took us to visit in Lebanon. They lived in an apartment building perched high on a hill just outside Beirut. Their veranda, where we spent many an evening, offered a stunning view of the sea. Before climbing into the family SUV, Zayn and Nabil loaded the back with meat and vegetables for a barbecue later.

Our first stop was the port city of Tyre. We wound our way through the city's weekend traffic—local families on outings, shoppers, and tourists from the Gulf. Our destination was *Al-Mina*, a tourist site of Roman- and Byzantine-era ruins. We parked the car and bought admission tickets. The price was based on nationality, with Lebanese paying the least, those from other Arab countries getting a discount, and "foreigners" paying the highest price. Zayn purchased two Arab tickets and one foreigner admission. When I explained the difference to Amira, she beamed her pleasure at getting the Arab price.

Amira and Zayn walked hand-in-hand, ahead of Jamila and me as we strolled among the remnants of ancient baths and a marketplace. Taking in the view of Amira and her father from behind, I stopped and stared: Sauntering among the relics of colonnades and cisterns, their backsides, with the same bubble shape, shifted from side-to-side in an identical clipped rhythm. I never knew that two people could *walk* the same way. I shook my head and laughed aloud.

From there we continued southward toward Naquora, Nabil's home village. Along with a large swath of southern Lebanon, Naquora had been occupied by Israeli forces from 1982 until Hizballah forced their withdrawal in 2000. Between Beirut and Tyre, we passed through one checkpoint manned by Lebanese and Syrian soldiers, a reminder of Syria's part in the civil war.

The checkpoints appeared more frequently and were more heavily manned the farther south we drove, with the red, white and black Syrian flag all but edging out the cedar tree-emblazoned emblem of Lebanon. We wound along a road that hugged the coastline. Pictures of young men who died fighting the eighteen-year Israeli occupation dotted the landscape. The turquoise water crashed against rocks and eggshell-colored beaches empty of human activity. We eventually reached a fork in the road at the base of a large hill that afforded a sweeping view of the intersection. About halfway up the hill, an imposing billboard dominated by Hizballah's yellow-and-green insignia stood like a broad-chested sentry. "Liberated territory: Enter Peacefully and Safely," declared the huge letters.

"How to get Americans to understand this?" Zayn observed, shaking his head and gesturing toward numerous Hizballah flags fluttering on the rooftops of modest, working-class homes we passed as we drove south. "America sees this and declares these people terrorists, Islamic fundamentalists. They don't see simple people who only want for their children schools where they can be educated and medicine for them when they're sick. These people want to live their lives without a foreign occupation. Hizballah gave them this, and so they fly the Hizballah flag. Will America ever understand what this flag means to these people?"

His words swirled in my head as I gazed out of the window. People were going about their daily lives. Men peddled wares from street carts, or hunched over work benches wielding tools and sweating, always sweating; women brought in their laundry from clotheslines or their children from play. And children were everywhere: mischievous little boys raced battered bicycles festooned with colorful streamers and trinkets salvaged from the neighborhood streets; and straight-backed, dark-eyed girls walked together and talked. I tried to imagine what life had been like under this Israeli occupation. Thousands had been imprisoned, tortured, or killed during that time. I wondered to what lengths I would have gone as a mother to protect my children. To whom would I express gratitude for my husband walking through the door every night? Whose flag would I fly?

Soon we were in Naquora. The town was the headquarters of the United Nations Interim Forces in Lebanon (UNIFIL), first established in 1978 to confirm the withdrawal of Israeli forces after their first invasion; two more followed and the UNIFIL mandate was adjusted accordingly.

Nabil's family lived in a sleepy village outside of the main town. Ambient sounds were as likely to come from crowing roosters or braying donkeys as they were from cars. Old stone houses and newer ones the color of biscuits stood watch over clusters of olive trees. Nabil maneuvered through the village road, the SUV's girth hanging over the side like a middle-aged paunch. We pulled into a clearing next to a simple stone house. An old woman sitting on a stool outside struggled to her feet. She smiled, turned toward the house, and appeared to say something to someone inside.

Nabil hopped out of the car and waved to her, smiling the same smile.

"*Marhaba, ya ma.*"

"*Ahlan wa sahlan, ya ibni. Ahlan wa sahlan.* Welcome, my son," her voice, scratched with age, drifted toward us.

We got out of the car and unloaded the food Nabil brought. His sister Amina appeared in the doorway, nodding and wiping her hands on a towel. Nabil introduced us, and then brought chairs from the house and arranged them on a patio under the shade of a large mulberry tree, its scattered fruit leaving red stains like tiny paw prints on the stone tiles. We drank cold juice while Zayn and Nabil prepared the barbecue. After a meal of glistening meats grilled with tomatoes and onions sweetened by the charcoal heat, everyone settled under the tree with glasses of mint tea.

"What is the name of this tree in Arabic?" I asked Zayn.

"*Toot,*" he replied, eyeing the other men lighting up cigarettes, which he had given up in the intervening years.

Nabil looked up at the tree and smiled.

"I had already moved to Beirut when the Israelis invaded in 1982. During my last visit here before the invasion, this tree was just a sapling, not much taller than Amira is now." He took a long drag on his cigarette. "It was impossible to visit my parents during the entire time of the occupation. When I was finally able to visit in 2000 after the Israelis withdrew, the tree had 'grown up.'" Nabil sat up in his chair and raised his hand above his head, like a parent bragging about a child's growth spurt. "I couldn't believe it when I saw it," he sighed, leaning back again and shaking his head. "Eighteen years."

After the tea and then Arabic coffee, we got back in the car and headed a bit farther south. *Ras al-Naqoura* (the head of Naqoura) was the Lebanon-Israel border point where UNIFIL troops were stationed to monitor the no-man's land between the countries. On a map, the southwest border of Lebanon is shaped like a nose; *Ras al-Naqoura* is its tip. Within a few minutes of leaving the village, signs appeared, replete with skull and crossbones, warning drivers about the possibility of off-road mines. The road ended at a white metal gate. A UNIFIL guard station stood behind it about ten feet away.

We got out of the car and stood in silence. Beyond the gate, beyond the UNIFIL soldier—from Fiji or Nepal or India—was Palestine. Zayn lifted Amira onto his shoulders and pointed.

"That's Filisteen, baba," he said, and was silent again.

This was the closest they'd ever been to being there together.

Seeing the country from this side was like looking in your own window. There was a gauzy familiarity but an unmistakable distance. The red-tiled roofs of the Rosh Hanikra kibbutz stood out among the greenness of the trees and the blueness of the sea. Twenty-two years earlier I had been in Kiryat Yam, twenty miles south. And one hundred miles beyond that—at the other end of the sea—was Gaza.

Near the end of our second week, we packed up Zayn's car for a return visit to Damascus. When Zayn had left Yarmouk for Beirut a few years earlier, he didn't sever his ties completely. Having a Plan B is always a good idea for a Palestinian. He had moved from the apartment we last lived in together and bought another near one of the main roads that bisected the camp. This was our destination.

Zayn had told me to get a Syrian visa before we left the U.S., but as it turned out I didn't need one. As we approached the land crossing at *Al-Masnaa*, Zayn suggested to us not to speak. He reached over to the glove compartment and pulled out some dollars that were rubber-banded together. He then rolled down his window and greeted the Syrian soldier who was waving us to a stop. He seemed to recognize Zayn. The soldier bent his head a little lower to indicate me.

"*Meen?* Who's that?"

"*Marati wa binti.* My wife and daughter," Zayn replied, not missing a beat.

The soldier glanced at Amira and then looked away. His camouflage pants, at least two sizes too big, were synched to his waist with what was once a belt but was now a thin strip of leather. He rubbed the stubble on his face and then leaned his forearms on the window slot, his hands dangling delicately on the inside of the car. Zayn slipped the wad of bills into them. The soldier straightened up and glided the money into his pants pockets.

"*Yalla,*" he said, his hand motioning slightly, fingers pressed straight, like they were standing at attention.

Seeing the city of Damascus again I understood why Zayn preferred it.

"Beirut is not an Arab city," he said by way of explanation.

Its commercial glitter of Western-style shopping malls and fast-food franchises stood in stark contrast to Damascus, where even outside the ancient walled city, shops and restaurants looked like they belonged there and not in the Milwaukee suburbs. Beirut's old city had been either bulldozed out of existence in the post civil war rebuilding frenzy, or "restored" into million-dollar flats that looked like models of old-style Islamic architecture you'd see in a museum. To be sure, the pressure of economic liberalization and development policies was evident in Damascus. Sections of the Old City had been lost to highways and high rises, but residents still struggled to remain part of one of the world's oldest cities. Damascus had seen its share of wars and foreign occupation—history that showed itself in the black-and-pink arches of basalt and limestone of the Umayyad Mosque, which was at one time a Roman temple to the god Jupiter and at another a cathedral that housed the head of John the Baptist—but Beirut-scale destruction would not be visited upon the country for another decade.

An hour and a half after leaving Beirut, we drove into Yarmouk. I immediately noticed two differences: the cement arches that stood at its entrance had been painted an already-chipped beige, and Hafez al-Assad's severe visage had been replaced by that of his son, Bashar. He had his father's distracting ears and wispy moustache, but less of a chin. The portrait posed him in an army uniform, although his military experience was limited to the quick-and-dirty training he received to groom him as his father's successor. When his older brother died after crashing his Maserati at the Damascus airport in 1994, Bashar was called back from London, where he had been training as an ophthalmologist. After his father's death six years later, he was anointed as the President of the Syrian Arab Republic.

Taking in Palestine Street, one of the two main arteries that diverged at the camp's entrance, things looked mostly the same. It was late morning and the street was jammed with traffic. The flamboyant store windows lured shoppers, who spilled out onto the street. Cart peddlers jockeyed for shade and the best corner. Blooms of black exhaust sprouted from the backs of buses. It was seeing them that I realized what was different: the lumbering, yellow 1950s Chevys that had served as taxis were nowhere to be found. They had been replaced by fuel-efficient Japanese cars a quarter of their size and minibuses with sliding doors and seatbelts. I was seized by an unexpected pang of loss.

From the moment we drove into Yarmouk, Amira drank in the hustle and bustle of the place. The last time we visited—seven years ago—she was only three, so it was essentially a new experience for her. The noise, the colorful fruits and vegetables piled in geometric shapes in the open-air markets, the eye-catching displays in the mom-and-pop shops, the street life winding well into the night—it all overwhelmed and excited her.

On that trip, Amira got to know the *saber* cactus fruit seller on Yarmouk Street who stood outside her favorite *shwarma* grill, hawking plastic buckets full of the prickly-skinned delicacy. When he saw her coming, he would pluck a grenade-shaped fruit as it bobbed in the ice-cold water and present it for inspection and approval. Then he'd pull a razor-sharp knife from his back pocket and with the precision of a surgeon separate the fruit's tough skin and thorns, sacrificing only a microscopically small part of the pulpy membrane that lay underneath.

Multiple visits to the "*saber* man" were often followed by glasses of *karkaday* hibiscus tea. The peripatetic tea seller poured the blood-red liquid by bending over and tipping the ornate, long-necked brass tea pot strapped to his back. A crimson stream shot into Pyrex glasses, and although I held my breath every time, he never spilled a drop. Between customers, he plied the camp's streets and clicked the empty glasses together in a remarkably complex rhythm, shouting, "*Azka karkadaaay!* The most delicious *karkaday*!"

Nearly all of Amira's shirts were stained orange and red after that trip.

About halfway down Palestine Street, we veered off to the right. Zayn stopped in front of one of the mushroom-colored apartment buildings that were stacked throughout the camp like cartons in a warehouse. We walked into the dimness of his ground-floor apartment, shuttered against the dust and heat. A hallway extended the length of the apartment from the front door, with the living room and one bedroom to the left and the kitchen and another bedroom on the right.

I followed Zayn into the living room, where he began opening the shutters and curtains. In one corner stood our plywood china cabinet, empty of dishes but full of my books. There was *In Search of Our Mothers' Gardens* and *A People's History of the United States*, two of the books that had made it out of Gaza. I opened the cabinet and took out *People's History*. I turned the cover page and there was my name, written in a relaxed, curvy handwriting that I barely recognized as my own. And there, pushed into a corner of the room, was the orange sofa that we had shared in our house, a layer of dust muting its bright fabric.

"*Ahlan was sahlan. Uqudee,* have a seat," Zayn said, motioning to the sofa.

He left Amira and me there and busied himself with opening up the rest of the house. Even with the apartment opened to the outside, there was an unsettling stillness about the place.

As soon as we finished unpacking our things, Zayn's attention turned to feeding Amira.

"Would you like some Syrian bizza, *ya baba*?" he asked her, his eyes lighting up.

"I guess," she responded, interested in "pizza," I could tell, but not quite sure what "Syrian" meant as a topping choice. I knew it meant sliced olives, peppers, and kernels of corn— not exactly what she was used to from Golden Crust Pizza in Mt. Airy. Before I could suggest something else, Zayn was out the door with a, "I'll be back in a few minutes."

This is going to be interesting, I thought to myself. I just hoped he wouldn't have his feelings hurt.

Zayn returned a while later with three small cardboard boxes and several bags of produce and groceries he picked up returning from this neighborhood's pizzeria. He handed me the boxes and took the groceries to the kitchen. He reappeared with three plates and three cans of soda. At least enjoying the rare treat of a soda would blunt her "Syrian bizza" experience.

"*Sahtayn, ya baba,*" Zayn said, handing her a plate.

Amira opened the box in front of her. She looked at the colorful array of vegetables and then she looked at me.

I leaned over toward her and said, "Let me cut it for you, honey." As I did I whispered, "It's okay, just try it."

Amira took a tentative bite. Then another. And one more. I watched in amazement as the entire thing disappeared in a few minutes.

Zayn laughed at her clean plate.

"Do you want another one, *baba*?"

"I'm sure she's pretty full, Zayn," I interjected so Amira wouldn't have to answer.

"Is there more?"

I turned around and looked at her. She smiled at me with a mouth extended by streaks of tomato sauce at the edges. I sat back in the old scratchy sofa and smiled back at her.

"*Sahtayn, habibti,*" I said to her.

❧

Back in Lebanon we spent our remaining days at the beach or in the mountains, escaping the city's heat. Amira took turns sleeping with me some nights and other nights next to her father on the living room floor, where they would line up two foam mattresses alongside each other. When they shared the living room floor, I could hear them whispering into the night. Sometimes Zayn's notorious belly laugh would erupt in the darkened house, with Amira's little girl giggle bouncing along underneath. At other times their conversation went to a different place: competing staccato bursts and then sudden silence. Amira would then spend the next night with me.

For years a light sleeper, I was always up before them. I would quietly take my coffee and yesterday's newspaper to the balcony off of the living room, tiptoeing around the sleeping Amira and her father. The shuttered room was redolent with the smell of warm bodies, the air softly punctuated by the sound of their breathing. As I shuffled toward the balcony one particularly early morning, they stirred and rolled over—first Zayn, then Amira. Thinking I was waking them, I froze and then turned around. Without opening his eyes, Zayn opened the palm of his hand, raised it to his mouth, and licked it.

❧

Amira and I would return for several more trips. But things wouldn't always be this easy between her and Zayn. Over the years our visits grew tense, as Amira entered puberty and the toll exacted on Zayn by exile became more apparent with time. And now he was living alone in a country that was perhaps more alien to him than to us. Lebanon continued providing many more opportunities to experience the disorienting overlay of Western culture on a land that is so often viewed as inimical to it. A memorable instance of this was seeing the musical *Chicago* performed at the Roman-built Temple of Jupiter in the Beka'a Valley.

Much of our time we spent swimming in that magnificent sea and visiting Zayn's office, where we met new colleagues and caught up with old ones. I always looked forward to tracking the progress of the *toot* tree in Nabil's village.

We passed many hours in the company of Nabil and Jamila at their apartment in Beirut. The neighbors across the hall from them had a daughter Amira's age who spoke fluent English. Dina and Amira became good friends as the years progressed, and by the time they were teenagers, they were planning get-togethers at Dina's and outings without the adults.

During one stay when we were all visiting Jamila and Nabil together, the girls were ensconced in Dina's bedroom across the hall as we sat on the veranda talking and drinking tea. After we had once again watched the sun in its slinking, flamboyant glide into the sea, Amira and Dina reappeared. With one look at Amira, I could tell that she had something in mind.

She sidled up to me and whispered, "Can I have a sleepover with Dina?"

By that time in Amira's life, it was the odd weekend when a sleepover wasn't part of her plan. But this felt like a different kind of milestone. With each successive visit to Lebanon, Amira increasingly preferred spending time at Zayn's apartment watching television, to doing just about anything else, much to the puzzled annoyance of her father.

Happy that she felt so comfortable with friends there and trying to hide my surprise, I replied, "Of course, honey, if it's okay with Dina's parents."

"Her mom said it was fine. But do you think it will be okay with Baba?"

I looked over at Zayn who was bent over his teacup loudly relaying an office story to Nabil and Dina's father.

"I don't think he'll mind," I replied. I could tell that Amira was thinking about our departure in a few days and how little time remained to be together.

"I'll talk to him. You can go back to Dina's, and I'll come let you know after I do."

She turned back to Dina and they hurried across the hall, whispering and giggling. Zayn glanced over and gave me one of those *time to go?* looks. I got up from where I sat and crossed the veranda toward him. He rose and met me halfway.

"Amira wants to spend the night with Dina. Is that okay with you?" I asked.

"Of course. Why not? She's free to do what she wants."

This had become his standard response to Amira wanting to watch television rather than going on outings he planned during our visits.

"But she's afraid that you'll be upset since we're leaving in a few days," I made clear.

"Really, Rebecca, I don't mind. I'm glad that she has a friend here. These people love her very much. You know that."

I did indeed know that.

I went across the hall to reassure Amira that everything was fine and then returned to help Jamila clean up. I walked a tray of dirty teacups into the kitchen and stacked them in the sink. Jamila's spotless kitchen window looked out onto the Beirut night. The view from this side of the building was of an undeveloped part of the neighborhood, so there was more darkness than light. I could see sun-parched scrub waving and tumbling, blown by the breeze coming up from the sea. A smattering of lights from an unknown source flickered in the distance. It hit me that Zayn and I would be alone together for the first time since I left Syria nearly a decade and a half earlier.

Zayn and I said goodbye to our hosts and kissed our daughter goodnight on the way out.

"*Tisbahee 'ala kheir,* wake up to good things, Amira," Zayn said.

"You are among them, Baba," Amira replied. "*Wa inta men ahlo.*"

In the car on the way back to his apartment, I turned on the radio to silence the quiet. It was late on a weekday, so the streets in Zayn's neighborhood were deserted, save for the odd car and stray cat.

We rode the elevator up to his floor. As the metal cage lumbered up the six stories, Zayn whistled through his teeth and kept pressing the "6" button, its clicking noise blending with his whistle. He unlocked the front door and made a bee line for the television. The sounds of his nightly wrestling show filtered in through the bedroom walls while I changed into my pajamas. Brushing my teeth in the bathroom, I stared at my reflection in the mirror. I could no longer push away the thoughts skulking around the edge of my consciousness.

Was something going to happen between us?

What would I do if he initiated something?

Throughout the years, I had dated off and on, and had even been in a serious relationship or two. I had no idea of Zayn's "relationship status," although the older Amira got, the more she tried to pull it out of him. One day at the beach he had greeted a woman, but uncharacteristically didn't stop to chat.

"Who's that, Baba," Amira immediately asked him.

"A friend," he replied.

"Your girlfriend?"

In snippets of telephone conversations overheard back home, I knew Amira had been encouraging him to find someone to be with.

Zayn shifted in his beach chair and glanced out at the sea.

"Not exactly. She's a kind of…she was someone I…"

"It's complicated," I interrupted, not being able to bear Zayn's discomfort.

"Yes, it's complicated," Zayn said.

I shot Amira a look. She shot one back and went off to swim.

I don't remember if at that time I was in a relationship. All I remember was that I didn't want anything to happen with Zayn that I would regret. But I wasn't sure what it was that would be regrettable.

I finished brushing my teeth and went out into the living room to say good night.

"Tisbah 'ala kheir, ya Zayn."

Zayn turned in his chair. It had been more than fifteen years since I had turned around to see him in that Gaza taxi and had been taken with those dancing eyes. Now they receded into cavelike hoods, their verdancy dimmed to a dull gray.

Behind him a Speedo-clad wrestler jumped off of the ropes, his long hair flying behind him like a cape. He landed on his opponent with a *thud*. The crowd roared its approval.

"*Wa inti men ahlo,* you are among its good, Rebecca," he answered.

The bedroom door clicked shut, and I turned off the light.

Postscript
#birthrightstruggles

It wasn't a message that surprised me, but reading it seemed to fill the room with a menacing thickness.

"The Israelis are holding me at the border. They've been asking me questions about everything in my life for an hour and a half. They have my passport."

It was October 10, and Amira was crossing the Allenby Bridge into Palestine for the first time since I took her to visit when she was one year old. It was also my fiftieth birthday. She was studying in Jordan for the fall semester during her junior year at university, and this was her first holiday break. The school was observing *Eid Al Adha,* the Muslim Festival of the Sacrifice, which commemorates Abraham's willingness to sacrifice his first-born, Isaac, to show his devotion to God.

The *blip* of the Skype message refocused my attention.

"They asked for Baba's phone number. I gave it to them. Should I have not?"

Zayn was in Gaza, stuck there by the political fallout of the summer 2013 Egyptian military coup, which resulted in the closure of the Rafah border. He had been traveling between Gaza and Beirut via Egypt since the Israeli military evacuation of the Strip in 2005.

How to respond? My first thought was, "*Oh, no!*" But I didn't want to add to her anxiety.

"Who knows?" I wrote. "It doesn't matter now. Are you okay?"

As she typed a response, I tried to get in touch with Zayn to warn him that he might be getting a call. There was no response on Facebook, Skype or to the phone numbers I had. I found his niece Leen on Facebook and asked her to get the message to him.

He had purchased a one-dunam plot of land in the northern part of Gaza, where he spent much of his time tending a new garden. That is where he would be.

"I'm okay. Katia is with me," Amira wrote of one of the three friends traveling with her.

God bless Katia!—Katia, from Houston, whose family was from Mexico, knew about the pain of crossing borders.

"The others already crossed and are waiting on the other side."

Amira was the only Arab in the group.

"Will Baba be upset about the phone number?"

"Don't worry," I reassured her, not quite knowing the real answer. "I'm getting in touch just to let him know what's going on."

Leen had reached Zayn on his Gaza cell phone number and had written that he would call me as soon as he was back home.

"How are they treating you?" I was afraid to ask.

"The woman was very nice and polite. She asked about everything in my life—school, family, friends, interests, finances."

Amira Zayn Omar Majdalawi. The fear of the Israelis was that she was coming to stay, adding another Palestinian body to the "demographic threat."

"Did you tell them I'm Jewish?" I asked.

"I was afraid they'd be angry. I told them you were Christian."

Remembering reactions ranging from confusion to anger from soldiers who had stopped me in the Occupied Territories and had seen my Jewish last name in my passport, that was a good decision.

How had we ever gotten to this point?

A family history of Jews hiding. A world history of Jews compelled to hide the fact that they were Jews in order to survive. And now my daughter standing at a border crossing, facing a soldier of the "Jewish state," hiding the fact of her mother's Jewish heritage so as not to anger her inquisitors.

Three hours had passed since they'd started questioning her.

"Have you eaten anything?"

Jewish mother question. Arab mother question. Mother question.

"We ate around four," she replied.

It was nearly eleven now.

"Katia and I just shared a banana."

Trying to inject some levity, I was typing out a quip about their getting enough potassium, when another message came through.

"Mom, I have my lucky charms with me."

The precious stones.

In her lovely hands that reminded me of his, the tiny map of Palestine and the heart with our initials, which he had carved in Ansar prison.

Then as suddenly as she had appeared on Skype, she was gone.

I noticed Zayn was on Facebook.

"She's no longer on Skype. Do you know what's going on?"

I furiously tapped out a message to him, the staccato sound of my typing reverberating like gunfire. It was now almost eleven-thirty there. I didn't know what time they would close the bridge crossing, or what would happen to Amira if they did while she languished in this border purgatory.

"I just talked to her. She is all right." He had reached her on her cell phone.

He then disappeared from Facebook.

I sat staring at the computer screen; it blinked back. The technology that, moments ago, had allowed me to communicate with my ex-husband in the Gaza Strip and with my daughter at a desolate border crossing had abandoned me.

I spent the next twenty minutes trying to reach friends I knew who had crossed the bridge or had similar experiences, including one Palestinian-American, a Quaker who had been detained and questioned for eight hours at the Tel Aviv airport.

"Just tell her to remain calm," she told me.

It was close to midnight there. I propped my elbows on the edge of my laptop, cupped my face in my palms, exhaled and inhaled, attempting to cut through the heavy air that had descended with the first message.

Another *blip.* I looked up again at the computer screen. It was 4:59 p.m. eastern time in the States, 11:59 p.m. in Jordan. A message from Zayn's new wife, Sherene.

"Amira entered."

"She's in Palestine?" I nearly gasped.

"Yes," was the response.

Mine was a big yellow :>)

I leaned back in my chair, my arms stretched out wide on either side of my body.

She made it. Amira's in Palestine.

Sitting alone in the nonprofit office where I worked, a memory of hearing Zayn's voice tell me, on a distant Damascus phone line, about his visa denial suddenly rolled in like thunder on a sunny day. That denial ended the family we'd hoped to be. The fear and tumult of groping for what would replace it for Amira had weighed on me ever since.

She was now a young adult—almost the same age I was when I first arrived in Ramallah after losing my father. Nothing could ever compensate our daughter being separated from hers. But family needs the desire for connection to grow and be sustained. Contemplating those three words—*Amira's in Palestine*—I somehow felt I had done what I could to turn over some fertile ground. And the good luck charms from Zayn had become initials of her love and steadfastness—her own desire and commitment to nourish belonging in this world.

The next morning, I immediately opened Facebook. Among Zayn's photos proudly displaying the bounty of his new garden—grapes defiantly bursting from their arbor, a rainbow of flowers with blossoms as big as hands—I saw his most recent post.

> *Amira finally entered Jerusalem safely after being held at the bridge for hours. And discovered, not for the first time, what it means to be a Palestinian, even if you're an American.*

And Amira's.

> *After being detained for 4 hours at the Israeli border crossing and questioned multiple times, finally made it to Palestine.*
>
> #notsurprised #birthrightstruggles